Berkley Prime Crime titles by Erika Chase

Cover Story

ERIKA CHASE

BERKLEY PRIME CRIME, NEW YORK

THE BERKLEY PUBLISHING GROUP
Published by the Penguin Group
Penguin Group (USA) Inc.
375 Hudson Street, New York, New York 10014, USA

Ⓟ

USA | Canada | UK | Ireland | Australia | New Zealand | India | South Africa | China

Penguin Books Ltd., Registered Offices: 80 Strand, London WC2R 0RL, England
For more information about the Penguin Group, visit penguin.com.

COVER STORY

A Berkley Prime Crime Book / published by arrangement with the author

Berkley Prime Crime Books are published by The Berkley Publishing Group.
BERKLEY® PRIME CRIME and the PRIME CRIME logo are trademarks of
Penguin Group (USA) Inc.

For information, address: The Berkley Publishing Group,
a division of Penguin Group (USA) Inc.,
375 Hudson Street, New York, New York 10014.

ISBN: 978-0-425-25211-6

PUBLISHING HISTORY
Berkley Prime Crime mass-market edition / August 2013

PRINTED IN THE UNITED STATES OF AMERICA

10 9 8 7 6 5 4 3 2 1

Cover illustration by Griesbach / Martucci.
Interior text design by Laura K. Corless.

ALWAYS LEARNING   **PEARSON**

Acknowledgments

Many thanks, yet again, to everyone who had a hand, or eye, involved in this third Ashton Corners Book Club Mystery!

I'm truly amazed at how wonderful and talented the team is at Berkley Prime Crime, from my editor, Kate Seaver, and editorial assistant, Katherine Pelz, to the effervescent publicity person Kayleigh Clark, the copyeditor and the awesome artists who've produced yet another purrfect cover!

Closer to home, many thanks to my readers Lee McNeilly (aka my big sister!), Diane Walker (bookseller extraordinaire), and Mary Jane Maffini (longtime cohort, conspirator, and go-to gal). Thanks to my writing group (aka the Ladies Killing Circle), known to all as Joan Boswell, Vicki Cameron, Barbara Fradkin, the aforementioned M. J. Maffini, and Sue Pike. We've had a memorable year, one of many in the twenty-plus years we've been together as a group, and as friends.

It's a pleasure, as always, to be in the company of the wickedly mysterious bloggers at Killer Characters, a source of support and clever ideas. Writing groups are invaluable in the support department also, so thanks to Sisters in Crime, Guppies, Capital Crime Writers, and Crime Writers of Canada.

And, a ginormous thanks to readers. I value the comments I receive and treasure the fact that you enjoy reading this series.

Chapter One

◇◇◇

Read, read, read. That's all I can say.

THE SECRET OF THE OLD CLOCK—CAROLYN KEENE

"The thing about friendships," Molly Mathews stated then paused to take a sip of her iced tea, "is that they're as cozy as an old chenille bathrobe that you crawl into when you're feeling down, or have a bug, or just want to feel good all over.

"Teensy Coldicutt and I were best friends all through our school years," Molly went on, smiling as her mind made the trip down memory lane.

Lizzie Turner leaned forward in the patio chair to better hear Molly's voice, which had softened with the reminiscing. This was the most relaxed Lizzie had seen her friend in months, and Molly's attempts to contain her excitement were noticeable.

Molly glanced around her spacious backyard gardens before continuing. "She used to wear pedal pushers when all the rest of us had to wear dresses, and her hair in ringlets, Shirley Temple style, which incidentally she hated."

"I don't think I've heard you mention her before."

"Probably not." Molly shook her head, looking regretful. "We'd lost touch over the years even though we were best of friends. That is, until Teensy met John Coldicutt at our senior prom. My, oh my, it was love at first sight . . . for them both. Wouldn't you know she'd go and marry him right after graduation? Her folks were plenty mad but there was nothing they could do about it."

"What happened then?" Lizzie fanned herself with her napkin. No breeze today and the July Alabama temperature had hit the midnineties. Even her yellow cotton sundress felt too hot. But it was relaxing sitting out on Molly's patio so she wasn't about to complain.

"Well, John wasn't from around here. He was visiting some relatives, I think. He came from Georgia, so that's where they lived after getting married. And then they moved all the way to Tucson. Teensy came back to Ashton Corners to visit a few times but her folks never really forgave her, so finally she stopped coming. And then many years later, she gave up on writing to me."

Lizzie noticed the brief flash of sadness in Molly's eyes. "You must have been so pleased when you learned that Teensy had moved back here."

"I was delighted," Molly agreed, clapping her hands, giving Lizzie a glimpse of the younger girl. "I couldn't believe it when she just showed up here at the front door. And I recognized her immediately. She really hadn't changed much, just gotten a bit older. Well, quite a bit. But then, so have I." Molly took a long drink of her tea and then chose a cinnamon pecan twirl from the plate on the table.

Lizzie nodded but, as usual, found it hard to think of Molly as being in her seventies. Her hair, though gray, always framed her face with a soft halo and what lines had embedded themselves around her mouth and eyes gave her a look of perpetual laughter, not of haggard age. Her sense of style also made it understandable when others pegged her as at least ten years younger. Lizzie sighed, hoping she'd look that amazing in later years, then helped herself to a second tea cake.

"Why did she move back now?" she asked.

"Her husband died of cancer last year and I guess she just found it too hard to stay on her own in Tucson." Molly pushed the long sleeves of her filmy blouse up to her elbows now that the sun had shifted away from her. She kept her wide-brimmed white linen hat on, though.

"That's sad but very nice for you."

"Yes, it is. But I haven't told you the best part. Teensy wrote a book, sort of a historical saga, she calls it, with a mystery element. So I told her the Ashton Corners Mystery Readers and Cheese Straws Society would be delighted to include it on our fall reading list. It will be my choice for September."

"I think that's great. We could have her as a guest at that meeting, too. It always adds another layer to the book, meeting the author and getting her take on it all."

"I'm glad you agree, Lizzie." Molly finished her tea and suddenly looked serious. "But I've gone a step further, and I'm hoping you'll be on line for this, also." She gazed straight at Lizzie, her face unreadable.

Lizzie waited to hear more. Molly seemed to be enjoying ramping up the suspense.

"Well, Teensy was devastated to hear that the Book Bin

closed and we don't have a bookstore in town any longer. But I assured her I'd help her market her book. She didn't go the traditional route of publishing, you know. It's a local vanity press so Teensy has to beat the bushes now that the book's available. I'll hold the launch right here in my house and arrange some signings in town for her, too. She's sure to attract a lot of attention, being an Ashton Corners gal and all."

"I think that's great. What's the catch?"

"I'll need some help . . ." Molly let the statement just dangle there.

"Uh-huh. You're meaning me, aren't you?"

"Well, honey, you are in charge of the book club." Molly gave the brim of her sun hat a slight adjustment.

Lizzie nodded. "Of course I'll help. But is it possible we can do all of this in the next month before school starts? I'll be fairly busy working with the teachers for the first few weeks after that."

"Well, surely. That shouldn't be a problem then. And I'll contact the printer and order the books. I think it would be a good idea to call the rest of the book club and maybe set up a little meeting, a patio party, I think, this Sunday and get them all involved, too. Do you think they'll all agree?"

"I think that's guaranteed." Lizzie thought it through. "I'm happy to do the promotional stuff. And Sally-Jo would be a whiz helping with the organizing and planning a menu. You are going to have food, I'd imagine?"

Molly nodded.

"And Stephanie would take pride in selling the book," Lizzie went on.

"We'd have to ask Andrea to watch over baby Wendy in that case," Molly added. "Stephanie can't be tending to her child at the same time as counting out change."

"That would work. But I'll bet Andie could also help with the selling and, between the both of them, keep an eye on the baby, too."

Molly seemed to be considering the possibility and finally nodded her agreement.

"I'll just sweet-talk Bob into handling the operations portion," Molly said with a twinkle in her eye. "You know, moving the books around and such. I daresay that will appeal to his orderly tendencies, as in law and order."

"Sweet-talk him? Molly, you devil." Lizzie laughed, stretching her legs out and into the sun that was creeping past them on the patio. "Jacob will be certain to help with that, too, I'd think. Or maybe we could put his lawyerly skills to good use elsewhere. Dealing with the publisher, maybe? Do we need a contract or two?"

Molly leaned over and squeezed Lizzie's hand. "I know Teensy will be so pleased. I can't wait for you to meet her. She's larger than life."

"I look forward to it and I'll bet everyone in the book club will be happy to take part. After all, we're always up for a mystery."

And, it would be good to not have a murder on their agenda, except, of course, between the covers.

Chapter Two

<small>◇◇◇</small>

Our appreciation of things is relative to our circumstances.

MOTOR CITY SHAKEDOWN—D. E. JOHNSON

Lizzie looked around at the members of the Ashton Corners
Mystery Readers and Cheese Straws Society seated
around the large Martha Stewart table on Molly's patio on a
humid Sunday afternoon. Sally-Jo Baker wore a yellow tank
and brown Bermuda shorts, her auburn hair even shorter in
the new pixie cut. She didn't look much older than some of
the students in the evening literacy classes she and Lizzie
taught.

Molly looked equally cool in a blue-and-white-striped
cotton sundress that fell in soft folds to midcalf length.
Andie Mason and Stephanie Lowe each wore cutoff jeans
and white T-shirts, although Andie's had a black skull mid-
center on the front of hers. The older male in the group, Bob
Miller, had his usual plaid cotton shirt on but his jeans

looked brand-new while Jacob Smith's green golf shirt with beige chinos looked straight out of a Nordstrom catalogue.

Molly waited until everyone had a glass of wine in their hands, and sixteen-year-old Andie, a glass of punch. She raised her glass. "I'd like to make a toast to our new season, the second year of the Ashton Corners Mystery Readers and Cheese Straws Society. May we enjoy many good books."

"And no real murders," Sally-Jo added.

Everyone nodded. "Cheers to a bloodless year," Jacob said, clinking his glass against Sally-Jo's.

Lizzie caught Molly's eye and raised a glass to her. "How wonderful of you to host this, Molly. Not having a book club meeting all summer means we've missed the schmoozing. But having a planning party before we start up is a great idea."

"Hear, hear . . . I second that," Bob Miller cheered and finished off his wine. He walked over to the bottle sitting on the buffet table and poured himself a refill.

"I'm glad y'all think so," Molly admitted. "And I've got a wonderful suggestion to start off our year," Molly continued. She made sure she had everyone's attention, waiting until Andie looked up from playing with little Wendy, Stephanie's seven-month-old baby daughter.

"My dear old friend Teensy Coldicutt—you'll remember her, Bob—has just moved back to town and she's published a book. There's a mystery element to it so I asked Teensy to talk to us at the first meeting."

"Sounds like a good start," Bob agreed. "I haven't seen Teensy since high school days and she was a Perkins at that time. Pass the cheese straws please, Andie. That's a girl."

"That's a girl? Really, Bob, you're starting to sound sexist in your old age," Molly stated as Andie grinned.

"Old age? Might I remind you, young lady, that you are older than I?"

"Barely," Molly said under her breath. "Wait . . . there's more. Since we no longer have a bookstore in town, I've offered to host a book launch for Teensy and also to set up a few signings. I'm hoping I can count on y'all to help with all these events." She glanced around the circle of friends, pinning each of them with a look that spoke volumes.

Andie bolted upright in her chair. "Awesome. I could, like, sell the books." Her short, spiky black hair had orange streaks illuminating it, a change from the usual blue or red she favored. She turned to her left and touched Stephanie on the arm. "Steph, we both could do it."

Stephanie nodded. "Yeah, that would be fun. I'd have to see if Mrs. Sanchez could do some extra babysitting for me. She did say when I went back to work that she was fine for the shifts I'd got but not much else. I've been putting it off, finding someone else to do the other times if need be. Y'all have been so kind about watching her whenever I've needed someone. Well, most of you." She grinned shyly at Bob and Jacob.

Bob turned beet red. "I haven't done that stuff for way too long, Stephanie. I'd be plumb afraid of dropping her or something like that."

Stephanie laughed. "I'm just teasing you and Jacob. I wouldn't expect either of you to do any babysitting."

Lizzie jumped in. "Besides, you'd have to arm wrestle the women at this table for a chance. I think Stephanie and Andie would make a fine bookselling team. And the rest of us can pitch in and help as needed."

Bob made his way over to the small table that had been set up at the right end of the patio to hold the refreshments. "I'll take charge of moving the boxes. I assume that's how the books will be packaged. How's that? What's the title of this book anyway?"

"*The Winds of Desire*," Molly replied.

"Am I correct in guessing it's not a police procedural?" Bob asked.

"You would be."

"No big surprise there. Guess we'll all have to wait until November to sink our teeth into the Michael Connelly I've picked."

Molly kept a straight face as she said, "The wait will be hard."

Stephanie stood and walked over to the baby carrier she'd placed on the porch. She checked on baby Wendy, tucking the blanket under a tiny fist, and returned to the table.

"How will we get copies to read? Is it in the library?"

"No, it's not. It's just been printed and is sitting at the Riverwell Press warehouse out on Beaufort Road. I'll just give them a call tomorrow and order enough books for us and for the launch and have them delivered here. I'll let y'all know when they arrive and maybe you can stop by to pick up your copies."

"How will you know how many books to order?" Andie asked, her eyes on a gray squirrel darting around the lawn.

"Excellent question, Andrea. I'll want to make the launch an invitation-only event so I'll have to come up with a guest list and then add extras in case people want to buy several copies. They'd make good gifts, don't you think—signed books by a local author? Let me just grab a calendar and we'll make some decisions." Molly swept into the kitchen and Bob got up to refill everyone else's wineglasses.

"She's really excited about her friend moving back, isn't she?" Andie asked.

Bob sat back down. "She should be. They were inseparable, those gals, when they were real young. Thought they were something, they did. Not concerned about what the other girls thought of them, just banding together and having fun. There were five of them, thick as molasses."

Molly reappeared carrying an Alabama Scenes wall calendar. "I heard that, Bob Miller. But you're right, we certainly were."

"Tell us about them, Molly," Sally-Jo suggested.

"Well, we met in the first grade and Teensy's name was Theodora Kathleen Perkins. That was, oh my, about sixty-seven years ago. As Bob said, there were five of us who used to chum around for the longest while until Rae-Sue Watson's daddy got himself a big promotion and they moved to Atlanta. But those first few years, we stuck like glue to each other. We even formed a secret society and chose our special names. The rule was, you had to use the first letter of your given name. So, Theodora became Teensy and that stuck from then on."

"What was your name?" Lizzie asked, eager to hear more about her friend's childhood, something Molly rarely talked about.

"I chose Mopsy—you know, from the Beatrix Potter books. Susanna Quinn was Su-su. Joyce Blaney, Joyful—not very original but we let her keep it because that's what she wanted. And Rae-Sue became Racy."

"So, did you have a secret handshake and things like that?" Andie asked.

Molly chuckled. "Honey, we had everything you could think of and it drove our folks mad. We called ourselves the Jitterbugs . . . you know, after the dance. Well, maybe you don't, being so young and all. We thought the dance was the cat's pajamas, an expression that is also from that era, even though we were way too young to go to dances. When we got into high school, we even had our own rating code for the boys, although none of us went steady or anything like that. We usually hung out in groups of girls and boys." Molly paused, remembering.

"That sounds like so much fun," Stephanie said, a wistful look on her face making her appear much younger than her nineteen years. "I didn't have myself many friends growing up."

Molly leaned over and patted Stephanie's hand. "Well, I can tell y'all that Teensy's really excited and doesn't want to wait too long to have this launch even though I think in the fall we might get a better turnout." She looked at the calendar she'd dropped on the table. "Do you think we could put it all together for the first Sunday in August? That's only two weeks away. Say, from two to four P.M.?"

Everyone nodded.

"Lizzie, you said you'd take on the publicity duties, maybe talk to George Havers at the *Colonist* and make sure we get a story in the paper before the event and that he has someone here covering it. That should get the whole town interested in the book. I'll gladly pay for an ad about the book."

"Happy to. And I think it would make sense if we had some public events lined up at the same time, to make better use of the ad. How about a book signing at some stores and the library?"

"Excellent idea. Would you kindly take care of that, too?"

Lizzie nodded.

"Can I sell the book at the library event, too?" Andie asked.

"Certainly, if they're in agreement." Molly looked around the table slowly, focusing on each of the members. "Bob, you agreed to take care of logistics. Jacob, how about you giving him a hand when it comes to moving all the boxes of books around?"

"Sure thing, Molly."

"Then we're all agreed?" She looked around the table, and when they'd all nodded, added, "Then we're in the book-launching business. Now, if you think of any folks who should be on the invitation list for the launch, call me with their names tonight. I'll be making out a guest list and tomorrow I'll order the books."

"I thought we had a dinner date tonight, Molly." Bob sounded like his feelings were hurt.

"Of course we do. And then we'll do the list." Molly beamed. "This is a group activity and we're all going to have ourselves so much fun. I can feel it."

Chapter Three

◇◇◇

To say my stomach felt like it had jumped on a roller coaster and was doing a loop-de-loop was an understatement. Panic zipped through me.

CLOBBERED BY CAMEMBERT—AVERY AAMES

Lizzie picked up the phone on the third ring. She'd just come inside from the driveway, where she was washing her car, and had rivulets of water running down her bare legs. Her denim shorts were soaked, the result of a renegade hose. Of course, her two Siamese cats, Edam and Brie, were quick to rub along her wet legs, leaving stray fur attached. She recognized Molly's voice immediately.

"I was just beginning to think no one wanted to talk to me today," Molly said. "It took me three tries to finally reach Orwell Rivers over at Riverwell Press this morning. He didn't even have an answering machine. Said it was not working. How can he run a business like that? Anyway, I placed an order for one hundred fifty books and they'll be delivered in two days, on Wednesday morning."

"That sounds like a lot of books, Molly."

"Well, I got to thinking, I might as well get some extras in. I have room to store them in the garage and you never know when you'll be able to line up an impromptu signing or some event."

Lizzie chuckled. "You're really getting into this. Maybe you should go into business."

"You might be right. I've been thinking I need something extra in my life. And I always did have a good head for numbers. I just might give it some thought."

That surprised Lizzie. She'd been kidding. It sounded like Molly was not. The only problem was, how many published authors were there in Ashton Corners? Not many, she was certain.

"Okay," Lizzie said, "I'll do my bit and call George Havers this afternoon and line up an appointment to see him. Maybe he can send a reporter out to interview Teensy this week sometime. Do you think she'd be up for that?"

"I'd guarantee it. I'd like you to meet her, too. How about coming for dinner Wednesday night? You can pick up your copy of the book then. I'll just check if Teensy's available."

"I'm good. Let me know if there's anything else I can do before then."

"Thanks, honey. I'm starting to draw up lists now. You may hear from me real soon."

Lizzie lifted the two bags of groceries into the trunk of her car, returned the cart to the front entrance of the Piggly Wiggly and drove slowly out of the lot, pointing the car toward Molly's. A quick call to Molly had confirmed that Teensy's book had been delivered on schedule, and although Lizzie would be having dinner at Molly's, she wanted to get her copy before that. She hoped to give it a quick scan before meeting Teensy.

She'd not had any luck making an appointment with George Havers at the *Ashton Corners Colonist* when she phoned. He was out of town for a few days but his wife had promised to pass on the message. So, she might as well concentrate on what she'd be promoting.

Lizzie parked in front of the huge triple garage that had been added in the midfifties. Molly's 2008 silver Audi coupe was parked farther along the circular drive. The 1964 Corvette that was the pride and joy of her now long-deceased husband, Claydon, a car that Molly had kept but never drove, took up a small portion of the garage. So Lizzie knew there was a lot of remaining space to store several boxes of books.

She went up to the front door of the stately antebellum mansion and rang the bell. After several minutes with no Molly answering, she walked around to the back of the house, taking a few minutes to enjoy the beauty of the backyard. The thick green maze beckoned from the edge of the lawn that surrounded the flagstone patio. She hadn't had a wander through it in quite some time, although it had long been an oasis of calm at the most turbulent times of Lizzie's life. She'd have to come do that real soon. She knocked on the back door, still looking at the yard and taking in deep breaths of the fragrant air. When she turned to glance through the back window, she gasped, then screamed Molly's name.

Molly lay crumpled facedown on the kitchen floor. *Heart attack*.

Lizzie's own heart was pumping as she tried the door handle and the door opened. Lizzie ran over to Molly, calling her name.

"Oh no. Let her be alive," Lizzie whispered as she felt for a pulse and found one.

She grabbed the phone off the counter and dialed 911. The dispatcher took the details and told her to stay on the line but Lizzie hung up when she noticed the dark blotch of blood mixed in with the grey of Molly's hair. She phoned police chief Mark Dreyfus's cell phone and he answered on the third ring.

"I just found Molly unconscious on her kitchen floor," she said breathlessly. "She may have had a heart attack. There's blood on the back of her head but I can't tell if she fell and hit something or what. I've just called 911."

"I'm on my way. Stay on the line with me."

Lizzie did as instructed and tried to keep calm and coherent, explaining to Mark how she'd found Molly. By the time she finished her story, the emergency sirens sounded like they'd race right through the house.

"I'm a block away," Mark said. "You can hang up now. I'll be there in a minute."

Lizzie opened the back door as the paramedics came around the corner of the house. She held the door open for them and stood back as they rushed over to Molly. Mark came in next. He squeezed Lizzie's arm and went over to take a look at Molly. After a quick glance around the room, he went back to Lizzie.

Lizzie folded her arms across her chest and started shaking. Mark pulled her into his arms and held her a few moments before easing her over to the bench at the banquette. They'd been dating for close to a year since meeting at another crime, in front of Molly's house, last fall. Even though she hadn't seen Mark since high school days, it hadn't taken long for her to fall under his spell again, despite the fact that he hadn't realized her feelings way back then.

Mark sat her down and went back to Molly. The young male paramedic checked vital signs and the female examined the wound. The male then slipped out the back door and grabbed the gurney they'd left outside. Together, they eased her onto it.

Molly groaned and Lizzie let out the breath she'd been holding.

"Will she be all right?" Lizzie asked.

"Better save that question for the doctors," the male answered.

"I'd like to go to the hospital with her."

"Sure," the female said, tucking Molly in.

"I'm going to the hospital with Molly," Lizzie told Mark when he returned.

"Okay. I'll be there shortly. Lizzie, it looks like Molly might have been hit over the head, but the house doesn't appear to have been ransacked. There's no sign of forced entry."

"Somebody attacked her? Who? Why?" Lizzie felt sick.

"Hopefully Molly has those answers."

Lizzie watched the gurney being wheeled out the door and grabbed her purse from the table. "I've got to go with Molly. See you later?"

Mark nodded and squeezed her hand. Lizzie followed the procession to the ambulance, her stomach tied in knots, and waited while they settled Molly inside before climbing in behind the paramedic. The second paramedic closed the doors and waited while an IV was set up and monitors were switched on. Then the siren erupted. *Please, God, let her be all right.*

When they arrived at the hospital, Lizzie was told to

stay in one of the waiting rooms and Molly was whisked down the hall. Lizzie started pacing, hoping to ease the ache and to clear her brain. What was this all about? Had she collapsed and hit her head? But Mark had thought she'd been struck. If that was the case, why had it happened? Why Molly? And, why had she mumbled something about books? Lizzie abruptly stopped and took a deep breath, trying to calm down and think.

Did she need to call someone? Bob would want to know. Teensy also, but she had no way of contacting her. Lizzie pulled her cell out of her purse and glanced down the hall in the direction the gurney had gone, hoping to catch sight of anyone who might have news. She punched in Bob's number and he answered on the first ring. Lizzie told him only that Molly had been hurt and was in the hospital. It sounded like he'd hung up as he was telling her he'd be right over.

The wait seemed interminable. Bob arrived and demanded information from the nurse behind the desk. When none was available, he growled and went to sit beside Lizzie.

"What happened?" he asked. His hair looked disheveled and he appeared as though he'd thrown a wrinkled cotton plaid shirt over a paint-stained white T-shirt. His jeans were well-worn and faded with ragged cuffs and a tear below the left knee.

Lizzie went through all the details again. As she finished, Mark strode through the automatic opening doors. He spoke to the nurse at the desk before joining Lizzie and Bob.

"Did they tell you anything?" Bob demanded.

Mark shook his head. "She's still in the treatment room. Lizzie, how are you doing?" He reached over and touched her arm.

Lizzie took a deep breath. "I think I'm going to burst if we don't hear something soon. Why did this happen, Mark?"

"I don't know. I've got a team processing the crime . . . uh, house. Any ideas, Bob?"

Bob continued to stare down the hallway. "You think she was attacked?" Mark nodded. "Was anything stolen?"

"Not that we could tell. Nothing disturbed in the rest of the house. Just the kitchen where the incident took place, and that was messy but not searched in any way."

"Why do you think she was attacked?" Lizzie wanted to know.

"Because of the wound. Where she lay. She wasn't close by anything that could have done that damage. Several things, Lizzie."

"Did you find any prints?" Bob asked.

"They're still checking but nothing so far. Whoever did this probably wore gloves."

"They had to be looking for something," Bob said. His voice sounded close to breaking. "No one would just beat up on Molly."

"It's very lucky for Molly that you stopped by when you did," Mark said to Lizzie.

"I hadn't planned on it. I just decided since I was out, I'd pick up my copy of Teensy Coldicutt's book."

Mark looked puzzled.

Lizzie explained. "Our book club is reading it and copies delivered to Molly's house this morning. Molly mumbled something about books in the ambulance. Did you happen to notice them in the garage? There would have been several boxes because she's also throwing a book launch."

"We didn't find anything like that."

"I called Molly this morning and she said they'd been delivered."

"We'll keep searching to see if we can find some way of identifying the perpetrators. The books may be somewhere around. I'm hoping Molly will have some answers when I'm able to talk to her. You know we'll do everything we can to figure this out," Mark said.

"You'll post an officer at Molly's door?" Bob's question sounded more like a command.

"Of course," Mark answered.

Lizzie swallowed hard. Bob nodded. They all stood abruptly as a green-clad doctor walked toward them.

"I'm Dr. Nasmith," he said, looking at Mark. "You're here about Molly Mathews, Chief?"

"How is she?" Lizzie blurted out. "Will she be all right? Was she hit? Was it a heart attack?"

The doctor looked at her and then Mark, who nodded. "No. Her heart's just fine. It looks like she was struck from behind with a blunt object. We did a CT scan and there's no serious head injury. She should recover nicely but that's one hell of a headache she'll have tomorrow and a bit of bruising around the eyes to go with it. We stitched up the wound and we'll keep her in overnight in case of a concussion."

"She couldn't have fallen and hit her head?" Mark asked.

The doctor seemed to consider it for a few moments. "It's unlikely. The size, the roundness and the location of the wound wouldn't fit that scenario. Not unless she fell backward and her head hit a hammer just lying there."

"She was facedown," Lizzie whispered.

"Exactly," Mark said.

"Can we see her?" Bob asked.

"I'm going to have to ask her a few questions," Mark said. "Is she up to that?"

Dr. Nasmith folded his arms across his chest. "Only for a few minutes. She needs rest and she's been medicated, so she may just fall asleep on you. We're moving her to a private room shortly but you can see her in the examining room." They followed him to the end of the hall and into a large room with curtains dividing the beds.

Lizzie's heart was pumping in her chest. Her throat felt dry. She gasped when she saw her friend lying there, pale and with a large bandage around her head. "Molly," she whispered. Molly's hair was flattened and clung to the sides of her face. Her eyes were closed and tubes snaked into her right forearm. An oxygen mask perched close to the headboard gadgets.

Bob stood stock-still. Lizzie could hear his breath coming in short rasps. Mark walked over to the bed and gently said her name. After a couple of seconds, Molly opened her eyes to half-mast. Mark held his hand out to keep Lizzie back.

"Molly, what happened at your place?" Mark asked.

Molly took her time answering. It came out in a hoarse whisper. "I'm not sure. Two big men. They barged into the kitchen. Guns. They had guns." She closed her eyes and swallowed hard. "They wanted the books."

"Teensy's books?" Lizzie asked.

Molly opened her eyes. "Lizzie, you here, honey?"

Lizzie went over beside Mark and grabbed Molly's hand. "I'm here."

Molly nodded then grimaced. "I said I didn't know what they were talking about." She took a deep breath. "One of them hit me. That's the last I remember."

A nurse appeared and told them they'd have to leave. Lizzie gave Molly's hand a squeeze and kissed her on the cheek. "I'll be back real soon to see you."

The three of them walked out to the parking lot. "I don't get it," Bob finally said. "Is this about Teensy's book? What the hell did she write about?"

"That's a good question," Mark said. "Do you know, Lizzie?"

Lizzie couldn't stop shaking. Even though a hot breeze wafted across the parking lot, she felt cold to the bone. "I have no idea, except for the title, *The Winds of Desire*."

"Could it be some other books they were looking for? Does Miz Mathews have a valuable collection or anything like that?"

"Not that I know of. No, I'm pretty sure she doesn't."

Mark looked away. "What are you thinking?" Lizzie asked.

He looked from Lizzie to Bob. "What if it's something to do with that mess Claydon Mathews was involved in? That came back to haunt everyone after decades. Maybe there are parts of it still not resolved. What if all that ruckus got some other folks to adding two and two, and the four meant they'd been swindled? There could have been other endings that were just as bad."

"You don't really think that, do you?" Lizzie asked.

"We'll have to track down those books that were delivered this morning and then we'll have one answer, anyway."

Mark's cell phone rang. He stepped away from them and took the call. Lizzie and Bob just stood there, silent. Lizzie's mind raged. What was happening? Who had hurt Molly? Would she be all right?

Chapter Four

◇◇◇

Somewhere in the ocean, a shark was missing its cold eyes because this man had them.

THE LOCK ARTIST—STEVE HAMILTON

"That was Officer Craig. Theodora Coldicutt has just arrived at Molly's house," Mark informed them.

"We were invited for supper," Lizzie said and glanced at her watch. Five o'clock. The entire afternoon had gone by.

"Let's get over there," Bob said. "Maybe now we'll get some answers."

Mark cleared his throat. "I'll take care of it. Lizzie, you come with me. Bob, I'll be in touch."

Bob looked like he was about to argue but turned abruptly and walked back into the hospital.

"He's taking it hard," Lizzie said.

"And that's why I don't want him messing around in this. I'm hoping you'll be able to help with Miz Coldicutt in case she's in any way reluctant to talk about her book. I told them to ask her to wait." He gave his head a shake. "Bob's right about one thing. If that's what's at the bottom of this, it must be some book."

They found Teensy pacing the length of the front porch of Molly's mansion. Lizzie almost stopped in her tracks. At no time had she pictured Teensy as the full-figured woman who came rushing over to them. Her bright red hair was obviously out of a bottle, not the natural shade of Sally-Jo's color. The mass of curls was held back by a wide silver and lime green headband. She wore a billowing chiffon blouse in greens and oranges, white leggings and white sandals, bejeweled and with six-inch stilettos. Her nails flashed a bright orange as she held out her arms to encircle Lizzie in a hug.

"Oh my goodness gracious, sugar. What's happened to our wonderful, poor Mopsy? How is she? Is she seriously hurt?"

Lizzie wasn't able to answer. In fact, she couldn't breathe until Teensy released her and stepped over to face Mark.

"And what, young sir, are the police doing to catch the hooligans who attacked her?"

Mark looked at Lizzie, his eyebrows raised questioningly.

"Why, everything we can, ma'am. I'm Chief Dreyfus by the way, and I'm hoping you'll be able to help us out."

Teensy turned and with a flourish of sleeves, teetered over to the front door. "Of course, Chief. Anything I can do to help my dear Mopsy. Can we go inside, though, please and get out of this heat?"

Mark held the door open for them and gestured to the library on the right, the same room where the book club held its monthly meetings. Lizzie looked slowly around the room, wishing she'd see Molly sitting on a chair and everything was all right.

Teensy headed over to the brocade settee. She looked at Lizzie and patted the space next to her. "Now tell me, how is she? The officer here wouldn't give me any details."

"The doctor thinks she'll be fine. It looks like she was hit on the back of the head and fell to the floor. She'll be sore and bruised and need to rest," Lizzie said, trying not to stare at Teensy close-up.

Teensy took a deep breath. "Well, I'm certainly relieved to hear that." She paused and dabbed at the corners of her eyes with a tissue. "And I'm just so pleased to be finally meeting you, Lizzie, although this is not the way I'd have wanted it. I knew your mama when she was a youngster and I must say, you're every bit the beauty she was. Now, what do y'all want to know?"

Lizzie was flabbergasted. She rarely was called a beauty. Good-looking, with her long dark brown hair, oval-shaped face, blue eyes and slim figure. But not a beauty by a long shot. Or so she felt. The fact that Teensy had also known her mama, Evelyn, took her by surprise.

"Excuse me, I know this is a shock for you, Miz Coldicutt," Mark said, steering them back to his questions, "but we're trying to find your books that were delivered here today."

"My books? What do they have to do with anything? They were delivered. Molly called all excited around ten this morning and said they'd just been delivered. I told her to get on with it and open a box and have a read. There'd be questions at supper tonight." Teensy sniffed. "That's what I said to her . . . there'd be questions. Oh, Mopsy."

Lizzie reached over to pat Teensy's hand.

Mark sat down in a burgundy velvet club chair facing Teensy. "The perpetrators asked Molly about the books before hitting her, and there are none of your books on the property. I've sent Officer Craig out to talk to your publisher in case he knows something about this, so we may have some answers soon. We need to know if that's what the attack on Miz Mathews is all about, although it seems awfully strange that would be the reason. But I'm wondering, if the books were stolen, why? What did you write about?"

Teensy stood up with as much flourish as a five-foot-two person could manage and started pacing again. "I've no idea why they would be stolen. That's so absurd. It's just a little— well, four hundred pages, so maybe not so little—romance and mystery. A sort of contemporary *Gone with the Wind* with all the glamour of Southern belles and the like."

Lizzie couldn't help but ask, "But Miz Coldicutt, what did you do about the civil war plot?"

Teensy stopped in front of the floor-to-ceiling windows overlooking the front lawn and spread out her arms. "Why, sugar . . . sex trumps war in any plot. I just filled it with lots of hot, steamy sex." Lizzie realized her jaw had dropped. She took a quick look at Mark, but he appeared about to burst into laughter. That wouldn't do. Lizzie didn't want Teensy's feelings to be hurt.

"And do call me Teensy, sugar. I don't feel much like a Miz these days."

Lizzie nodded. "Well, I don't see how that could make the books the target of a thief, do you?" she asked Mark.

He cleared his throat. "No, I don't. Are you sure you haven't told someone's deep, dark secret in it?"

"I, sir, would not do that. I am a lady." Teensy sounded affronted but in an instant, she burst out in mischievous laughter. "It's all fiction, every last word of it, but I did have so much fun writing it. And doing the research." Her eyes twinkled as she sat back down next to Lizzie.

"That doesn't sound like the type of book someone would steal, but they must have taken the books, because they're not here," Lizzie said, feeling like she was stating the obvious.

Mark shook his head. "Thank you for your help, Miz Coldicutt. I'll see you ladies to the door now."

"Is your mama Priscilla Kearns?" Teensy asked as they were leaving. "I think I'd heard she'd married Kenny Dreyfus."

"Yes, ma'am."

"How is she doing? She used to babysit my next-door neighbor and she'd often be out in the backyard. We'd talk sometimes."

"She's just fine," Mark said, his mouth twitching downward. "Thank you, again."

As the door shut behind them, Lizzie turned to Teensy. "You know, Molly is so delighted you've moved back to town. And she's really looking forward to planning lots of events for your book." She felt a moment's panic, wondering if that would be such a smart thing to do after all that had happened.

Teensy folded her hands together. "Thank you, sugar. I'm truly pleased to hear that. I missed Mopsy very much. I don't know how much she's told you about our younger years but we were inseparable growing up. We could finish each other's sentences, we knew each other so well. When I left to get married, I had a harder time leaving Mopsy than anyone or anything in this town. It was my own fault that I let the years go by without any contact . . . and I truly regret that. I was hoping we could get the friendship back on track for our later years. She will be all right, won't she?" Teensy asked, a sob escaping her lips. "I didn't leave it too long, did I?"

Lizzie could see the tears forming again in Teensy's eyes. Deep down Lizzie dreaded the thought that Molly might be more injured than she'd been told but she wouldn't let on. "Molly will be just fine. They're taking good care of her so don't you worry. Would you like to come over to my place and I'll make us some sweet tea?"

Teensy shook her head. "No, sugar. I do appreciate the thought but right now I'd kill for a Bourbon so I'll head on home. I'm renting a house on Lee Road while I look around for something more permanent. I'll try to get over to the hospital and visit Mopsy tonight, if they'll let me. And why don't you give me your phone number and we'll talk tomorrow."

Lizzie wrote it down on a small pad in her bag and passed the note to Teensy as they walked over to their cars. Teensy turned and gave Lizzie a big hug and kiss on the cheek, then got in her car and drove off.

Lizzie stood in place for a few minutes, absorbing it all. Teensy Coldicutt came across a bit over-the-top and some- what ditzy but she was all heart when it came to Molly. That made Lizzie happy. She knew Molly needed more in her life these days.

Chapter Five

◇◇◇

Famous last words? I hoped not. I really wanted her
to be right.

A SHEETCAKE NAMED DESIRE—JACKLYN BRADY

"**W**hat?" Sally-Jo sat down with a thud. She stared at
Lizzie across the counter in her kitchen and asked
again, "What are you talking about?"

"Molly is in the hospital with a possible concussion and
it looks like Teensy's books are missing. Someone attacked
Molly after they'd asked about the books. And now Teensy's
books have vanished," Lizzie explained.

"Is Molly going to be all right?"

Lizzie nodded. "They believe so. But they're keeping her
in overnight for observation and will decide tomorrow when
she can go home."

Sally-Jo just sat there with her mouth open, shaking her
head. "I can't believe someone would hurt Molly. And for
a bunch of books? It just doesn't make sense. Are you sure
nothing else was stolen?"

"Only Molly can tell for certain but it doesn't appear so."

The front doorbell rang and seconds later, Jacob Smith walked into the kitchen. "Hi, Lizzie. I thought that was your car in the driveway." He gave Sally-Jo a quick kiss on her cheek. "What's up?"

Lizzie went through the story again. Jacob's reaction was much the same. "I just hope she'll make a quick recovery," he added. "Someone her age . . ." He stopped abruptly when Sally-Jo gave a quick shake of her head.

"I know," Lizzie groaned.

"But she's going to be just fine," Sally-Jo said, sounding almost cheerful. "You know how determined Molly can be."

"Of course she will," Lizzie said quickly. *She'd better.*

"This surely can't be about the books. Has Mark talked to the publisher yet?" Jacob asked.

"Officer Craig went out there but I haven't heard anything."

"There's got to be some reasonable explanation."

Sally-Jo went over to the cupboard and pulled out three glasses along with a bottle of red wine and poured them each a glass. "I think we could use this."

Lizzie smiled her thanks and took a sip. "I think I'll head back to the hospital. Molly said the books had been delivered but I didn't ask if she'd actually seen the book and made sure it was Teensy's. Would you mind calling Stephanie and Andie to let them know?"

"I'll do that for sure," Sally-Jo said. "But why don't you stay and have some supper with us. We're having sautéed squash and tomatoes along with garlic shrimp, and it's ready. There's plenty. You really should have something to eat."

Lizzie smiled. "You sound like Molly. Okay, I'll gladly stay for your cooking but I'll eat and run, if you don't mind."

"Not a problem. Jacob, would you mind setting the table and I'll dish everything out from here? Lizzie, you just sit and enjoy your wine."

Lizzie cleared a pile of magazines from the chair beside the wall, sat and watched while Jacob found the cutlery and plates with ease. She knew he and Sally-Jo had been seeing a lot of each other but had no idea at what stage they were in their relationship. She hadn't heard anything more about the wife he had separated from nor if these two had made any plans for the future. They both looked happy so that was all for the good.

Lizzie could see through to the living room where the furniture was shoved into the center with huge drop cloths covering it all. She knew the archway into the main hall was being repaired and a built-in bookcase added to one wall but that was the extent of renovations for that room. A paint job was also slated. The sixty-two-year-old house had already received an updated kitchen opening onto the new dining area, which gave the rooms a bright, airy feel. Sally-Jo planned to tackle the upstairs in another year or two.

"How is Teensy taking the news about her books? She must be in a real panic," Sally-Jo commented, setting their plates on the table. She turned back to the counter for her own.

"She's as shocked as everyone else. And she's crazy with worry about Molly."

"It just doesn't make a whole lot of sense that someone would do this in order to steal the books." Jacob was still working through the problem. "What if two different things happened very close together in time? What if the wrong books were delivered to Molly and the publisher had them picked up again for some reason? Maybe a printing error was found and they needed to be redone. And their disappearance had nothing to do with the attack on Molly."

"But Molly said they asked about those books," Lizzie pointed out. "And, she didn't say that the original shipment had been picked up."

"Well, maybe Teensy really did write about a big, dark secret and whoever was involved didn't want it made public." Sally-Jo added a dish of watermelon salad to the table and sat down with them. "Remember what happened to Derek Alton last winter."

"Wouldn't that be too weird?" Lizzie asked.

Jacob shrugged. "Stranger things have happened."

Lizzie wanted to ask, *Like what?* She ate a shrimp instead. "Yum. This is delicious, Sally-Jo. I'm glad I stayed."

"You and Jacob are my best fans. It's a pleasure to cook for you. I was wondering, though, about Molly. Is she safe in the hospital?"

Lizzie paused, her fork in midair. "Mark's leaving an officer on guard at her door. I'm really hoping the danger is over."

When she finally made it to the hospital, Lizzie found Bob in Molly's room, sitting in a chair beside her bed, holding her hand and talking softly to her. He looked over at Lizzie as she entered the room, a slight red coloring spreading across his face.

Lizzie smiled at them. "I'm happy to see you're awake, Molly. But I'll bet you're feeling awful."

"I'm feeling pretty groggy is what it is." A faint smile hovered on her lips. "They give good drugs here."

Bob laughed. "Well, enjoy them, missy, 'cause you earned them."

Lizzie pulled over a second armchair that had been pushed against the wall. The orange Naugahyde seat had seen better days. "I just had supper with Sally-Jo and Jacob and they send you their love. None of us can get over what's happened."

"I'm dumbfounded, also. I hear the boxes of books were actually taken. I just can't believe all this happened because of some books."

"Did you get a chance to see if it was Teensy's book in the boxes?"

"Yes, I opened one of the boxes."

Bob looked at Lizzie sharply. "Where are you going with this?"

Lizzie explained Jacob's theories.

"What I do know is the delivery van did not come back to pick up the shipment," Molly said, her voice a big stronger.

"What about your own personal collection of books? Are there any valuable first editions in it?"

"No, honey. Their only value is of the sentimental variety."

Lizzie took hold of Molly's hand. "Molly, I'd like you to come and stay with me for a few days once you're released."

"Thank you, honey, but I'd feel so much better in my own home. I would welcome your company, though."

"Done. I'll ask Nathaniel to feed the cats." She felt Bob's eyes on her. She glanced at him, at his raised eyebrows and quick gaze toward the door, and got the message.

"I guess I should be going," Lizzie said. "I'll stop by after breakfast and see if they've decided when to release you."

Bob said, "No need to, Lizzie. I'll come by, and if she's ready to go home, I'll give you a call with an ETA and use the Bob Miller taxi service."

Lizzie grinned. "I hear it gives good service to special clients." She walked over to Molly and kissed her forehead. "I'll see you tomorrow. Sleep well."

She gave Bob a small wave and left. She stopped by the nursing station to see if she could find out anything else about Molly's condition but they couldn't, or wouldn't, add to what she already knew. She looked back at the police officer sitting on a chair to the right of the door. He nodded. She tried to smile but turned instead and walked to the elevator, tears in her eyes.

Chapter Six

Uh-oh. Not again.

BEHIND THE SEAMS—BETTY HECHTMAN

Lizzie found Mark slumped on her love seat, his feet on her brown leather hassock. She knew it had been a long day for him, too. Last night he had a city council meeting to attend and it had gone on well past the usual finishing time. She was debating whether to wake him or let him sleep, when his eyes popped open.

He grinned and reached out to her. "Hey, come here, you."

She sank onto the love seat beside him and curled up in the crook of his arm. She felt like one of her cats. Totally content. Until she thought about Molly.

"Did you go back to the hospital?" he asked, as if sensing the path her thoughts had taken.

"I stopped by after having supper with Sally-Jo and Jacob. Bob was there. I think he's been there the entire time."

She felt Mark nod. "It's a big shock for everyone. Hard to imagine anyone hurting Molly Mathews."

"Did you find out anything new, Mark?" Lizzie sat up and looked at him. She could hear how shaky her own voice sounded.

"Miz Coldicutt's books were delivered all right. Officer Craig spoke to the publisher and he confirmed the details. He has no idea why anyone would want to steal them, though."

"Jacob wondered if the wrong books were delivered and they were then picked up again."

"Craig didn't ask him specifically but he would have told us if that were the case, I'd think. He's as puzzled as anyone, and Craig said he really got upset when told about the attack. I'll talk to him myself tomorrow morning."

Lizzie sat upright to face Mark. "There's got to be a reason."

"Oh, there is. There always is a reason for violence and that's why I don't want you going poking around in all this. Okay?"

Lizzie shook her head. "I can't promise that, Mark. Molly is family. Someone tried to hurt her. That's more important than the books. But the books are the reason. Maybe there's a way the book club can help."

"You've been lucky in the past, Lizzie. The worst that's happened was you being shot in the arm."

"Grazed."

"Whatever. We don't know what we're dealing with here and I don't want you becoming a target again. So no nosing around."

Lizzie leaned forward and kissed him. "Understood. But . . ."

"No 'but's." He shook his head. "I've got to get back to the office. I've still got some paperwork from the meeting last night that has to be finished. Will you be all right?"

She nodded and smiled. She didn't want him worried about her on top of all his workload.

Mark stood up and pulled her with him. He gave her a long, deep kiss. Her toes tingled and she had to fight off the urge to push him back onto the love seat. He was right. That would have to wait.

He hooked his finger through her belt loops, gave her a shorter version of the kiss and walked to the door. "I've gotta say it, though. This is one for the books."

As she closed the door, Lizzie's earlier fatigue gave way to an urge for cleaning house. She was all nervous energy and anxiety pushing to keep busy. She started by dusting then progressed to vacuuming the main floor, followed by washing the kitchen floor. She glanced at the clock before carting the vacuum upstairs and was shocked to see it was well past midnight. She felt like she could go on for several more hours but knew how foolish that would be. Instead she opted for a cup of chamomile tea and a good book.

Her two Siamese cats, Brie and Edam, raced by her on the way upstairs and had pounced on the bed, each staking out its claim by the time she walked into the bedroom. She left the window open, hoping to take advantage of the soft evening breeze, crawled under a light sheet, the only bedding she used during the summer, and selected from the top of a pile of paperbacks and hardbacks on her bedside table the copy of *Clobbered by Camembert* by Avery Aames. She'd been wanting to dive into it for a while. Now would be a good time to start, and if she fell asleep reading, so much the better. She could always start again at the beginning the next time.

She couldn't concentrate. Her mind kept looping back over what had happened to Molly. She set the book on the bedside table, turned out the light and slid down under the cover.

The next thing she knew, her radio clicked on its usual early morning hour. She liked to get up at the same time all year round, finding it much easier on her body rhythms. She started a mental checklist for the day when her mind suddenly clicked on Molly. She scrambled out of bed, found the phone number for Mercy General Hospital and called the information desk, since there was no phone in Molly's room. When they couldn't give her an update, she asked for the nurses' station on the seventh floor. After several rings, the phone was answered and Lizzie asked about Molly. She breathed a sigh of relief on hearing Molly had a restful night and would probably be released later that afternoon.

Lizzie let out a whoop after hanging up, which startled Edam and Brie. They leapt off the bed and were poised at alert at the top of the stairs, beating her to the bottom when Lizzie started down.

Lizzie wondered about her next move. She'd told Mark she'd stay out of it. Well, technically she had just acknowledged she understood his asking. That wasn't exactly the same thing. And if she were to drive out to Riverwell Press to pick up a copy of Teensy's book, and if she just happened to ask Orwell Rivers some questions at the same time, that couldn't be construed to be deliberately nosing around.

She liked that plan. And she could fit it in this morning in plenty of time before she had to go to Molly's. Lizzie ate a breakfast of spoonfuls of almond butter to top off bites of banana, quickly ran upstairs to change into a red sleeveless cotton blouse and white crop pants and was headed to Riverwell Press by nine o'clock. She hadn't thought to wonder if it would be open at that hour. She shrugged. She'd just have to hope for the best.

She pulled into the parking lot twenty minutes later. The lot was empty and the building looked dark. Not so good a start. She tried the front door but that was locked, even though the posted hours on the door were weekdays eight to four. She walked around to the back and noticed an older blue Ford Taurus parked next to the rear entrance.

Frustrated, she peered through the windows. At first she couldn't see anything but outlines of large objects. Slowly her eyes adjusted and she noticed a large file cabinet to the right of the window, and next to that, jutting out into the room, a wide gray metal desk. And on the floor, next to the desk, what looked like a crumpled body. There was just enough light from a desk lamp to show a dark stain emanating from under the body.

Lizzie crouched down and tried to slow her heart rate. *Oh no . . . not another body.* Would the book club get pulled into yet another murder? There'd been too many bodies in too short a time.

She wondered if the attacker had left or lurked just inside the door. Without a look back, she darted around the front to her own car, jumped in and locked the doors. With a shaky hand, she pulled out her cell phone and punched in 911.

The dispatcher advised her to stay locked inside her car until the police got there. It was a short wait until two police cars and an ambulance arrived in tandem. She rolled down her window and told the officer what she'd seen. One car drove around the back followed by the ambulance. The other car was just about to pull across and block the entrance to the parking lot when Mark pulled in.

Lizzie got out of her car and managed to stay calm by leaning back against it.

"I don't believe it," Mark said in an exasperated voice. "You're first at a crime scene again? Didn't I tell you not to get involved?" He looked at her and then wrapped his arms around her, whispering in her ear, "Are you all right?"

Lizzie gently pulled away. "Yes, I am. But whoever is inside sure isn't."

"You wait here. And I mean it. I'll be right back."

Mark signaled to the officer at the other cruiser to keep an eye out and he walked around back of the building. About ten minutes later he came back. "The body is that of the owner, Orwell Rivers, and he's been murdered. Did you see anyone else when you were arriving?"

"No. The lot was empty and I don't recall passing by any cars heading into town from this direction. Not once I got on Beaufort Road."

"What are you doing out here anyway?" He sounded sterner now, although see couldn't see his eyes behind his shiny reflective sunglasses. He'd left his police hat in the car and perspiration glistened on his forehead. She wanted to tell him he'd better put the hat on but thought better of it, looking at the set line of his mouth.

"Honestly, I just came out to get a copy of Teensy's book. I wanted to read it before I see her again. And I hoped to make arrangements for the delivery of more books. I know Molly would want that done right away."

Mark sighed. "When a suspect starts out a statement with the word 'honestly,' I know it's most certainly anything but."

"Suspect? What am I suspected of?"

"Meddling. Now, did you call him this morning before heading out here?"

"No, I just took a chance he'd be here. And he was." She swallowed hard. "I couldn't believe it when I saw him lying there. Don't you think it's suspicious that this would happen the day after Molly was attacked? And they both had something to do with Teensy's book?"

"That may not be the only connection between the two. Or there might not be a connection at all. There doesn't have to be. These could be two very separate incidents. But yes, it is suspicious. And now even more dangerous. Which is why I'm telling you to stay out of it." He ran his hand across his damp forehead and removed his sunglasses. "Have you heard how Molly is doing this morning?"

"She had a good night. I'm still hoping she'll be released this afternoon."

"Well, shouldn't you be at home preparing or something?"

"I'll be staying with her at her place." Lizzie was about to tell him she wasn't going anywhere just yet, not while they were still searching for clues, but decided against it when she noticed the dark look in his eyes. He was quite serious about this.

"Good. Now I'll watch while you drive away from here to make certain you're not being followed." He kissed her on the forehead and opened her car door.

He's kidding, isn't he?

Chapter Seven

◇◇◇

And he never saw his killer.

DOG TAGS—DAVID ROSENFELT

Lizzie glanced at the dashboard clock as she stopped at the next intersection. Noon already. She'd meant to stop in at the school board office this morning and check if the books she'd ordered for the first term had come in but that would have to wait. She decided to stop at the hospital and just make sure Molly would still be released as planned. Of course, she had no intention of burdening her with the news of the death of Orwell Rivers.

"How are you, Molly? You're looking much better," Lizzie said with relief once she'd passed through the gauntlet of medical staff and police guard. "Hey, Bob."

Molly waved the observation away. "I'm feeling great and I can't wait to get out of here."

"Molly, you'll never guess what's happened," Lizzie

began then realized this was exactly what she'd pledged not to do. She tried to backpedal. "I thought I'd just check in and see if it's a go this afternoon."

Bob stood and walked around the bed to stand next to Lizzie. "It is and she's doing quite fine. Of course, she'll have to be watched. The doc said he'd give me a list of things to be aware of. Now, what's going on?"

Lizzie sighed. "I hadn't meant to bring this up here but . . . Anyway, I went out to Riverwell Press this morning to try to get a copy of Teensy's book. And, well, I found Orwell Rivers's body."

Molly gasped. "By body, you mean that he's dead?"

"Murder?" Bob asked.

"It looks to be," Lizzie answered. "I didn't stick around very long after the police arrived so I don't have many details."

Bob went back to his chair. "Now, that's right puzzling. Just too many things connected to Teensy Coldicutt's book. Do you know any more about its contents?"

"Just what Teensy said, and she swears there's nothing in it that would result in all this. No secrets revealed, for instance."

"Well, something's going on. Molly, maybe you should just stay right here in the hospital for a few more days. The police might have some answers by then." The look on Bob's face reflected the concern in his voice.

"Don't talk nonsense," Molly retorted. "I'm not in any danger. They've had their go at me. And they've got the books, so I couldn't be safer. But if you're concerned, Lizzie, you don't need to stay with me."

"You can't get rid of me that easily, Molly. What time do you want me over?"

Molly looked at Bob, who shrugged and checked his watch. "What, say, three?" Molly nodded.

"Okay. I'll be there." Lizzie gave Molly a quick kiss on her cheek and waved good-bye to Bob.

Out in the hall she thought about Bob's suggestion. Was Molly still in danger? Maybe Mark would post a guard at her house. *Here we go again.*

L izzie sat in her car in the hospital parking lot for several minutes trying to decide what to do next. She wanted to head right back out to Riverwell Press to see what the police had found out but she knew Mark would get angry. Of course, she could just cruise by and if his Jeep wasn't in the parking lot just stop in and see if Officer Craig was there. She seemed to be more approachable since the police staff party last Christmas. And Lizzie really did want to know if there were any copies of Teensy's book in the warehouse. She needed to get her hands on a copy and decide for herself if the reason for the attack and theft lay in the book.

She kept telling herself all the way back along Beaufort Road that she had a right to be inquiring about the book. She was in charge of PR, after all, and they needed to get some books for the launch. That is, if they still went ahead with the plans. Would it be too dangerous? Maybe they should delay the launch until the case was solved.

She pulled over to the shoulder as she neared the parking lot. She couldn't see Mark's Jeep but maybe he'd parked it around back. What to do? She'd put her PR hat on and walk right up to the front door, that's what.

She hadn't counted on the officer who stopped her before she'd walked halfway across the parking lot. He looked vaguely familiar, probably from the party, but his name escaped her.

"You can't go in there. I'm sorry, there's a police investigation in progress," he said, not sounding at all sorry.

"Is Officer Craig around?"

He looked startled. "Nope."

"I just need to talk to whoever is in charge, please"—she peered at his name tag—"Officer Vicker. My name is Lizzie Turner and I'm the one who found the body earlier."

Vicker's gaze swung to the right behind her. She heard footsteps approaching across the gravel lot. From the look of satisfaction on Vicker's face, Lizzie knew she was busted.

"I thought I told you not to get involved," Mark said, grabbing her left arm as he came up to her side.

Lizzie tried to look contrite but figured it wasn't working since Mark definitely appeared upset. She sighed. *Remember, Ms. PR.* "I just need to know if Teensy's books are here. I was so flustered earlier, I never thought to ask. That was the reason I came out here, after all."

Mark folded his arms across his chest and stared at her a few seconds before answering. "Yes, there are quite a few boxes in the warehouse with Miz Coldicutt's name on them. I assume those are the books, but they're part of an investigation now, so I can't let you have them."

"Oh, come on, Mark. Molly needs them for the launch that's coming up. The book club needs to get reading them. They're not the murder weapons, after all. Can't I take a few boxes with me?"

"I know you'll think this is being picky but the funny

thing about the law is it can come back to bite you if proce-
dures aren't followed. Now, they're present at the scene of
a crime and so they have to be logged into the reports. I'll
need to see a receipt from Miz Mathews's purchases and
then I might be able to release the books to her."

"Don't you think you're being just a tad pigheaded
about this?"

"Do you recall my telling you about the new DA? And
about how he's being a stickler for every 't' being crossed
and 'i' being dotted?"

Lizzie huffed. "Maybe we could invite him to the launch.
That way he'll have to give us the books."

Mark grimaced. "You must be desperate."

"I am."

Mark gave her arm a light squeeze. "I'll see what I can
do. But I do want you to leave now. Go home and write out
your statement and I'll come by to pick it up later. You know
the drill."

"I'll be at Molly's."

Mark nodded and turned away to answer a question from
one of his officers.

Lizzie felt dejected. This wasn't promising. She knew
Mark wasn't to blame but she wished he could plead their
case to the DA and get those books released. Was this new
guy on a power trip or what? She took a deep breath and
forced herself to concentrate on the road.

She decided to go home, write out the statement and pack
a few things in her overnight bag. She'd ask her neighbor
Nathaniel Creely to feed the cats tomorrow morning
so she wouldn't have to rush home. She knew he'd be willing. Hopefully he'd be home. He'd been spending so much
time with his new love interest, Lizzie was never sure when

she'd find him around. The fact that he was also Lizzie's landlord guaranteed he would appear at some point.

His brand-new bright red Chrysler 200 sedan sat parked in his driveway. He'd bought it not too long after he'd started seriously dating Lavenia Ellis. Lizzie took it as a symbol of his new outlook on life. He was moving on. After all, his wife had been dead for over seven years. Lizzie parked and went up to his front door. It opened before she was able to knock.

"Lizzie, my dear, you startled me," Nathaniel said, then added with a twinkle in his eye, "but such a pleasant way to be startled."

"Sorry, Nathaniel. Are you on your way out?"

"Yes. Lavenia and I are attending a meeting of the Horticultural Society at the public library this afternoon. That's where we first met, you know." His smile showed he was very pleased with himself. His wire-rimmed glasses were pushed up on his forehead and his thinning white hair had been recently cut, no longer hanging straight and on the long side. It now was layered and shaped around his ears, shorter in the back, too. He looked years younger, Lizzie thought.

"I remember. I just have a quick favor to ask. Could you please feed the cats tomorrow?"

"I can and will. Gladly. Happy to help out. You'll be out of town?"

"No, I'm going to stay with Molly. I'm not sure for how long. She's getting out of the hospital this afternoon and needs someone to keep an eye on her."

"I'd heard about that dreadful incident. She's going to be all right?"

"Yes, thankfully. She was tied up and hit on the head but the doctor says she'll be fine."

"That's good," Nathaniel said. "I also heard it had something to do with Teensy Coldicutt's book?"

"Yes. Did you know Teensy before she moved away?"

"I didn't know her; rather I knew of her and that group of Molly's friends. I was several years older, you know. Still am." He chuckled. "They were quite the gals as I recall. Fearless and always pulling pranks. Oh, nothing serious or anything that would hurt anyone. Just enough to get a bit of a reputation. And now she's back and has written a book and next thing you know, Molly gets hit on the head." He shook his head.

"Not only that," Lizzie said. "I went out to Riverwell Press today, out on Beaufort Road, to pick up some copies of the book, and I found the body of Orwell Rivers."

"Orwell Rivers is dead? My, that's not good."

"You knew him?"

"Again, I knew of him. It's hard to live in Ashton Corners all your life and not know someone who's done the same."

"I suppose so."

"What I don't like is the fact that you're once again mixed up in murder. That could be too dangerous, Lizzie. I hope you'll take care. Is there anything I can do other than feed the cats?"

"Not that I can think of. Thanks for asking and I do appreciate it. I'll let you know how long I'll be staying if it's longer than overnight. Enjoy your meeting." Lizzie grinned, resisting the urge to wink.

Nathaniel nodded and pulled the door shut, locked it and walked down the stairs and over to his car. Lizzie walked to her place, an extension at the side. It was a two-story white clapboard house with wraparound porch, and the two-bedroom addition made an ideal, cozy home for her and the two cats. The colorful patches of dahlias, sunflowers, hibiscus and green ferns made a welcoming first impression on visitors.

She quickly packed an overnight bag, throwing in a change of clothes, pajamas and toiletries before refilling the cats' dishes. It really did seem like too much of a coincidence. Molly, Orwell Rivers and Teensy's book. That had to be the key. Maybe Teensy would lend her a copy of the manuscript if she had to wait much longer for the books to be released.

Lizzie rummaged through her purse and found the piece of paper with Teensy's phone number. Feeling sudden pangs of hunger, she grabbed the jar of almond butter from the cupboard and had a couple of mouthfuls before giving Teensy a call. What she was going to say, she had no idea.

A slightly breathless Teensy answered on the fourth ring. "Hey, Lizzie. I'm so glad you called. I was thinking I'd like to stop in at Molly's this afternoon when she gets home from the hospital. I know you'll be staying with her. Do you think it's all right if I come by?"

Lizzie wondered if it was wise to have too many people there at once. Surely Bob would want to stay. But it wasn't really up to her. Molly could tell Teensy if she needed some quiet time. "I'm going over to Molly's for three o'clock so how about sometime after that?" She could also ask Teensy her questions at that time.

"So, what was it you wanted, sugar? I just sort of jumped right in there like my mouth's overloaded my tail. Oops, wait just one itsy minute. There's a police car in my drive and an officer of the law at my door. Maybe I'd just better hang up and I'll see you later today."

"Bye, Teensy." Lizzie wondered if Teensy was about to

be given the news about her publisher. And she hadn't even had a chance to ask Teensy to bring along her manuscript. She'd have to make do with blindly asking some more questions until she did read it.

Chapter Eight

◇◇◇

Even so, things were about to get very messy.

BURIED IN A BOOK—LUCY ARLINGTON

On the drive over to Molly's, Lizzie tried to focus on how best to question Teensy. If she'd written something inciting in her book, she was obviously unaware of it. Had she told the plot to someone or had someone read it over before having it published? That would be a starting point in her investigation, as she now thought of it.

She parked in front of the closed garage and used her key to let herself into Molly's house. It seemed strange to be there with no Molly calling out to her. She left her overnight bag out of the way in the hall until Molly told her which of the ten upstairs bedrooms she should use, and went to check on the supply of iced tea.

She hadn't been prepared for the sharp feeling of dread she experienced when she entered the kitchen. This didn't feel life a safe haven any longer. Was it wise to let Molly return home so soon? What if the attackers came back?

Lizzie shook her head and took a deep breath. Time to take control of her thoughts. The bad guys had gotten what they came for. The books were gone. They had no reason to come back. She knew that. Yet, a part of her seemed destined to remain in worry mode.

Lizzie pulled out the box of molasses cookies she'd bought earlier and was arranging them on a plate when she heard the front door. Bob held the door open with one hand and had a hold of Molly's left arm with the other as Lizzie hurried over to them and gave Molly a hug, trying not to stare at the large white bandage.

"It's so good to see you home."

Molly stopped and took a deep breath. "Believe me, honey, it's even better to be home." She took a long, slow look around and said to Bob, "Let's go on out to the kitchen and have ourselves something nice and cold to drink."

Lizzie poured the tea while Bob helped Molly settle herself on the banquette. "Shouldn't you go to bed?" Lizzie asked.

"I have been in bed since yesterday, and now that I'm up, I plan to keep it that way. Until I finish my tea, anyway. Thank you, honey," she added as Lizzie put down the glass in front of her.

Lizzie wondered how Molly felt about being back at the scene of the attack, but aside from wincing as she'd entered the room, Molly didn't say a thing about it. The window in the door had been replaced. Bob had seen to that and he'd cleaned up the debris, too.

Bob pulled out a chair and settled on it. "I'll have a quick stay and then I need to get a few errands done. But I'll be back for a while, early evening, if you'll let me. You won't get rid of me that easily, Molly."

She gave a light laugh. "I'm not trying to, Bob. You've been so good. I should think you need to get on with your own life."

He colored slightly, then took a bite out of the cookie he'd chosen.

"Teensy called and asked if it would be all right to stop by for a brief visit. I thought you might want to see her," Lizzie said.

"I'm glad she's coming over. I'm very curious about what's going on," Molly replied.

"Well, just don't let yourself get carried away being curious," Bob jumped in. "I have a few questions about her book, too. Maybe I'll just hang around until she gets here."

"You just go on and do what you have to, Bob. Lizzie here will ask all about the book, I have no doubt."

Lizzie nodded, her mouth full of cookie crumbs.

The doorbell rang at that moment. "I'll get it, and if it's Teensy Coldicutt, I'll just keep on going in that case," Bob said. "I'll see you later." He gave Molly's hand a squeeze and nodded at Lizzie.

They heard him answer the door and Teensy's high-pitched voice laughing, then the door closed and high-heeled shoes sounded through the hallway. She pushed the door open and swooped over to Molly, her long pink and blue sundress swirling around her calves, and gave her a big hug.

"Oh, sugar, I'm so upset about what's happened. Are you sure you're all right? Shouldn't you still be in the hospital?"

"I'm not that fragile, Teensy. Now sit down, have some tea and cookies. It's good of you to come over."

Teensy gave Lizzie a quick hug and then sat while Lizzie fetched a glass and filled it with tea.

"Now, just what did the doctors say? Are you concussed? Shouldn't you be in bed? Just when do they think you'll be right back to normal?"

"Normal? Teensy, you're making me feel like I'm some sort of weirdo here. I do have a very mild concussion but it should be just fine in a couple of days at most. Lizzie here is staying with me overnight, on doctor's orders, just to make sure everything's fine." She winked at Lizzie. "I'm actually looking forward to a girls' pajama party and so didn't put up a fuss when he mentioned it."

Teensy bounced out of the chair and started pacing in her white stiletto sandals. "I just can't get it out of my head that this is all my fault. If it wasn't for that damned book. But that's just it . . . I don't have a clue why that book would be causing all this trouble."

"Teensy, just sit down and calm down," Molly said, her voice a lot firmer than before.

Teensy did as she was told, sitting on the edge of her chair, ready to leap up again if needed, it appeared.

"What's the plot of the book, Teensy?" Lizzie asked.

"The plot? Well, it's set on an old plantation just outside Alexander City." She leaned forward, eyes sparkling. "You know, Tara-style. There's an aging beauty, a Southern belle who inherited it all from her daddy, and this oh-so-handsome Yankee gentleman who shows up mysteriously and offers to buy the place, which will save her from the poorhouse. And then the body of her older brother, who died over twenty-five years before, is found when they dig up a dying magnolia tree. And so they solve the murder together.

That's it in a nutshell. Of course, there's a lot of steamy sex scenes in it. I mean, it just calls for it, don't you think?"

Lizzie bit back a smile. She wondered what a seventy-something's idea of a steamy sex scene read like. But then again, her thirty-year-old imagination might do no better. And what about Andie? She gave her head a mental shake; nothing shocked a sweet sixteen these days.

"And you're certain there's no mention of anyone from around here who might take issue with being written into the plot?"

"Well, as any writer knows, most of our characters do have a bit of basis in reality. I mean, I can't help but use some characteristics of people I know. But I haven't been mean-spirited at all. I didn't base the killer on anyone I know. And certainly not the hero and heroine. Although she might be a tiny bit like me."

Molly burst out laughing. "Oh, Teensy. I do have to read this for certain."

Teensy's cheeks colored slightly. "I have a vivid imagination, Mopsy."

"I'm also wondering how anyone around here would know what's in the book?"

"Well, Orwell Rivers knew. He published it, after all," Teensy said.

Lizzie wondered just how involved Rivers had been. "Did he also edit your book, Teensy?"

"Why no, sugar. It's one of those joint publishing books. I put up the money for half of it and we split the profits, although he does get a larger percentage 'cause of all he'll do, or would have done, with the distribution end and some of the promoting. The editorial content is totally under my control. He did tell me he'd read it, though, and thought it would be a bestseller. Oh dear, I wonder what will happen now?"

Lizzie shrugged, not having a clue about the book publishing business. "It sounds like Mr. Rivers would not have been one to let any tidbits from your novel be spread anyway. Did anyone else know or read it?"

"No. I wasn't living here at the time I wrote it," Teensy said, with a small apologetic smile.

"Do you think I could borrow a copy of your manuscript just to give it a read?" Lizzie remembered to ask.

"Why, sure thing. Maybe I should just email it to you. Would that be all right?"

"Absolutely."

"Why don't you see if the police will let you pick up one from Riverwell Press?" Molly asked. "They must have lots of copies on hand. At least, they better. We still need them."

"About that. After all that's happened, I'm a bit concerned about our going ahead with the launch at this time."

Teensy gasped. "You can't be serious, sugar. I mean, I know it's been absolutely horrid and we're mighty lucky that Molly wasn't hurt even worse, but all that's passed now. The police will surely find who did it. And this launch is so important to my career."

The fact that Teensy considered this a career had never entered Lizzie's mind. "I do hate to disappoint you, Teensy, but safety has to come first."

"Well, yes, of course it does," Teensy said, reaching for a cookie. Lizzie pushed the plate toward her. "It certainly does, but now that they have the books, what else could they want?"

"There's also the murder of your publisher, Teensy. That's a bit too close for comfort. And more than a coincidence, I'd say."

"Lizzie does have a point," Molly said gently.

"Tish tosh. I don't see how the two events can possibly be tied in. His murder certainly has nothing to do with my book. That's absurd. Why, I'll hire security guards for the launch if that makes it any safer."

Wow, she's serious. "Why don't I run it by Mark and see what he thinks? But there's also a slight glitch we'd have to deal with."

"And what would that be?" Teensy did not sound amused.

"Mark was saying the books need to be held in evidence during the investigation."

"What?" Teensy exploded. "They cannot do that. It's my book. I paid for it. Well at least half of it, so I should get at least half the books."

"That's a good point," Lizzie agreed. "Mark did say he'd see what he could do, but this new DA is a stickler for the rules."

"Maybe I could talk to the mayor. He called the other day to welcome me back to town." Teensy looked expectantly from Lizzie to Molly.

"What about the fact that I'd already ordered and paid for the books?" Molly asked. "Teensy and I agreed I'd handle this as a business venture. I'd purchase the books and keep the profit and then she'd collect royalties."

"How did you pay, Molly? By credit card?"

"No, check."

"Well if he deposited the check then that would be proof one hundred fifty copies are yours."

"I take it there's no record that I'd ordered them?"

"Maybe they'll come across it when they dig deeper. Let's wait and see what Mark can do."

"Mark, huh?" Teensy asked, a suggestive smile playing at her lips. "Would that happen to be police chief Mark Dreyfus?"

Lizzie nodded, feeling her cheeks grow hot. "An old high school acquaintance."

Teensy grinned. "As good a time of life to meet Mr. Right as any."

Chapter Nine

◇◇◇

"Who shot him?" I asked. The gray man scratched the back of his neck and said: "Somebody with a gun."

RED HARVEST—DASHIELL HAMMETT

By the next afternoon, Molly had assured Lizzie enough times that she was truly all right and no longer needed a babysitter. Lizzie finally agreed and, after making Molly promise to phone three times a day, headed for home. She was secretly relieved to be doing so, although she enjoyed spending time with Molly. And when Molly was resting, Lizzie had put those hours to good use. She'd finished outlining a proposed workshop for the Ashton Corners Elementary School teachers she'd planned for late September titled "Graphic Novels as a Teaching Aid." And, most of her handouts were ready to be dropped off at the school board offices for printing.

The literacy classes she taught on Monday and Wednesday nights would also be restarting, but not until the second week in September. However, aside from a general outline of what topics would be covered in the year, she liked to get to know the needs of the individuals in her class and then tailor the sessions to help them reach their goals. For most of them, that was usually a "pass" on their GEDs.

Lizzie loved the variety that came from teaching at night while working more with teachers during the day. Of course, as a reading specialist, she also worked with small groups of students to increase their reading skills, as needed.

When she'd enrolled in Auburn University right after high school, she'd planned on being a journalist like her daddy, but somewhere in that freshman year, she'd stumbled on teaching and eventually decided that the more special-ized role was something better suited to her abilities. It had been hard leaving Ashton Corners, with her mama tucked away at Magnolia Manor, the assisted living facility in town. But it was exactly because of the good care given Evelyn Turner that Lizzie could live on campus and be home in about an hour most weekends to visit. Usually she'd stay at Molly's house on those visits, having sold the family home to help pay for Evelyn's care.

Molly had been in Lizzie's life as long as she could remember, since she had been close friends with her grand-mamma and then a lifesaver when it came to dealing with Evelyn's increasing retreat from reality. That had started soon after her daddy, Monroe Turner, had died in a car accident when Lizzie was ten years old.

Lizzie had finished unpacking her overnight bag when the phone rang. She was surprised to hear Jacob Smith's voice.

"Lizzie, I'm at Bob's place and a body has been found. Do you have any idea where Bob might be? I don't want to call to Molly's and get her all worried so I thought I'd try you first."

"No, I don't. He was at Molly's for a visit this morning but he left shortly before lunch. He said he had a lot of errands to take care of. Who is the body, Jacob?"

"The police don't know at this point. They'll have to check his fingerprints. There's, uh, not much in the way of facial features left to identify him by."

Lizzie felt sick to her stomach. "It's not Bob, is it?"

"No. That much is for certain. Wrong build entirely."

"Who found him?"

"Our letter carrier, Oscar. He decided to go around back and just have a short rest on Bob's deck and he found the body. He came running over next door to my place after that."

"Should I take a drive through town and look for Bob's truck?"

"No need. The police are doing that right now. I just thought, in case he was at Molly's, it would be good to ask. I don't like to see her getting upset right after what she's been through."

"No, you're right. That's very thoughtful of you. What's going on, anyway?"

"Good question, Lizzie, but no one has any answers as yet. I'd better get going. Bye now."

Lizzie hung up and sat down at the table, staring out the kitchen window. Two bodies within as many days. Not that they were necessarily related. But poor Mark would be run off his feet. And why was this dead person at Bob's place anyway? Maybe it had something to do with a case when Bob was police chief. If so, Bob would know the guy or have some ideas. But where was Bob? She gave Molly a call, just in case Bob had stopped back in there. He'd been doing that a lot over the past couple of days. Lizzie hadn't really needed to stay there, except overnight.

"He's not here, Lizzie. Why would he be? He just left a couple of hours ago."

Lizzie smiled. Molly hadn't yet clued in to the frequency of his visits. Lizzie didn't want to break the news about yet another body, especially since, as far as she knew, there was no tie-in to the earlier events.

"But now that I have you on the line," Molly continued, "let's talk about Teensy's book launch. We need to get moving on it, you know. You saw how important it is to her. We should have been talking about it all the time you were here. I don't know why we didn't do that. Oh well, my mind wasn't working as it should, obviously. Has Mark said anything about getting me those books?"

"I haven't had much of a chance to talk to him, Molly. He's been so busy with the murder." *And now, with another one, I'll have even less of an opportunity.* "Let's work around them for the moment. What's next on the list to be done?"

"I've been making some notes since you left. Let me just fetch them." Molly put down the phone and Lizzie could hear her bustling around the kitchen. Maybe it wouldn't hurt to continue with the planning and make the final decision once they knew more about where the investigation was heading. Or once she'd read the book. That was now the priority.

"Here now . . . I've got the guest list on the go. I'll also give Sally-Jo a call and confer on a menu, or maybe the two of you could come by here and we'll do that?" She sounded like she was thinking out loud, so Lizzie didn't answer. "Would you mind drafting a press release? And remember, you said you'd stop by and talk to George Havers at the *Colonist* to try and get some publicity. Have you also given some thought as to where else Teensy could do a signing?"

"I'm on it, Molly. Now don't you forget to take a rest at some point, too. I'll check with you later on and let you know how my list is progressing."

"You see, now you have a legitimate reason to call me without seeming overly—and do I emphasize the *overly*—concerned about my welfare." Molly chuckled and hung up.

Lizzie smiled. Molly sounded back to her old self. And Lizzie had a task. She'd quickly write out a short press release, or what she figured one would look like, and take it down to the *Colonist*. She might even take a quick drive around town, particularly by Bob's favorite hardware store, and see if she could spot his blue pickup. Couldn't hurt.

After writing her two-paragraph press release, which had taken much longer than she'd counted on thanks to Brie sauntering back and forth across the keyboard, Lizzie printed it out, checked on Edam, who was sound asleep on her bed as usual, locked up the house and drove over to the Main Street offices of the newspaper. Luckily she found a parking spot right in front of the *Colonist*'s offices. She eyed the police station parking lot adjacent to the offices but Mark's Jeep wasn't parked in it.

George Havers looked up from the Chinese takeout he was eating at the front desk when she walked in. He tried to smile but his mouth was too full. Lizzie said, "Just go on ahead and finish. I love watching people eat."

Havers took a swig out of the water bottle on the desk and smiled at her. "Sorry about that. I let Kevin go have lunch with his girlfriend and I'm covering the front, but I'm also hungry. Now before you even ask, I don't have anything on Orwell Rivers's murder."

Lizzie's mouth gaped. "What do you mean?"

"Well, the only time you come to my office is when you want information about a murder. And the only one recently is Orwell Rivers. So . . ."

"Humph. That's really the only time I come here? Well, I'm changing my pattern. I'm here to give you a story. I have a press release for you about Teensy Coldicutt's new book, *The Winds of Desire*, and the launch being held at Molly Mathews's house." She handed him the page. "We're hoping you'll send out a photographer to the event and maybe do a story beforehand. Something about local woman returns home and writes a blockbuster novel. Along those lines."

Havers laughed. "You sound exactly like a PR person. And I'd be happy to do both those things." He read through the press release. "Wasn't Orwell Rivers her publisher?"

"Yes."

He sat straight up and looked closely at Lizzie. "And did the mugging of Molly Mathews have anything to do with Miz Coldicutt's book? I'd heard some books went missing."

"It appears so."

"Huh. Imagine that. Looks like I'll have to do a quick rewrite of that story now."

"The police hadn't told you that?"

"They didn't give me all those details. Do you think Miz Mathews would mind if I called to interview her? She's home from hospital, I gather." Havers put the lid back on the now-empty food container and wiped his mouth with a white paper napkin.

"She just got home yesterday. Maybe you could wait until tomorrow?"

"It'll have to be first thing in the morning then, in order

to meet my deadline. Can you ask Miz Coldicutt to give us a copy of her book and I'll have someone review it?"

"I'll bet she'll be delighted." Lizzie glanced around the room before asking her next question. "Have you had any information about the murder?"

"Aha. That's more like it. Not beyond the bare details. And you know those because you found the body, right? Care to give me a quote?"

Lizzie made a face. "I presume you were writing the story without that quote, so I'll just skip it, please."

Havers laughed. "All right. It wouldn't really add anything to the story anyway, unless you have an idea of who the killer might be."

"I was going to ask you the same thing."

"Nada. Neither do the police, I take it. Well, I certainly hope Molly Mathews is all right and that's the end of it."

"That makes two of us. And thanks for agreeing to do the story on Teensy." Lizzie hitched the strap of her purse over her shoulder and turned to go. "By the way, George, I also have a tip for you. There's been another murder."

Chapter Ten

◇◇◇

Light reading is not light writing.

MARGERY ALLINGHAM

Mark's Jeep was still nowhere to be seen in the police parking lot so Lizzie spent a few hours doing errands and then headed home. The cats came scrambling down the stairs as she deposited her purse on the kitchen counter. She glanced at the clock. Dinnertime all around.

Edam and Brie sat in front of their dishes, patient for a change. *Just like well-trained dogs.* She wondered if Mark was able to take a break and feed Patchett, his year-old hound. When a murder investigation took over his life, Mark often found it hard to get around to the normalities, like meals, sleep and his dog. She checked the phone, just in case Mark had left her a message. Sure enough, he had, asking if she could walk and then feed Patchett. She had a key and knew the routine so it would not be a problem.

But first, the cats. After topping up their dry food dishes and taking a few more moments to stroke their gleaming beige fur, she grabbed her purse and keys and drove to Mark's house, just five blocks away. Her own dinner could wait.

Patchett started his long, morose yowl the minute she stepped on the front porch. She braced herself as she unlocked the door, commanding him to stay when she shoved it open. Much to her delight, he sat down, although within inches of the door, allowing her just enough room to squeeze through. All those hours in dog-training classes had paid off for her. Mark had been saying for many months she should attend them along with him but it never happened. When he finally asked her to take his place for a few sessions, she knew their own relationship was on solid ground. It had to be love to allow your girlfriend into that sacred man-dog union.

They walked for half an hour and then she let him off leash at the high school football field and threw a grungy tennis ball for him to retrieve. When her arm started feeling sore, she hooked him up and they went back home for his meal. Although she was first and foremost a cat person, Patchett, with his long, sloppy ears and hangdog look, had won over her heart. She left him slurping water and went home.

She sent Mark a text letting him know all was well with his dog, and then gave Molly a quick call.

"How are you feeling? Are you in bed? Did I disturb you?"

"Good. No and no." Molly laughed. "You sound a bit breathless, honey. What have you been up to, or should I even ask?"

"I've been walking Mark's dog, that's all. Now that he has two murders, he'll have even less time than before for other things, be it four- or two-legged." She paused, wondering if Molly had heard about the other body. Should she have even mentioned it? She hadn't meant to but, as usual, there it was.

"I know. Bob is over here. He picked up some takeout and we're just about to eat. He's very upset that the body was found right out in his backyard, such as it is."

"Did he know the guy?"

"He said they haven't been able to identify him as yet. The face was apparently damaged."

Lizzie could hear the revulsion in Molly's voice. Better to have this discussion with Bob.

"Well, I'm glad he's there with you for a while. Enjoy the evening and I'll call you tomorrow morning."

"Thanks, honey. I look forward to that."

Lizzie wondered if Molly meant the morning phone call or the evening with Bob. She fixed herself a tuna salad and sat down to read. Teensy had emailed her the manuscript as promised. She turned on her iPad, checked the page count and groaned. She'd be reading all night, maybe all week.

Her meal was long finished and the light in the room starting to fade when the phone rang, pulling her out of the plot.

"Lizzie, it's Mark. I thought I'd take a short break. Do you have the fixings for a cheese sandwich if I stop by?"

"Toasted?"

"Uh-huh. I'll see you shortly." She hung up and turned on a table lamp in the living room, then went into the kitchen to start fixing the sandwich. She also pulled a Coors out of the fridge. One beer wouldn't hurt, even though he was still working.

She'd flipped the sandwich out of the grill and onto a plate as the back door opened. Mark entered and walked over to where she stood at the counter with her back to him. He wrapped his arms around her waist and nuzzled her neck on the left side.

"Hey. I hope you're Mark and not some housebreaking lowlife because I'd hate to have to report you, that feels so good."

Mark laughed. "Fickle woman. Umm. That smells good. Thank you." He spotted the beer on the counter and flipped the tab off. After taking a long drink he poured the rest into a glass.

Lizzie set his plate on the table and sat down across from him. He smiled and started eating. After a couple of bites he stopped long enough to say, "Tastes as good as a steak."

"There must be a reason for such a hallucinatory statement. When did you last eat?"

He shrugged. "Morning sometime. So my pal Patchett at least had a date with a beautiful gal tonight."

Lizzie felt herself blushing. *Come on now, you've slept with the guy and you're still blushing?* "He was very well behaved. We walked then he retrieved for a while. And then he ate. His table manners still need polishing up."

Mark nodded and got back to his own meal, not talking again until he was finished. "Thank you, ma'am. I needed that."

"Thank you for the 'ma'am.' Now I feel fifty years old."

"Not you. Not with that body."

"Oh my, kind sir. How long did you say your break was?"

He stood up and pulled her out of her chair, giving her a

long, deep kiss that left her breathless. "Not long enough,
I'm afraid."

"Time for a quickie? Espresso, I mean."

He grinned. "Yeah."

Mark sat back down while Lizzie made them each a cup.
When she'd set it down in front of him she asked, "What's
this about a body being found at Bob's place?"

"I suppose the entire town knows by now. His prints are
in the system but we're not releasing any information as yet
except that he was killed sometime midmorning. The postie
found him around noon. There's not much traffic on the road
that time of day and most of the neighbors are too far apart,
or not at home. It was pure luck Jacob Smith had taken the
day off. Says he was helping Sally-Jo with some of her renos
and had gone back home for a tool he needed."

"It's weird, don't you think . . . two bodies in two days?"

Mark nodded. "Now don't go trying to make a connection, because at the moment, there is none. And it's just one
big puzzle."

"Any other pieces?"

Mark looked at her a long time before answering. "Now,
I know you enjoy reading mysteries and are a naturally
curious woman, so I will tell you, but since this has nothing
at all to do with you or your book club this time, treat it as
strictly information. Okay?"

"Fine."

"Officer Craig found several twenty-dollar bills in the
victim's pocket."

"And that's a clue because . . . ?"

"They're counterfeit."

Lizzie wasn't sure what to say. Of all the things Mark

could have mentioned, that had never occurred to her. She thought about it for a few minutes.

"Is this all coincidence? Molly's being attacked; the stolen books; Orwell Rivers's death; and another body found at Bob's?" she finally asked.

"You're forgetting to add the counterfeit to that list."

"That's just too bizarre. How do you think it ties in?"

Mark shook his head. "Damned if I know. Yet."

"Changing the subject, just slightly, Molly's all keen to get on with Teensy's book launch. Do you think that's wise? Might they still be in danger?"

Mark gave it some consideration before answering. "I don't really know, Lizzie. It appears that Molly's attackers got what they came for so she should be fine. The murder of the publisher may or may not be tied in to that. And we still don't know why they wanted the books, but Miz Coldicutt seems convinced she hasn't written anything damaging or controversial. Have you read it yet?"

"I've just started it."

"Well let me know, and soon, if you find anything, please."

"What about Teensy's books? I'm going ahead at this point with the planning of the launch and it's scheduled for the last Sunday of the month. Books are usually an integral part of a launch. Although, I suppose if worse came to worst, we could hold a 'non-launch'. Actually, that's not a bad idea." She sat forward on the couch, warming to the direction her mind was going. "We could have Teensy read some chapters from her manuscript, blow up a huge copy of the cover, which I'm hoping she has, and take orders for the book." She smiled, pleased with herself.

Mark chuckled. "I think you may have a future in public relations. Give me another day or so. I'll make a point of stopping by the DA's office and try to sort it out."

Lizzie smiled. "Thanks, Mark. That would mean a lot to two old friends."

"It's the younger friend I'm trying to impress."

Chapter Eleven

◇◇◇

I hate mornings. They start so early.

PLUM SPOOKY—JANET EVANOVICH

Lizzie was just crawling into bed after spending the rest of the evening following Mark's visit by reading some more chapters of Teensy's book and then, for a change of pace, going over last-minute details for Teensy's launch. Mark had promised to make amends for all his working hours when he could. She'd played around with that notion for a while and wondered what she could do to speed up the solving of the murders. She wondered if the book club could come up with a plan.

The phone rang and Lizzie glanced at the caller ID before answering it. Andie Mason. An odd hour for her to be calling.

"Hey, Andie. What's up?"

"Hey, Lizzie, I've got a big favor to ask you." She sounded out of breath. "It's a really big one."

"I need to know what it is before I can answer," Lizzie said, hoping it would be something she could help her with.

"Yeah. Well, my folks are going away again. This time on a two-week Alaska cruise—well, three weeks in total—and they won't let me stay here on my own. They want to ship me off to stay with an aunt who doesn't have any kids or even like them, in Michigan of all places. You can't let them do that to me, Lizzie. Not with only a few weeks more of summer vacation. I can't just dump my friends." The pleading brought Andie's voice several octaves higher.

"I can see why you'd be upset but I don't know what I can do," Lizzie said cautiously.

"Can I stay with you, please? I'll be real quiet; you won't even know I'm there. And I'll do absolutely everything you say. And I'll help around the house, do the dishes, vacuum, you know, things like that. Play with the cats, too. Please, Lizzie? You're my only hope."

Lizzie wanted to ask why she couldn't stay at one of her friends' houses but realized she'd probably already tried that and it wasn't going to fly. She liked Andie a lot; she sympathized with her and her predicament, but to have someone else staying that long, and a teenager to boot? Lizzie didn't think she could do it.

"Maybe I can help with extra things for the launch," Andie threw in.

"It's not as if that should be a priority for you, Andie, even though I certainly do appreciate your help. It's just that I'm not used to having anyone staying with me. Do you understand?"

"Totally." Andie didn't sound mad, just very dejected. Lizzie could picture her, with whatever color her hair was this week, slumped in a chair or facedown on her bed, tears close to shedding although Andie would be tough enough not to give in to that. Or maybe that was only her public face.

Lizzie had no idea what life was like in the Mason house. She'd never had a normal home environment since her daddy had died. But she did know that Andie often felt neglected, that the Masons placed far more emphasis on their social lives than on the emotional well-being of their daughter. *Oh boy . . .*

"Do you think your parents would agree to it?" Lizzie asked, wondering what she was getting into.

"I'd make them," Andie shrieked, sounding revived. "Oh, Lizzie, thank you, thank you. You won't be sorry. I promise."

"Well, you'd best ask them before you start packing. When are they leaving anyway?"

"On Wednesday morning."

"Oh."

"I'll ask them first thing in the morning. I'll get up early and nab Daddy before he goes to his golf game. I'll call you as soon as I know. Oh, thank you, Lizzie."

After they'd hung up, Lizzie sat shaking her head. Was that not just the craziest thing she'd ever done?

Lizzie was out the door by six A.M., hoping to complete her early-morning run before the heat of the day settled in. She knew several teachers who weren't bothered when the thermometer hit the high eighties but Lizzie knew her own limits. And to her, the exercise wasn't worth the discomfort.

She decided to cut through the football field at the back

of Stonewall Jackson High School and run along the path beside the Tallapoosa River. She fell in about thirty feet behind another female runner, pleased their paces matched and they could continue their own form of morning meditation. For Lizzie, it was a time to sort through a mental agenda and plan her day and then try to do the final couple of miles clearheaded and communing with nature.

When they reached Glendale Park in the town center, the other runner kept to the river path while Lizzie veered into the park and back out the main gates, looping back toward her home.

Her mind came to rest on thoughts about Andie. Lizzie wasn't used to having anyone around all the time, although knowing Andie, she'd be out doing her own thing a lot. Should Lizzie worry about that? She'd never had any reason to doubt that Andie was a sensible young girl who hadn't gotten into any trouble. But would Lizzie be responsible for Andie as long as she lived under the same roof? That was quite a commitment. Could she handle it? Maybe there was nothing to worry about. Andie's parents might not allow it in the first place. She thought that sounded reasonable and tried to finish her run in a more meditative state of mind.

After a quick shower she put on a pair of khaki Bermuda shorts and an orange T-shirt and padded around the kitchen in bare feet while getting breakfast ready. She ate a bowl of granola with fresh berries and checked the clock. A bit too early for the stores to be open but she could stop by the farmer's market that set up throughout the summer months in the parking lot of the old county office that was now a regional museum on Madison Street. She'd stock up on fresh veggies and buy three big bouquets of summer flowers, one she'd take to her mama when visiting her tomorrow, one for her date for dinner at her best friend Paige Raleigh's house, and the other she'd take over to Molly's house later today.

She was just about out the door when the phone rang. She grabbed it on the fourth ring.

"Lizzie, it's Molly. Teensy's just stopped by with some good news about the books. Could you come join us for some coffee and buttermilk scones with some delightful Stone Fruit Preserves she brought over? We can get on with the planning. Do you have time this morning?"

"Sure do. I'll be by shortly," Lizzie said and rang off. Wow. That was fast work if Mark had already been able to get the books released.

She decided to make a quick detour and stop at the market, and dashed into the first stall selling flowers and bought three bunches. She arrived at Molly's twenty minutes after receiving the phone call.

"These are for you," she said, handing one bouquet to Molly. "Fresh from the market this morning."

Molly hugged her. "How beautiful these are and how thoughtful. Thank you, honey."

"Do you mind if I just put these others in water until I leave? They're for Mama and Paige," Lizzie explained.

"Why, sure. Just find yourself a vase in the bottom cupboard. Then come on and hear all about Teensy's news."

Lizzie followed Molly into the kitchen, where she took care of the flowers, and then out into the sunroom. Teensy sat at the green wicker table and chair set, a big grin on her face. She bobbed up to embrace Lizzie and pulled out the chair next to her.

"You just sit right down here because I'm just bursting to tell you my good news," Teensy said, tucking her flowing paisley cotton skirt behind her as she settled back into her seat. The crimson red top with wafting sleeves matched perfectly and she'd added a red headband to hold her unruly hair back from her face.

"I'm all ears," Lizzie said, taking the cup of coffee Molly offered her and choosing the largest scone from the plate in Molly's other hand.

"Well . . ." Teensy suddenly looked all coy. "I decided that if this here DA was going to be stonewalling us, I'd just have to go over his head. So, I made an appointment and went to see Mayor Harold Hutchins and I gave him an invitation to my launch. Then I told him, if he wanted to come, he had to guarantee my books would be released by the police."

Lizzie's couldn't hide the look of surprise from her face.

Teensy chuckled, her voice a high-pitched cackle. "Now don't you go looking like that, sugar. I believe that sometimes a gal's just got to go out there and press a few buttons. And you know what?"

"It worked?"

"It certainly did. The DA's assistant called me and we'll have access to my books on Monday. We'll need to see just how many are in stock and then haul them out of there. Lizzie, sugar, I'm wondering if you'll be able to go there with me and do that?"

"Sure, I can do that. Let's just see how many boxes there are and if we can manage on our own. We might have to ask Bob to help."

Teensy looked quickly at Molly. "We'll see. Well, thank you, sugar. And my other news is that I am going out to dinner at the Golden Goose tonight with the mayor."

Lizzie grinned. "Wow, you are some slick worker, Teensy. I'd say you charmed the mayor all around."

Molly nodded. "Teensy always did get whatever she wanted. Even as a little girl. If we wanted to stay out later, we just sent Teensy in to coax the parents. If we wanted to play hooky and not get caught, Teensy made it happen." Molly reached over and squeezed Teensy's hand. "You certainly haven't lost your touch."

Teensy smiled. "Why thank you, Mopsy. It might come in quite handy to have the mayor at my side at some of these book events you have planned. Speaking of which, what are you planning?"

Lizzie pushed away the feeling of unease that had sprung up with talk of the launch. She quickly filled them in on her visit to George Havers and the fact that the *Colonist* would be covering the launch and sending out a reporter to do an interview in advance.

"That's wonderful, sugar," Teensy said. "You've been right busy. I'm so very grateful."

"And I still plan to set up some book signings."

Teensy clapped her hands. "Oh, this is so exciting. I never ever saw myself as being a famous author—and I know that having a few signings in Ashton Corners doesn't make me famous, but it does give me a certain cachet, don't you think?"

"And there will be more," Molly added. "I've left a message for Abe Jorgens at the Ashton Corners Historical Society. I think you might add a bit of spice to their oh-so-boring annual general meeting in September."

Teensy laughed. "Oh, I promise to do that. It's a nice homecoming for me, don't y'all think?"

Molly nodded and got up to refill their coffee cups. At the same moment Bob appeared at one of the floor-to-ceiling windows on the west side of the sunroom. "Would you mind going and opening the back door for him, Lizzie? I swear that man knows when there are freshly baked biscuits on the table."

Teensy winked at Lizzie and gathered her purse from the floor. "I'll let him in, Molly. I need to run along now. I have a hair appointment with Willetta at ten o'clock. I do want to look my best tonight." She gave Molly a hug and patted Lizzie's shoulder as she walked past.

In moments Bob was seated where Teensy had been. "Coffee and a buttermilk biscuit, what a good way to start off a weekend. And is that plum preserves I spy?"

"Of course it is."

"You're looking in fine health this morning, Molly." Both her eyes were bloodshot and the predicted left black eye was becoming noticeable. However, her hair was pulled back and secured with a large pink bow that matched the long-sleeved floral top she wore. White slacks completed the outfit. Compared to Bob's camouflage green T-shirt and faded jeans, she looked positively elegant.

"That's because I am. And now that we're back to planning Teensy's launch, I've got things to keep me busy. It's always good to have something on the go."

"Is there a message there, Molly?"

"Of course not. Don't be so sensitive. Now, have another scone."

"So that means y'all are lining up work for me to do?" Bob asked.

"You'll see," said Molly, the tease back in her voice.

Lizzie finished off her coffee and asked, "Any news on the body they found at your place?"

"Well, he's been identified, although I haven't been told his name. And I understand they're still awaiting forensic results, although I'm sure they won't tell me that, either." He shook his head. "I can't imagine what he was doing at my place."

The front doorbell interrupted him. "I'll get it," Lizzie said and left them. A few seconds later she was back, Officer Amber Craig trailing her.

"She's asking for Bob," Lizzie said and stepped aside.

"Would you like some coffee?" Molly asked.

"No, thanks, ma'am. I need to talk to Mr. Miller." Officer Craig took a quick glance around the room and focused on Bob, still at the table. She'd removed her police hat and held it in her left hand. She wore her long blonde hair in a ponytail and her uniform of charcoal pants and light gray shirt looked crisp even in the already sweltering morning heat. "I'd like you to accompany me to the station, please. We have some further questions for you."

"What's this about?" Bob asked.

"I'm not at liberty to say."

"Who is it?" Lizzie asked then realized this wasn't her conversation. "Sorry."

Craig shook her head. "I can't release that information at this point. Now, Mr. Miller . . ."

"Is he under arrest, Officer Craig?" Molly asked. Lizzie could hear the desperation in her voice.

"No, ma'am. We just need to ask him a few questions." She looked pointedly at Bob until he put his hands on the table and pushed himself upright.

"It's all formality, Molly. Don't you worry now. I know this procedure thing inside and out." He reached out and squeezed her hand. "Thank you for the coffee and eats." He nodded at Lizzie and left through the back door, Officer Craig following.

"Oh my . . . that doesn't sound good, does it?" Molly said,

watching them until they disappeared around the side of the house. "Do you think I should call Jacob at least?"

"That's probably a good idea. Jacob will know if he should go down to the station or not. Do you want me to call?"

"Would you please, honey? I think I'm just going to have a small rest. There's been much more excitement this week than I'm used to. You don't have to wait around, Lizzie. I know you have things to do. Just give me a call later."

Lizzie gave Molly a hug and watched as she walked slowly out of the room, shoulders sagging. She quickly dialed Jacob, and when he didn't answer, left a message. Then she locked the door behind her and went to her car thinking about all that was happening.

It was only eleven in the morning. She still had lots of time to run into town and do her errands. But her first stop was at the Piggly Wiggly to pick up some boxes of tissue that were on sale. She'd also indulge in some Very, Very Dark Chocolate ice cream as a treat. She missed her usual weekend jaunts to the bookstore and now had to rely on buying the latest mysteries at one of the grocery stores, a big box outlet or online. She still preferred to actually pick the book up and thumb through it before buying. She also did not own an e-reader, her tiny rebellion at the decreasing availability of the printed page.

She couldn't help buying yet another potted hibiscus plant for herself, this one a brilliant orange color. She'd keep it inside, to brighten the kitchen. Her home phone was ringing as she struggled inside with her purchases. It was Molly.

"I'm so sorry to keep pestering you, Lizzie, but I haven't heard a thing from Bob and I'm getting worried. I can't reach him or Jacob for that matter. Have you heard anything by any chance?"

"No, I haven't, Molly. I've been out running errands. Look, why don't I just pop by the police station and see what's going on? I'll call you when I know something."

"All right, if you wouldn't mind. And to make it worse, even his sister Lucille has been calling here trying to track him down. I just sit here and get to worrying."

"Did you have a nap?"

"Yes, I did. I guess I was even more tired that I'd thought. Thank you, Lizzie. I'll wait to hear from you then."

Lizzie hung up and quickly checked to see if she had any messages. Nothing. Not that she thought Jacob or Bob would call to update her. She was curious, though, and Molly was worried. That couldn't be healthy for someone who'd recently suffered a concussion. That decided it. Lizzie refilled the cats' dishes with dry food and then headed for the police station.

Chapter Twelve

◇◇◇

"A very peculiar case," he said disapprovingly. "Freakish, you might say. Silly. Except for the corpse. Corpses," Mr. Fox observed with severity, "are never silly."

A WREATH FOR RIVERA—NGAIO MARSH

Lizzie knew that the part-time officer staffing the main desk at the police station was tight-lipped at best. No way she'd get any information from Officer Hailey Yates. She decided to go directly to the top. She asked for Mark but was told he was busy and she could leave a message.

"Can you tell me if Bob Miller is still being questioned?"

"No, ma'am."

"No, you can't tell me, or no, he's not being questioned?"

Officer Yates let out an exasperated little sigh. "I can't give you that kind of information."

"Thank you, anyway. I think I'll just wait awhile." Lizzie walked over and sat in a heavy-duty plastic chair, selecting from the end table a *Southern Living* magazine from the previous November to thumb through. After thirty-five

minutes and six magazines, Jacob walked into the lobby.
Lizzie stood quickly and waited until he'd reached her before
asking about Bob.

Jacob lowered his voice and pulled Lizzie toward the
front door. "Do you have time for a coffee and I'll explain?"

Lizzie nodded and they walked across the street to the
Cup 'n Choc. They each ordered an iced cappuccino and
took their drinks to a table at one end of the room. It was
fairly crowded as most patrons chose the air-conditioned
comfort as opposed to the few hardy souls who sat at the
bistro tables out front in a small area cordoned off from the
sidewalk by a three-foot white trellis.

"What's happening?" Lizzie asked after they'd both had
sips of their drinks.

Jacob shook his head. "The dead guy was an ex-con that
Bob had locked up on several occasions. His name was Cabe
Wilson. Bob says he has no idea what he was doing out there.
He hadn't seen him in years. However, Wilson had some
counterfeit twenties in his pockets and there were also some
of the same strewn around the yard. Bob denies knowing
about the money and there's no motive or a weapon, so he's
free to go, but he's topping their suspect list since there's no
one else on it."

"Bob's not a killer. He's still too much a lawman."

"We know that. I think the police believe that also but
they have to follow all leads. But as Bob says, he's been a
cop for so long, if he'd killed someone he'd know how to
make sure the body was not found. Especially in such an
incriminating spot."

Lizzie grinned. "He's right, isn't he?"

"I'd say so." Jacob took a long sip. "This doesn't add up
at all. And if someone's trying to frame Bob for the murder,

which is a possibility, what does the counterfeit money have to do with it? And where did it come from?"

"It's quite unreal. Two bodies and now counterfeit money. Ashton Corners doesn't seem so far removed from the big, bad cities anymore. Is there anything I can do?"

Jacob shook his head. "Not a thing. I'm going to keep on top of this. But I think they may find the murderer quickly once they get on with the investigation. In fact, I'll give a colleague in Montgomery a call. His name is Kenneth Stokes and he's a criminal lawyer. I'll ask him to stand by in case he's needed."

Lizzie shivered. "I hate to tell Molly what's happened but she phoned me because she couldn't reach Bob or you."

"We'll all keep positive about this. There's got to be some explanation. We just don't see it yet."

Lizzie glanced at the clock above the huge stainless steel espresso machine. "I should be going. I've got to get ready to go out tonight. Will you keep me in the loop?"

Jacob nodded. "Of course." He stayed behind to finish his coffee and pulled out some papers from his briefcase.

Lizzie called Molly as soon as she got home and filled her in, trying to reassure her and emphasizing that Jacob was on top of it. Then she got ready to go out to dinner at Paige's house, choosing white cargo pants and a red floral sleeveless cross-wrap top to give her a lift.

Paige Raleigh opened the door an instant before Lizzie knocked, as if she'd been lying in wait.

"Good to see you, girlfriend," Paige said and gave Lizzie a big hug. She wore her long blonde hair piled atop her head, held with a clip, but not securely enough to keep in check a bevy of tendrils that fell in a frame around her face. Her cheeks were flushed. The turquoise cotton tank she'd chosen fit snugly and Lizzie was happy to see it looked like her friend had gotten over being self-conscious about the few pounds she'd gained after the birth of her second daughter.

Lizzie managed to save the bouquet of mixed fresh flowers she was holding from being crushed. She laughed. "These are for you, hostess with the mostest, and the wine is for Brad but really for all of us."

"Thank you and thank you. Now, they're all out in the back. Grab a glass of wine on your way through the house. I need to flip the chicken breasts in the marinade and then I'll join you."

Lizzie did as she was told, pouring herself a glass of Shiraz from the open bottle on the counter. She could hear the sound of Paige's two young daughters, Jenna and Cate, shrieking outside.

Paige grimaced. "If you have any say in the matter, choose to have boys. They yell. Girls shriek. Yelling is easier on the nerves, believe me."

Lizzie laughed. "If I ever get to that point, I'll see what I can do about it. You sure I can't help with anything?"

"No. But if you're staying inside with me you can fill me in on your week." Paige pulled a tall vase out of the cupboard and filled it with water.

Lizzie sighed as she sat on a bar stool at the kitchen counter. "Not a good week, I'm afraid."

"What's happened since the book incident? Is Molly fully recovered now?" She played with the floral arrangement, cutting the stems at various lengths, then carried the vase to the table.

"Yes, she seems to be just fine. But I can't quite get past the feeling when I found Molly lying on the floor. I've always thought of her as being so infallible. And to think it could have been so much worse. She could have been . . ."

"Don't go there, Lizzie." Paige put her arm around Lizzie's shoulders and gave her a quick hug. "I know how much she means to you but she did recover so just don't go there."

Lizzie nodded and took a sip of wine.

"And no more bodies?"

"Well, actually, yes. But I didn't find this one. It was found in Bob's backyard." Lizzie filled Paige in on all that had happened since then and took a long sip of her wine.

Paige shook her head. "I cannot believe all that's been happening here in Ashton Corners. And what about Mark? He must be pulling his hair out. Oops, forgot. He doesn't have any." She giggled and Lizzie joined in.

The back door opened and Brad Raleigh walked in. At six-foot-five, he towered above the two of them. "Is everything funny to the two of you?" He smiled as he put an arm around Lizzie's shoulder and gave her a kiss on the cheek. His dark brown beard tickled and she ran her hand along the side of his face.

Lizzie grinned. "Just nervous reaction, I think. Paige will tell you all about it later. I see she hasn't talked you out of the beard yet."

He chuckled and shook his head. "Not going to happen, either. I let her have her way with everything else around here . . ."

"Since when?" Paige shrieked.

He continued, "But my face is my decision."

"You go, guy. No decisions for me tonight. I'd just like to relax and eat." Lizzie held up her drink. "And drink."

"Well, you've come to the right place," he answered. The front doorbell rang. "I'll get that."

Lizzie raised her eyebrows at Paige. "Don't know," Paige answered. "Brad was on the phone and said there'd be one more for dinner."

Lizzie broke out in a smile when she saw Mark following Brad into the kitchen. Mark gave her a kiss and said, "I'm afraid it will be eat and run but Brad said that wouldn't be a problem." He handed a box of chocolate pecan fudge to Paige.

"Happy to have you here for any amount of time, Mark. Especially when you're bearing my favorite indulgence."

Lizzie wrapped her arm around Mark's waist.

"Why don't we move the show outside," Brad said, grabbing the wine bottle, "and I'll conjure up some of the best chicken you two have ever eaten."

"I don't know," Mark shot back. "I've seen you flipping meat before. Maybe I should offer my services."

"I think you'd better save your services for later on," Lizzie said, reaching for the plate of shrimp and bacon appetizers Paige passed over to her.

Brad hooted and Mark grinned as he held the door open for Lizzie and Paige. By the time they finished their meal, Lizzie could see that Mark was back in work mode.

"I'm real sorry to eat and run," Mark said glancing at his watch.

Paige started stacking the dishes. "Nonsense. It was fun having you here. We don't get to see much of you these days."

"No one does," Lizzie said softly.

Mark looked at her and held out his hand, drawing her

out of her seat. He gave Paige a kiss on her cheek and shook Brad's hand. "Thanks, man. Best breast, chicken, I mean, that I've ever eaten."

"Yeah, right," Paige chuckled, watching Lizzie and Mark walk toward the corner of the house.

"It was a very pleasant surprise having you here tonight," Lizzie said when they'd reached his Jeep.

"Totally unexpected. Brad called and said to come on over, so I did. And I'm glad I did." He pulled Lizzie into his arms and kissed her. He leaned his forehead against hers and said, "By the way, the boxes of books that were stolen from Molly's have been found."

Lizzie pulled back to watch his face. "Where? Are they all right?"

Mark dropped his arms and leaned back against the Jeep. "They were found by a man climbing down the riverbank at the side of Highway 2. Said he was going fishing but when he saw all the boxes, he figured someone must have ditched the load so he called us."

"How bizarre. How come they weren't found sooner?"

"The trees and underbrush are real dense there. Unfortunately, a lot of the boxes had broken open and gone through that night of rain we had on the weekend. I'm not sure how many are sellable. And, it looks like three boxes are missing."

"That's not good news, although it is good they've been found. When can we take a look at them?"

"Whenever you want. We searched through them and then transferred them back to the Riverwell Press warehouse."

Lizzie leaned into Mark. "Thanks for letting me know.

I'll tell Teensy and Molly." She tilted her head up and he kissed her again before leaving.

Why couldn't those jerks just leave the boxes nicely piled under cover somewhere if they didn't want them? But why did they take them in the first place?

Chapter Thirteen

◇◇◇

Oh, woe to the woman who sticks her nose in a book and forgets that real life is not always destined for Happily Ever After.

WITHERING HEIGHTS—DOROTHY CANNELL

Sunday morning was hot as ever. Seventy-nine degrees already according to Lizzie's outdoor thermometer, with a high over ninety predicted. She was out running before six again. That didn't work out too well. Standing under a tepid shower for several minutes after the run helped somewhat.

The cats followed her around the house until she took her espresso into the living room and sat on the love seat. Both cats jumped up on her and vied to be the one to curl up in her lap. Brie won while Edam leapt up to the top of the backrest and settled there. Lizzie read a couple of sections of the *Birmingham News* then displaced Brie so that she could make some breakfast. By the time she'd finished her fruit salad, the cats were sitting on the front window ledge nattering at the birds.

Lizzie donned a fresh pair of shorts and a tank T-shirt

then pulled the vacuum out of the closet. She spent the next two hours cleaning the house then poured a glass of water and went outside to sit on her small wooden deck.

After another quick change, this time into a blue and green sundress, she drove out to Magnolia Manor to visit her mama. She parked in what looked like the last vacant spot. Something must be going on. Although people were usually seated at the groupings of wicker chairs on the front porch of the large white antebellum mansion, today it was surprisingly empty.

The first person she ran into once she'd entered the building was the activities director, who told her she'd find Evelyn Turner in the dining room where the residents were celebrating a birthday party. The room was full and Lizzie noticed that many in there were guests. A frail white-haired woman was standing behind a large slab cake with white and pink icing, having her picture taken. A white and black banner decorated the wall behind her, stating, "Happy One Hundredth Birthday, Gertrude!" Balloons were taped at intervals around the walls of the room.

Lizzie spotted her mama at a table for four, across the room and next to the window. She managed to thread her way through the tables without too much distraction and reached her goal just as everyone started singing "Happy Birthday." She joined in then pulled a vacant chair over beside Evelyn.

"How are you today, Mama?" Lizzie asked, leaning close to her ear. Evelyn continued staring out the window, oblivious to the festivities around her. Lizzie helped her with the slice of cake that had been set on the table, trying a bite for herself, and attempted some small talk, finally giving up when the hum of voices became too loud.

When most of the cake had finally disappeared, Lizzie suggested they take a short walk outside. The weather was surprisingly cooperative with a gentle breeze helping to keep things comfortable. They sat for a while on a bench overlooking the colorful flower beds at the side of the building, and when Lizzie had finished telling Evelyn all about her week, she guided her back inside to her room.

"Why don't we read some more of *Emma* today, Mama?" Lizzie picked up the book and sat across the small coffee table. After three chapters, she turned the radio on low, gave her mama a kiss, took a deep breath and left.

All the way home she replayed the visit in her mind, as she always did, searching for signs that Evelyn was having a good day or maybe had recognized her. At least she'd seemed content. That would have to be enough.

Mark called as she walked in the door. Lizzie had been hoping he could make it over for supper but he had to beg off, saying there'd been a break-in at the Sheridan Performing Arts Center and of course, it being a summer weekend and being short staffed, he'd taken the call.

She decided it was a good evening for reading. She eyed her to be read pile in the front room: *Iced Chiffon* by Duffy Brown; *The Diva Digs Up the Dirt* by Krista Davis; Jacklyn Brady's *Cake on a Hot Tin Roof*; and the latest from Ellery Adams. No, they'd have to wait. She had to finish Teensy's manuscript. Only two hundred pages to go and so far, nothing that could be considered remotely as a motive. By the time she reached the end, she felt like she was going cross-eyed and decided bed was a good option. She was sure of one thing, though. Teensy's book had nothing to do with all that had been happening in town. Unless it was written in code or had some other mysterious meaning unknown even to Teensy.

The cats followed her upstairs after finishing off their evening treats. The phone rang as she was brushing her teeth. She caught it just before it went to message, hoping it was Mark, but was surprised to hear Teensy's voice instead.

"I'm sorry to be calling you so late, sugar," Teensy said, "but I wanted to confirm that you're still planning on going to Riverwell Press tomorrow morning to help me pick up those boxes of books and move them on to Molly's."

Lizzie glanced up at the ceiling. *As if I'd forget.* "Of course, Teensy. I haven't forgotten. By the way, did the police tell you they've recovered the missing books?"

"They sure did, sugar. That's good news, although it sounds like maybe a lot were damaged so we'll also have to sort through them tomorrow."

"No problem. What time?"

"How about ten?" Lizzie could hear music playing in the background. It sounded like Wagner. Interesting.

"Fine. See you then."

She gave Mark a quick call before turning out the light. She told him what she'd discovered, or rather had not discovered, reading the book. Nothing. He sounded half asleep so she didn't prolong the conversation. Glancing at her bedside clock radio she realized why. It was after one A.M.

She'd meant to tell Teensy about finishing her book but maybe it was best not to mention that unless asked. She'd have to come up with a tactful way of complimenting Teensy. It really was quite the accomplishment, finishing writing the tome. It just . . . well, hopefully others would gush over it. Thank goodness for differences in reading tastes.

Chapter Fourteen

◇◇◇

There were far too many questions and not nearly enough time to find the answers.

CAKE ON A HOT TIN ROOF—JACKLYN BRADY

Lizzie pulled into the parking lot at Riverwell Press at ten on the nose the next morning. She had a brief flash of déjà vu and butterflies in her stomach, which eased when she noticed another car parked in the lot, a silver Lincoln. Teensy's shiny yellow Cadillac pulled up next to her. They waved at each other and got out of their cars.

"I'm so excited," Teensy said, her voice a higher pitch than normal. "The first time I get to see my printed book. It's like a dream."

Lizzie smiled. Teensy was acting like a teenager on her first date.

"Well, you'll be pleased to know I finished reading your book, Teensy, and I don't see how it's involved in any of this."

Teensy grabbed Lizzie in a bear hug then held her at

arm's length. "And, what did you think about it? Did you just love it? Go on now, sugar . . . you can tell me the truth."

As if. "It's all you said it would be, Teensy. A lively plot, great setting and lots of steamy romance."

Teensy hugged her again. "Oh, thank you so much, sugar. I'm just thrilled."

"By the way, how was the dinner with Mr. Mayor?" she asked as they fell in beside each other walking to the front door.

"He's a real charmer, he is. I can see how he made mayor. I'm sure he got the votes of all the women of Ashton Corners. Perhaps present company excluded since I wasn't around at the time. Although I'm certain I would have voted for him," she added. "He was a real gentleman, too, not talking so much about himself but asking a lot about me. In fact, we're going out again tonight."

"That's great, Teensy." They'd reached the front door. Teensy grabbed the handle and gave it a turn. Lizzie followed her inside.

A tall balding man with glasses riding low on his bulbous nose walked toward them, hand extended. "I'm Roger Emerson, Orwell Rivers's lawyer. I'm just here to assist you in looking through everything." His grip was surprisingly weak for someone with such a strong voice. Lizzie concentrated on his round face, complete with jowls. She thought he resembled Patchett and hid a smile.

"A pleasure, Mr. Emerson," Teensy said. "Don't you worry none, we're taking only what's already been paid for. Now, where are my books?"

Lizzie looked sharply at Teensy. Her tone had changed to total businesswoman with a tinge of snippiness, if Lizzie wasn't mistaken. Mr. Emerson had obviously rubbed her the wrong way. She confirmed it as they followed him into the back.

"He thinks we're going to try to run off with all the books, I'll bet," Teensy said in a loud whisper. "Did you see how his eyes narrowed and got all beady there? As if I need to steal my own books. The nerve."

"It's probably a good idea he's here, though. I'd hate to have something else go missing and we'd be accused. Not that it would. But you just never know," Lizzie offered.

Teensy harrumphed and made no further comment until they walked into the massive storage area.

Emerson came up behind them and said, "Those are the books that were salvaged." He pointed to metal shelving at the right. "Now, you need to sort through those and take what you want. I've already been through them and disposed of those in worst condition. I also did a tally for the DA."

Teensy didn't answer but walked right over to the shelves and started carefully checking books, placing them in the cardboard boxes that were positioned on the floor. Lizzie moved to the far end and started doing the same. Half an hour later, they met up in the middle. They'd managed to salvage half of the books from the original shipment then moved over to the section where the remaining books had been stored.

"The boxes say there are thirty books in each. Do we believe them?" Teensy asked, frowning as she pulled a box out from the bottom shelf and eased it onto the floor. She had flung her billowing lime green lightweight cotton scarf over her left shoulder. The sleeveless fuchsia caftan swirled around her ankles.

"Let's check one box and we'll assume the others are

correct. I guess we should take three of them even though that will bring us over the original total," Lizzie said, kneeling down and already slashing at the taped top with a box cutter. "We'll let Mr. Emerson know, of course." She pulled them out and handed them to Teensy, who piled them on the floor, both of them counting as they went along.

"That's thirty," Teensy said. "I guess we'll trust the others." She pulled two other boxes off the shelf and carried them over to the trolley they'd commandeered from the corner of the room. "I wonder how many more there are? I should just buy them all up and make sure they don't disappear or something. Who knows what's going to happen to this place now."

"We could count the boxes and then you'd know what amounts you're dealing with."

Teensy grunted as she stood up. "Good idea. It doesn't look like there's too many."

Teensy started pulling the boxes at the front of the three-tiered shelf off and onto the floor while Lizzie went around to the side to push some forward from the back. The open sides of the shelving made it easy to maneuver the boxes.

The last one she pushed forward was the same sized box but had a couple of red stripes along the edge of the box. The printing looked identical to the other boxes—the top line listed the quantity of books, the next line the title, the bottom line the price and the publisher information—except for two dollar signs that had been added with felt pen to the price of the books.

Lizzie allowed her curiosity to win out and slashed the top of the box open. "This is odd. Come take a look, Teensy."

"What's up, sugar?"

Lizzie put her hand in the box and lifted out a bundle

wrapped in newspaper. She carefully unwrapped it and gasped.

"Oh my Lord. Did we uncover some hidden treasure or something?" Teensy asked in awe.

Lizzie held the money for a minute, thinking before speaking. "Not a legal treasure. I think this is all counterfeit."

"Counterfeit? What makes you think so?"

"Firstly, it's an odd place to stash so many bills, all the same currency, or so it appears. Secondly, there have been some counterfeit twenties discovered in the last few days." She was reluctant to tell Teensy about the money being found on Cabe Wilson's body.

"I'd better call Mark." Lizzie put the money back in the box and pulled her cell phone out.

"What about Mr. Emerson?" Teensy asked.

"We'll let Mark explain it to him." She reached Mark on the second ring and explained what they'd found. After a couple of minutes, she hung up. "He's on his way. We're not to touch anything else until then."

"Oh my. What if they confiscate these books all over again?" Teensy was almost in tears.

Lizzie looked around quickly and pointed to the boxes on the trolley. "Let's get those stashed in the cars. We'll have to make two trips, I think. We'll say we found this box afterward, which we did."

Teensy nodded and they rushed the trolley to the door. "Will Mr. Emerson get upset about that?"

Lizzie stopped, her hand on the door handle. "Yikes. I hadn't thought about that. I guess we'd better let him see them first. Let's move them to the lobby anyway and leave them there. That way the police might want to look through them but shouldn't have to hang on to them. Why don't you go get Emerson from the office out back and I'll take these to the lobby?"

Teensy nodded and rushed off down the hall. Lizzie managed to work the trolley through the door and out to the waiting area. Teensy and Emerson arrived just as two police cars pulled into the parking lot.

"What do they want?" Emerson asked, sounding exasperated.

"I called them," Lizzie said. "I think the chief had better explain it to you."

Mark was first through the door. He nodded at Teensy and Lizzie. "Mr. Emerson. You're here also?"

"I was Orwell Rivers's lawyer, Chief. Just protecting the interests of his estate. These ladies were collecting Miz Coldicutt's books. I'm not quite sure what this is all about, though." He gestured at the three police officers who had crowded into the room.

Mark said, "I'll just have a talk with Ms. Turner back there in the warehouse and then I'll fill you in." He gestured to the door and Lizzie went in first.

She led the officers over to the shelves and pointed at the box. "We were trying to determine how many of Teensy's books were left once we'd taken the ones Molly had ordered. I noticed this box was marked a bit differently so I opened it. And that's what I found."

Mark reached in and pulled out the bundles of twenties. He then emptied the box. One of the other officers let out a low whistle.

"Are there any more boxes like that?" Mark asked.

"I haven't checked the rest of the back line yet."

Mark directed an officer to do so. They waited in silence

until he'd shoved the boxes around and pulled out two with identical markings. Lizzie handed him her box cutter and he sliced them open. All were filled with bundles of twenties.

"That makes about ninety thousand dollars," Mark said. "This isn't good." He looked around the room. There were three more sets of shelving. "You're sure the boxes you moved out to the waiting area are totally books?"

"We didn't check two of them but we will. They don't have the same markings as these. The rest are from those that were recovered."

"Yost. Vicker. I want you two to search all those boxes along that wall. Make sure we've found all the money." He looked at Lizzie. "Let's go tell Emerson. I'm sure it won't make his day."

Lizzie was almost afraid to voice her concerns. "Do you think these are tied in to the money found on the body at Bob's?"

"Lizzie, I just don't know. I'll head on over to see him when I've finished here. What are you going to do with those books?"

"We're taking them over to store at Molly's. Do you think that's safe? Was it the money the guys who attacked Molly were looking for?"

"It could very well be. They may have gotten it when they killed Rivers. I don't know if they know some is still here but I've had officers posted since the murder so they wouldn't have gotten in. I'll let it be known that some money was found and is in my custody. That should ensure Molly's safety."

Chapter Fifteen

◇◇◇

The tension in Iris' chest built up unbearably. By rights, the hooks on her bra ought to snap.

DOG EAT DOG—MARY COLLINS

"Bob would in no way be involved with anything illegal, especially counterfeit money," Molly declared as she helped shove the final box into place in her garage. She leaned over, stretching her side, then did the same with the other.

Teensy threw up her hands in the air. "I'm just telling you what we found and what I heard, Mopsy."

Lizzie's glare was lost on Teensy. She might be Molly's long, dear, lost friend but Lizzie was steaming that Teensy had dared to pass along what she'd obviously overheard of Lizzie and Mark's conversation. Sometimes that woman just didn't have a clue.

"You're absolutely right, Molly," Lizzie said soothingly. "Bob is one of the most honest people I know. He would not get involved in any illegal activity."

"I like Bob as much as the next person," Teensy said, doing a discreet minor adjustment to her bra strap, "but that body was found at his place, as was some counterfeit money. Don't they always say 'follow the money' on those TV crime shows?"

Molly turned to Teensy and put her hands on her hips. "Teensy, I will not allow anything disparaging to be said or even thought about Bob in my presence. Got that?"

Teensy looked shocked. "Got it, Mopsy. She winked at Lizzie. "And I get it." Fortunately, Molly missed seeing the wink. "Now, what should we do next?"

Molly shooed them out of the garage, closed the door and locked it. "I am going over to Bob's house just to check on things. Maybe we can get together tomorrow and finalize the launch plans."

Teensy nodded. "That's all right by me. I think I'll just stop by Willetta's and see if I can get a manicure." She hugged them both and got in her car.

As soon as Teensy had driven off, Molly walked briskly to the house. "I'll go with you, Molly," Lizzie offered.

"It's not necessary, you know. I am fine and can drive myself."

"Yes to all the above. But I'm still going." Lizzie planted her feet and stood still.

Molly looked back at her before opening the back door. "All right. I'll just lock up and grab my purse. But you'll have to drive if you insist on coming."

Lizzie smiled to herself and slid into the driver's seat of her Mazda 3. She breathed a sigh of relief when she saw Molly, in complete control of her emotions, march out to the car and get into the passenger side.

They made the drive in silence. Lizzie parked on the verge of the road since a police cruiser took up the space in the driveway. Another one was parked farther along the road. She followed Molly up to the front door. Molly knocked and opened the door without waiting to be asked to enter. Lizzie stuck close to her.

"We're here to see Bob," Molly announced.

Officer Amber Craig stood up abruptly from where she'd been crouched in front of the TV stand. "Miz Mathews, I'm sorry, I'll have to ask you to leave. We are conducting a search of the premises."

Lizzie could see a second officer going through cupboards in the kitchen and she heard noises from down the hall. Craig nodded at Lizzie, a pleading look in her eyes.

Lizzie jumped in before Molly could answer. "Perhaps we could just wait out on the back porch?"

Molly shot Lizzie a piercing look that made her want to retract what she'd just said. Bob stayed put, leaning against the doorframe to the kitchen, a pinched look on his face. He hadn't said a word since they'd arrived.

Craig answered, "That would be fine."

Lizzie took hold of Molly's arm and led her out the door and around to the back. There were two Adirondack chairs, hunter green and chipped, placed so that the evening sunset would frame the river.

Molly chose the chair closest to the kitchen door. "I'm not happy having to wait out here, Lizzie. We should be in there adding moral support. And what does she mean, searching? What on earth could they be looking for? Bob's not a criminal."

Lizzie shook her head. "Molly, I know you're concerned but there's nothing we can do at the moment."

"I guess you're right. We'll sit and wait. They'll discover soon enough they've made a mistake."

I sure hope so. Lizzie kept her thoughts to herself and tried to enjoy the view. The Tallapoosa River looked to be under the spell of the heat and just lazed its way along. A slight shimmer skimmed the top of the water, if she looked at it the right way. The far shoreline didn't seem quite as vibrant a green today.

After about ten minutes Molly asked, "You don't think they're seriously considering Bob is involved in any of this?"

"I'm not sure who their other suspects are. If they don't have anyone else, they may be concentrating on him." It had to be said.

"Well, they should be out there searching for the real murderer. Bob wouldn't hurt a fly and there's no way he'd be involved in a counterfeit ring."

The door opened as she finished speaking and Bob joined them.

"Thanks for your support, Molly. And I swear to you both, I'm not involved. But it looks like the evidence is standing in line to convict me." He sat down on the top step and stared ahead. He ran a hand wearily through his thick gray hair and then adjusted the neckline of his camouflage-colored T-shirt.

"Well that's downright foolish," Molly said loudly. "What evidence? It seems circumstantial to me."

"Oh, Molly, honey, you only know the half of it," Bob answered, his voice a direct contrast to her volume.

"Like what, Bob?" Lizzie asked.

Bob turned sideways and leaned back against the railing. "For starters, there's the fact the body was found out here and I knew him."

"I didn't know that," Molly said. "Who was he?"

"An ex-con who'd been in and out of jail a lot over the

years I was police chief, and most of the times, I'd put him there. He was involved in mainly small-scale stuff. Some B and Es, fraud, shoplifting. Nothing violent. But I don't know what he was doing here. I hadn't seen the guy in several years."

"Maybe someone dumped the body, trying to frame you," Lizzie ventured.

"Could be. But then there's the counterfeit money. They found some twenties lying around the yard when they dealt with the body. And I hear there was lots more of that at Riverwell Press. Now they're inside with a search warrant looking to see if I have any stashed." Bob shook his head. "It's all got to be connected in some way. There are just too many things happening at once for any of them to be a coincidence."

"I did finish reading Teensy's book and I can't see how it could in any way be tied in to all that's happened," Lizzie offered.

Bob grunted but didn't comment.

"If they find any money, it could be planted," Lizzie persisted. "You don't even have a motive, after all."

"I think I'll just hire you as my lawyer," Bob said with a small smile. "If I am being framed, there'll be more bases covered, you can be sure of that." He shook his head.

"Well maybe you should just give Jacob a call right now and get him over here." Molly's spine stiffened as she said it.

"Trouble is, he's not a criminal lawyer, Molly. He has put me in touch with someone, though. Kenneth Stokes. I s'pose I should call him and let him know what's happening." He shook his head again. "Never thought I'd see the day. After all those years of keeping the peace and locking up the bad guys, here I am being treated as one."

He pushed himself up to standing and walked toward the back door when it opened. Officer Craig came out holding a bundle of twenty-dollar bills held together by a wide paper band. "Mr. Miller, you'll have to come down to the station with us, please. You have a lot more explaining to do."

Lizzie stood up. "Bob, do you want me to call your lawyer?"

Bob shook his head. "No, thanks. Looks like I'll be getting the opportunity to make that call myself." He planted a kiss on Molly's forehead as he walked past her.

Chapter Sixteen

◇◇◇

Life can be fortuitous, or it can smack you upside
the head with bad timing.

CLOBBERED BY CAMEMBERT—AVERY AAMES

Lizzie dropped Molly off at her house after extracting a
promise that she'd go and lie down for a while and had
to promise in return that she would try to find out what was
happening at the police station. Just how she would do that,
Lizzie wasn't quite sure. No way Mark would talk to her
about this right now. But she could give Jacob a call. Maybe
he'd have time to talk and, more importantly, some
information.

She did just that when she got home, catching Jacob as
he was about to leave for the station.

"All I'm asking, Jacob," Lizzie said, "is that you let me
know what's happening and when they let him go home."

"I'll try to remember, Lizzie, but I've got a lot to be on
top of right now. I've also got Lucille Miller calling me at
all hours. Don't you worry, though. I'll do my best for him."

Jacob rang off and Lizzie put the phone down in frustration. She wished she could actually do something to help.

She realized the most she could do at the moment was to give some thought to Teensy's book and all the promotion involved. She grabbed a pad and pen, poured herself an iced tea from the fridge and sat at the kitchen table, determined to make a list of who to notify. But first she started by writing out a short announcement to be read on *Noella at Noon*, the local midday program on cable TV.

She was still deep in thought when her phone rang an hour later.

"It's Jacob, Lizzie. I'm at the station and I've just spoken with Bob. It seems that when the police searched his place, they found several stacks of counterfeit twenties hidden in his bedroom."

"Hidden? How?"

"They were inside a plastic bag that was taped to the bottom of his bureau. Now, a few stray bills outside in his yard are one thing. This is a bit more damning, although they're not sure how to tie it all together as yet. I'm calling that criminal lawyer I mentioned because I think it's getting too hot for Bob. In fact, they've passed the information about the counterfeit bills over to the FBI."

"The FBI? That's scary. It's one thing to deal with the local police but this really changes things, doesn't it?" Lizzie leaned on her right elbow and cupped her forehead in her hand. This was not good.

"I'll say. And I'd also advise you not to do any snooping this time."

"Hmm. I hear you, Jacob. But we have to do something to help Bob. You know he's not guilty of anything criminal in nature."

Lizzie heard some muffled conversation, as if Jacob had his hand over the telephone receiver. After a couple of minutes, he was back on line. "Sorry about that. They're letting him go and I'm going to drive him home. That's about all the news there is at the moment."

"Thanks for calling, Jacob. Molly's been pretty anxious to hear what's going on. I'll give her a call now."

She paused a few minutes before phoning Molly to think about what she'd been told. What did it all mean? It started with the books being hijacked and Molly being attacked. Then Orwell Rivers's body turned up. Then another body, that of Cabe Wilson, a con man, was found at Bob's place along with some counterfeit money. Some books were found along with boxes of counterfeit money at Riverwell Press followed by more counterfeit bills, this time stashed in Bob's house. There had to be a connection between all the events. But what was Bob doing mixed in there?

She'd meant it when she'd told Jacob that Bob wouldn't do anything criminal. It went against everything he'd stood for all his life. It wasn't possible. So, someone had to be framing him. How obvious was that! Surely Mark had thought of that.

Mark wouldn't like her asking, but she had to make sure he was checking that angle, too. She dialed the police station instead of Molly and asked for Mark. After a few minutes on hold, he came on the line.

"Hey, Mark. I know you're really busy so I won't take a lot of time but I wanted to assure myself that you're seriously considering the fact that Bob Miller was probably framed."

"Hey, Lizzie. Nice to talk to you, too. And, it's none of your business. I think I asked you to stay out of this."

"I know, Mark. But I'm just asking, that's all."

She heard his deep sigh. "My theory is that Bob has been set up but that doesn't mean that I can lightly pass over all the evidence. He has to be treated like a proper suspect. And in fact, two FBI special agents from Birmingham will be arriving tomorrow to take over the counterfeit money investigation. Bob will have to put up with some fairly onerous questioning by them. But I wouldn't worry about him if I were you. He is an ex-cop and he does know how the process works, well enough to make it work for him." Mark chuckled and Lizzie smiled.

Of course, Bob would be able to handle it. "Okay. Thanks for telling me that. It puts my mind at ease and I know Molly will feel better, also. Will I be seeing you at some point tonight?"

"It's not likely. I already took a short break and ate a burrito while walking Patchett. In fact, I brought him back to the station with me. Figure he can sleep under my desk as good as sleeping at home. I'm going to try to get out of here at a reasonable time. I'll need my wits about me tomorrow when those agents roll into town. And I've got the mayor breathing down my neck on this one. He doesn't like the idea that the FBI will be 'meddling'—his words, not mine—in his town." He sighed again. "I'll talk to you sometime tomorrow."

"All right. Good night, Mark."

So it was true, the FBI was getting involved. She dialed Molly's number, dreading having to pass along the information.

The next morning, Lizzie felt in need of an extra-long run to rid herself of too many frustrating thoughts about all the mysterious goings-on. She couldn't shake the foreboding feeling that enveloped her whenever she thought about Bob and the money. And if she felt that way, she was certain Molly would be in stress-overload. After breakfast, she planned to visit Molly and try to help allay some of her fears.

She ran along Broward past the old Carnegie Library, across the town square, over to the bike path along Sawmill Creek, through the park and turned toward home. There was a warm breeze that helped keep her comfortable. She tried to focus on her surroundings and take a time-out from thinking about what was happening, but to little avail.

On her way back along Madison, she heard a car slow down behind her. When it pulled up even, she glanced over and was surprised to see Officer Amber Craig at the wheel of a police cruiser. The car stopped and Lizzie did the same. Craig got out and walked over, taking a look up and down the street as she did so.

"Good morning, Officer. Want to go for a run?" Lizzie asked, remembering the last time that had happened just before Christmas.

Craig grimaced. "I'd rather be running right now than working, that's for sure. I just wanted to give you a heads-up. I'm not too sure how much the chief has told you or is allowed to tell you, but two FBI special agents are coming into town this morning to question Bob Miller."

"I know that." Lizzie's anxiety level rose as she wondered why Craig would feel it necessary to tell her. Or warn her.

"I'm concerned that once they get their hands on this case, Bob Miller might be a bit out of his depth. I know he had an admirable record as police chief, but from what I've been hearing him say, he doesn't seem to be taking the fact that he's a prime suspect as seriously as he should be."

"You're starting to scare me. We all know Bob's not

capable of committing any crime. He's the most honest guy I know. Present chief excluded, of course. He wouldn't get mixed up in murder or counterfeiting. Why would he? He doesn't need the money. What's his motive?"

Craig leaned back against the side of the cruiser and smoothed back a few strands of her long blonde hair that had escaped the tight bun, the way she often wore it when on duty. "I shouldn't be telling you this and if you let it slip to the chief it could mean my job."

Lizzie nodded and chewed on her bottom lip. "I have several sources around town. He won't know."

Craig took a deep breath. "Well, his sister Lucille Miller is in desperate need of money to pay back a second mortgage she took out on her house. She could lose it if she doesn't come up with the money by the end of the year. And it seems she told the bank that her brother was helping her to pay it back."

"That could mean anything," Lizzie protested. "Bob wouldn't get involved in something illegal even if she did need some money. I'm certain of that."

"Maybe you are but the FBI will see it as motive. I hope he actually has some viable means of helping her. If so, he hasn't told us about it."

Lizzie sighed. What could that mean? What if Bob had told Lucille he'd help her but didn't have a clue as to how to go about it? "Well, I know Bob Miller and I still say he's not involved. But thanks for the information, Amber."

"Oh yes . . . and the chief said if I came across you 'sticking your nose into any of this'—his words not mine— then I should tell him, and tell you to butt out of it." She winked.

"Don't worry about it. I never would dream of getting

involved. I know not to get mixed up in police business."
Lizzie gave Craig's arm a squeeze, mouthed a "thanks" and
started out again at a slower pace. She felt hot, tired and
worried. Thank goodness, only three more blocks to go.

She thought about what she'd learned the rest of the way
and almost missed waving to Nathaniel Creely as he backed
out of his driveway. So, no invitation to a freshly baked
scone and coffee this morning. Not that she needed either.

The cats sat at their dishes when she walked into the
kitchen. She'd been in such a tizzy this morning, she'd forgotten to feed them. She felt dutifully guilty as she filled
one side of their dishes with a teaspoon of canned food and
the other side with dried chow. Both Edam and Brie scolded
her in their totally different pitched Siamese nattering until
she finally put their dishes on the floor. She watched as they
attacked their meals, then she ground some espresso beans
and brewed a cup. She drank it while she glanced through
the newspaper then took the stairs two at a time up to the
bathroom to get ready for the day.

Freshly showered, dressed and having finished a breakfast of scrambled eggs with red and green peppers, she
grabbed her handbag and headed to the back door only to
be halted by the ringing of the phone. A hyper Molly was
on the other end.

"Lizzie, I want you to get right over here to Bob's house.
Right away. Okay? Please, honey?" She ended on a desperate
note.

"I'm on my way, Molly." Lizzie didn't take time to ask
what was up. She had a feeling she knew what, or who, she'd
find when she arrived at Bob's. She made it there in less than
ten minutes.

A black Ford sedan took up the driveway while Molly's

Audi was parked on the verge of the road. Lizzie pulled in behind it and hurried to the front door.

Molly must have been watching for her. She yanked open the door before Lizzie could knock. "Oh, thank God you came so quickly," she whispered. In a louder voice she said, "Why, Lizzie Turner. You are right on time for our meeting with the former police chief." She emphasized the last words and Lizzie had to keep from smiling. She spotted two men beside Bob in the center of the living room.

Molly grabbed Lizzie's elbow and ushered her over to them. "This is Elizabeth Turner and these here are two gentlemen from the Federal Bureau of Investigation."

Lizzie looked at the man on Bob's right. Medium height, brown hair just inches above a buzz cut, black-rimmed glasses framing two cold blue eyes, and muscles straining to break through the poorly tailored black blazer. He nodded at her and said, "Special Agent Greyson Ormes." Lizzie nodded back, trying not to cringe.

The second man stepped in front of Bob and stuck out his hand. At about six-foot-five, his black wavy hair and light blue eyes made a nice contrast to his partner. He wore a beige suit with a striped blue shirt and navy tie. "Special Agent Drew Jackson, ma'am. Pleased to meet you."

His grip was firm and warm and a bit too long. Lizzie tried for an impassive look, although it was hard not to react to the gorgeous guy in front of her. She managed a nod.

Molly jumped right in. "These men are here to question Bob. Now, isn't that ridiculous?" She turned to them both. "Just what are y'all hoping to achieve by doing this?"

"Now, Molly," Bob said, pushing past Ormes and reaching for Molly's arm. "We all know there's been some counterfeit money found here and that's their job. They need to track down where it came from." He turned back to them. "The only thing is, I don't know, myself."

Lizzie cleared her throat. "You do know that we found a couple of boxes of counterfeit money at Riverwell Press the other morning?"

Ormes looked at her in interest. "That was you who found it?"

"Yes. Teensy Coldicutt, the author, and I."

Ormes asked, "What were you doing going through a crime scene anyway?"

"I'm sure the chief has already told you or will. We were picking up boxes of Miz Coldicutt's books for her book launch. We had the permission of the chief and of the DA to do so." She straightened her back and glared at him.

Agent Jackson stepped in. "We were told that. Can you describe for us exactly where you found the boxes?"

"They were at the very back of the metal shelving, the middle row, right behind about ten boxes of books. The packaging was the same except for the red stripes on the side of the boxes, and the two dollar signs that had been written in black marker."

"And you opened them." It sounded like an accusation coming out of Ormes's mouth.

Bob stepped toward Ormes but Jackson put a hand out to stop him. "Thank you, Ms. Turner. We will probably need to be talking to you again and to Miz Coldicutt. Now, if you and Miz Mathews don't mind, we'd like to speak to Mr. Miller in private. You'll have to leave." He smiled and it seemed nonthreatening to Lizzie. *But it could be deceiving.*

She looped her arm around Molly's waist and pulled her gently toward the door. "Fine. We'll leave."

Lizzie could feel the fury in Molly's body as she led her down the sidewalk. "They have to question him, Molly. It's their job. We'll just wait in the car until they're finished. They can't object to that."

"It's not only that, honey. That Special Agent Ormes is a nasty fellow. I would have liked to have smacked his face when he was speaking to you."

Lizzie chuckled. "Good way to get thrown in jail."

Molly harrumphed. "You're probably right. I know they have to do it, Lizzie, and I know that Bob knows how to handle them. And I know that he's innocent. It's just that it worries me so." She eased into the front seat as Lizzie held the car door open for her.

Lizzie slid in behind the steering wheel. "Don't worry. We'll figure out some way to help him."

Molly reached out and squeezed Lizzie's hand. "I think I'll also have to keep an eye out for you, too. The way that Special Agent Jackson looked at you, he sure is sizing you up and not for handcuffs."

Chapter Seventeen

◇◇◇

Best to keep quiet about it and just hope that he never found out what they were up to, or the sparks would fly for sure.

MIND OVER MURDER—ALLISON KINGSLEY

Bob appeared at his front door as the two special agents drove off. Lizzie and Molly were halfway up the driveway when he joined them.

"Never did like working with the feds," he grumbled as he motioned them to the back.

The women chose to sit in the Adirondack chairs while Bob settled himself on the top step. His light green checked sports shirt was open at the neckline and tucked into his usual jeans. His feet were bare and his gray hair stuck out at angles, as if he'd just gotten out of bed. Lizzie felt a jolt of shock to see how much more the fatigue lines aged him. He must have felt her eyes on him because he quickly smoothed his hair into place.

Molly leaned forward from the bench. "I don't like the

Ormes fellow. I think he'd be very happy to cause you some trouble, Bob."

"Now, don't you go worrying none. I can take care of myself. And besides, I've got nothing to hide. I didn't have a thing to do with that counterfeit money and that's a fact."

"I know you didn't." Molly reached over and put a hand on Bob's shoulder. "But innocent people are always finding themselves behind bars. There must be something you can do. Or Lizzie and me. What can we do?"

"You'd best stay out of this one, Molly. You, too, Lizzie. I expect Mark's told you that already and I'm adding my warning to his. There's too many bodies right now and what with that counterfeit money, this isn't some small-time crook we're dealing with."

"I hear what you're saying, Bob. But there must be something we can do. I'll bet they've tapped your phone and your computer, if that's possible. That's what happens in the movies. Can I look something up for you on the Internet? Try to track down somebody or something? You must have some idea about who's behind this."

Bob chuckled. "You've been reading too many mysteries, Lizzie. I don't have any ideas about any of this, except that Cabe Wilson is dead. His body being found out here may be a warning to me, but for the life of me, I can't figure out why. I'm not a threat to anyone these days."

"But maybe someone thinks you know something that's tied in to Orwell Rivers's death and the counterfeiting and that it's just a matter of time before you realize what that is. They or he wants to stop you before that happens."

Bob cocked his head to one side. "All right, I'll allow you that but it still doesn't get us anywhere. My brain's not clicking on anything as yet."

Molly gave Lizzie a desperate look. Lizzie stood up and started pacing.

"Tell me about Cabe Wilson."

"Why? What do you have in mind?" Bob asked, looking suspicious.

"Maybe I can track down some information about him on the Internet, something that might make sense or suggest something to you."

Bob took a minute to think it over. He nodded. "Okay. I'll tell you as long as you promise to limit your inquiries to your computer, young lady. I know what kind of trouble you can get yourself into."

Lizzie leaned against the porch railing, her left hand in the pocket of her green cargo pants, fingers crossed. "Of course."

Bob grimaced. "I hope I don't regret this. Well, Cabe Wilson started his thieving when he was in his teens. Mostly petty stuff, lawn furniture that he'd then drive over to Holston County and sell from the back of his daddy's pickup truck. He was actually pretty inventive. Then he worked his way up to housebreaking, mostly electronics. Radios, TVs, cameras, items he could handle on his own."

"He doesn't sound like a mastermind of anything."

"Hardly. Although he was smart when it came to finding an angle. Last time I picked him up, he'd broken into the bank one night when workmen were in there doing repairs. No alarm to trip him up. Pretty smart, actually. He tried to get into the vault. His plans were to empty the safety-deposit boxes. But he couldn't find the right key to get him through the gate. So, he stole three small file drawers of customers' information. Thing was, the bank's surveillance cameras were still active. We caught him on tape and found the files in the basement at his mama's house."

Lizzie was intrigued. "What was he planning to do with the files?"

Bob shrugged. "I don't know if he'd rightly worked that out yet. He did say he was checking them for names of folks who lived in ritzy areas. What that would have gotten him, I don't know. All he'd have to do is drive through Remington Heights with a phone book beside him. Fortunately for the rich citizens of Ashton Corners, I don't think he had a plan of any value. And of course, we did catch him and lock him up."

Molly had been listening to all this. She asked, "Does this mean anything to you, Bob? Is there a reason in all that for him being at your place? Was he trying to implicate you in the money?"

Bob shook his head. "Not sure why he'd do that, Molly. None of this makes much sense to me."

"Was he married?" Lizzie asked.

"Not the last I saw him. He lived with his mama over on Tallapoosa. Her name was Clementine, as I recall. I believe she died a couple of years back. If he'd stayed out of jail, the house was probably now his home." Bob narrowed his eyes. "I'm certain Mark would know all this, Lizzie, and has searched his house, if that's what you're thinking."

Lizzie just nodded. What could it hurt to search it again? She made sure to keep her actions slow with no sign of anticipation so that Bob wouldn't quiz her on her intentions. She didn't want to get bogged down trying to convince Bob that she needed to do this.

"I think I'd better get a move on. I have a few errands to do this afternoon. Unless I can be of help here?"

Bob raised his eyebrows but shook his head. Molly, almost as if she were reading Lizzie's mind, gave her a sly wink and said, "Why don't you go on ahead. I think I'll stay a bit. That is, if Bob offers me some lunch later."

"Of course. My pleasure," Bob said, with much pleasure in his voice.

Lizzie waved good-bye and strolled out to her car. Her plan was to go home, search the Internet for anything on Wilson, check the phone listings for his house, then take a drive over.

After an hour of what Lizzie considered to be wasted time, it appeared that Cabe Wilson wasn't very noteworthy, at least on the Internet. No hits except for newspaper accounts of his various jail sentences and his murder, of course. She did manage to find a listing for his mother's house, still in her name. Lizzie checked Google directions, grabbed her handbag and drove over to the place.

There was no sign of police tape or anything that might keep her out. She had worried about that all the way over. However, she didn't want to be caught for breaking and entering. She parked on the street and walked with assurance up to the front door, just in case any neighbors were watching.

The front walkway needed repair and the shrubs lining the front porch had intermingled so badly it was hard to tell what each plant was. The dark blue paint job appeared new, as did the white trim around the windows and door.

She tried ringing the doorbell and knocking. When after a couple of minutes there was no response, she jiggled the handle but the door was securely locked. The living room window had a tall, narrow side window on either side of it. She checked but they also looked closed tightly. Maybe she'd have better luck in the back.

Again, walking as if she were on legitimate business, she

went along the driveway of cracked asphalt to the back chain-link fence. She closed the gate behind her and moved around a huge cedar bush to the back steps.

"Can I help you?"

Lizzie stopped in her tracks and looked at the woman sitting on a lounge chair on the small porch. She looked to be in her late forties, maybe even older. Stringy shoulder-length blonde hair that badly needed both a trim and a dye job was pushed off her face and held back with rhinestone clips. Brown-framed glasses did little to cover the dark circles under her eyes. Her cheeks were pink and puffy, and fuchsia gloss drew attention to pouty lips. She had on a sleeveless pink T-shirt that hugged a well-formed chest and faded cutoff shorts. Jeweled flip-flops dangled from her toes.

"Uh, my name is Lizzie Turner," she said, trying to come up with a good line. *I was looking for a way to search your house?* "Is this the house of Cabe Wilson?"

The woman looked suddenly stricken. "What do you want? Are you some sort of vulture? Trying to steal something or maybe get a house listing or something? He's dead, you know." She started sobbing.

Lizzie hurried to the top of the stairs. "I'm sorry. I didn't mean to upset you. I'm just looking for some information hopefully, something that will help find who was responsible for his death."

The woman drew in a deep breath and wiped her eyes. "You a cop or something?"

"No. But I am a friend of former police chief Bob Miller."

"Him. It's because of him that my Cabey is dead."

"I don't think so. Bob wouldn't hurt anyone."

The woman stared at her a minute. "I don't know about

that. But Cabey was on his way to talk to Chief Miller and that's the last I saw him."

"Do you live with him?"

The woman nodded. "I'm his fiancée."

"Did he tell you why he was going to Bob's house?"

She shrugged. "I know he was mixed up in something, even though he'd promised me he was going straight. I had told him, when you're straight, we'll get married. Anyway, he said that Chief Miller could help him get out of a bad situation. He'd know what to do." She started sobbing again. "And what did it get him but killed?"

"I'm so sorry." Lizzie gave her a moment to compose herself. "What is your name?"

"It's Urliss Langdorf. Cabe used to call me his baby-lips." That started more tears.

"Can I make you some tea or something?" Lizzie asked.

"Huh? No. Nothing will help."

"Do you know what Mr. Wilson was mixed up in?"

Urliss bit her bottom lip. "He wouldn't tell me. In fact he kept denying it but I heard him talking on the phone that last night, real hushed-like. He said something about wanting out."

Lizzie gave that some thought. "Did you tell the police about this?"

"Not about the phone call. They didn't ask. They just wanted to know if I knew why Cabe went to see Miller. I said I didn't know." She wouldn't look at Lizzie. "I didn't really know any of the details."

Bad move, Lizzie thought. It might help Bob's case if the police knew he was being asked for help. On the other hand, she didn't really want the police, namely Mark, to know she'd been here.

"I think you should tell the police about this but I'd really appreciate it if you didn't mention my visit here today to the police. Unless they come right out and ask you, of course. I wouldn't expect you to lie to them."

Urliss sniffed. "No problem."

"Is there anything I can do for you?"

She shook her head then reconsidered. "Well, you could find Cabe's murderer. That's what you said you were doing, right?"

Uh-oh. "I'll do what I can. I'd better get going." Lizzie touched her arm briefly. "I'm so sorry for your loss."

She walked away feeling lousy at not being able to offer any comfort but pleased that she knew Wilson had been going to Bob for help. Surely that cleared Bob of any wrongdoing. But the question was, how to tell Mark without letting him know how she knew, just in case Urliss didn't.

She unlocked her car door and slid in behind the wheel just as a big black Ford sedan pulled up to the curb. She cringed and wondered if it was too late to duck. Both special agents got out of the car and focused on her. Too late.

They walked over to her driver's window, which was open. "Ms. Turner," Ormes growled, "just what do you think you're doing here? You'd better not be interfering in a police investigation."

"I was just scoping out the neighborhood, looking for a new route for my run in the morning." She tried for an innocent smile.

Ormes scowled.

Jackson tried to hide a grin. "Hope you found what you were looking for."

He pulled Ormes toward the curb and they walked up the driveway Lizzie had just pulled out of. She breathed a sigh of relief and gunned it out of there.

Chapter Eighteen

◇◇◇

Maggie sighed. "There's only one thing I can do, find the real killer."

50% OFF MURDER—JOSIE BELLE

Lizzie had barely gotten the dinner dishes washed and put away when the phone rang. She saw Stephanie's name listed and immediately hoped the baby was okay.

"I'm sorry to bother you, Lizzie." Stephanie paused so long Lizzie wondered if she should have said more than it was fine.

"I'm not sure but I think someone's following me."

"What makes you think that?" Lizzie turned off the radio and sat down.

"It could just be my imagination. I don't really know for sure."

"Tell me all that's happened," Lizzie coaxed.

She heard Stephanie take a deep breath. "Well, I'm doing a month of noon to seven P.M. shifts at the Oasis Diner. I sort of like them because I have all morning with Wendy and I'm there to put her to bed at night, although I sure do miss her in the afternoon." She sighed. "I knew this wasn't going to be easy but it breaks my heart to leave for work. But it has to be done. I need to earn a living."

Lizzie heard the resolve in her voice. "Go on."

"Well the last couple of Monday nights there's been this old black pickup truck parked outside the diner. The first time it happened, the truck followed me when I walked home. It didn't come up close, just stayed back, real creepy-like. When I looked out the window, it was parked across the street. Last night, he was there again only he didn't follow me this time. But he was parked outside my apartment building when I looked outside a little later."

"Are you sure it's the same truck? There must be a lot of those around."

"I know, that's what I keep saying to myself. But I can see the outline of someone sitting in it whenever a car passes by. He stays inside it until I turn out my lights. Then he leaves. I'll tell you, it's really creeping me out."

Lizzie thought for a moment. Two times did not a stalker make. On the other hand, maybe it did. What did she know about that psyche?

"Do you have any ideas who it might be? Maybe baby Wendy's father?"

Stephanie drew in her breath sharply. "I had wondered. It's something he could pull but I'm certain he'd make sure I knew it was him. He'd have the power then."

"Hmmm," Lizzie said. Not very helpful, but she couldn't think of anything else.

"How about calling the police?"

"Oh, I couldn't do that. What if it is Wendy's daddy? I couldn't have her grow up knowing I'd called the police on him."

Why not? Especially if he's done something wrong. "Well how about if I mention it to Mark on an unofficial basis?"

"I don't think so, Lizzie. Thank you anyway. He'd then feel obligated to do something, I'm certain. Maybe it's just my imagination. I read an awful lot of mysteries, after all." She ended in a small laugh that turned into a whimper.

"Okay then, how about if I park in front of your apartment building next Monday night for when you get off work? I'll see if he shows up and we'll try to figure out who it is, maybe confront him?"

"I don't know about confronting him but I'd surely be grateful if you'd be there. Maybe you could just get his license number or something?"

Lizzie stood and walked over to where Edam sat staring at his empty food dish. She pulled a few dried treats out of the cupboard and he dug in.

"That's a good idea," she said, wanting to put Stephanie's mind at ease. "I'll be there for sure. Now, you try not to worry about it anymore, you hear?"

"Thank you, Lizzie. I'm feeling better already."

The next morning, Lizzie had just made it to the end of her street when another runner overtook her. She stopped in astonishment as Drew Jackson started pacing her.

"What are you doing here?" she asked.

"I'm a runner, myself. I was hoping you could show me some good routes, maybe over toward Tallapoosa Street." He grinned and started running at a faster pace, looking back at her until she caught up.

"Not this morning. I'm heading into town."

"Oh. Tallapoosa didn't prove to be a good choice?"

"You could say that," she hedged.

"Oh, there's a lot I could say about that. How about we get a good workout first?" He took off in the direction she'd been going, ramping up his speed. It took her until the end of the block to catch up to him and pass him by, although he looked like he hadn't even built up a sweat. His long legs carried him easily in a loping stride and the black stretch bike shorts showed off his muscular build.

She continued on her own route, not bothering to check if he was still with her when he fell back several times. By the time she'd finished the circuit and arrived home again, Jackson was by her side. She almost stopped in her tracks at the sight of Mark's Jeep parked in her driveway but Mark had already opened her front door and stood out on the porch.

"Hey, Lizzie. Special Agent Jackson," he said, his voice not giving away anything.

Lizzie could tell he wasn't thrilled seeing Jackson at her side. *Jealous?* The thought, brief as it was, pleased her, although she'd not really thought of Jackson as romantic material.

"Chief," Jackson acknowledged. "I was interested in Ms. Turner's running habits." He stopped at the bottom stair and did a hamstring stretch. "Especially seeing as yesterday she told me the reason she was at Cabe Wilson's house was to scope out a new running route."

Mark looked at Lizzie, who'd stopped just inches from him. He looked even less pleased than a few moments before.

"Would either of you officers like some coffee?" Lizzie asked as she continued into the house, leaving the door open behind her.

Mark was at her heels.

Jackson followed. "Some java would be great."

Mark spoke as she made the preparations. "Just what were you doing at Wilson's, Lizzie? I thought I'd told you to stay out of this case."

Lizzie knew she couldn't talk her way out of this one. "I got the distinct impression yesterday, after talking to the two special agents"—she paused and looked directly at Jackson—"that Bob might just stay in the prime suspect position. They seemed unwilling to hear any other explanations."

"And you thought you were the only one who would work at clearing Bob?" Mark asked.

Lizzie felt her cheeks glow hot. "Perhaps not, but you do have two murders on your plate."

"And a fully competent police department." He accepted the mug of coffee she handed over and sighed. "Lizzie, it's dangerous. As you said, there have been two murders. Just keep out of it, okay?"

Jackson came to her rescue. "Perhaps she could be of some help, Chief. Maybe we could use her as bait."

Lizzie tried not to sound as shocked as she felt. "Bait? Thanks a lot."

Jackson grinned. Lizzie caught on. He'd been teasing her. Mark caught on also.

"I don't have time to debate this any further, Lizzie. I have to meet with the mayor and give him an update." Mark finished his coffee and then leaned toward her and gave her a healthy kiss.

Lizzie's heart skipped a beat even though she knew the kiss was partially for Jackson's benefit. Mark was definitely alert if not full-out jealous.

"Can I give you a lift?" Mark asked Jackson.

"No, thanks. My car's parked around the corner." Lizzie raised her eyebrows. "I didn't want to spook Ms. Turner until I saw which direction she was headed."

"I'll walk you out, then," Mark said.

Jackson looked questioningly at him, then finished his coffee and thanked Lizzie before following Mark out the door.

Lizzie sat down to finish her mug. What had just gone on here between the two of them? Well, she was pretty sure Mark was showing that jealous streak again. Like last fall when Derek Alton had been shot in her living room. She had gone out to dinner with him and had been hanging mistletoe when he'd been shot at her house, and Mark had been none too pleased.

She really didn't think that Mark was the possessive, jealous type. She certainly hoped not. He definitely had nothing to worry about, especially where Jackson was concerned. And even though it had been Jackson who outed her on the Wilson visit, his presence had also spared her a much lengthier blast about keeping out of the investigation.

She finished the dregs of her coffee and jogged upstairs to shower and get dressed. The cats sat on the bed watching while she chose a short cotton cream-colored skirt and topped it off with a mossy green sleeveless cotton blouse. She pulled her hair back in a ponytail and added pewter hoop earrings.

"There," she told her image in the mirror and the cats, "I'm ready to do a little sleuthing. But don't tell Mark." She gave Edam a long, slow stroke along his back, and Brie a scratching behind the ears.

She also had some book signings to line up and thought she'd arrange them in person. *Should we really be going ahead with all this?* She gave her head a shake, trying to dispel the unease. *Treat them just like the launch. Set them up and cancel if necessary.* Besides, it would give her a chance to ask around about Riverwell Press. As the one and only publisher in town, Orwell Rivers must have had some contact with the outlets that sold his books. Perhaps someone knew something about his other business dealings. It was all she could think of at this point. Follow the books.

First on her list was the Winn-Dixie at the corner of Broward and Decker, just around the corner from where the Book Bin had been. Actually, the bookstore still sat there, books on shelves, but doors locked and windows papered over. She wondered what would become of it.

Lizzie asked to talk to the manager, and after a short wait, a slightly less glamorous version of Dolly Parton appeared. "I'm Eugenia Killick, the manager. You wanted to see me?" she asked, holding out her hand.

Lizzie shook it, introduced herself and got right down to business. "I'm a member of the Ashton Corners Mystery Readers and Cheese Straws Society. And we'd be so pleased if you would consider hosting a book signing for a local author, Theodora Coldicutt."

"Teensy? You've gotta be kidding, girl." Eugenia's face lit up and she started laughing. "You mean Teensy Perkins Coldicutt has actually gone and written a book? I'll bet it's a hot romance. I'd heard she'd moved back to town. Wow, imagine that. Of course I'll hold a signing here. Where can I get hold of the book? It'll be a blast."

Lizzie felt swept up by the enthusiasm. "That's great, Miz Killick."

"Oh, for heaven's sakes, girl, call me Eugenia. Now, when do you want to have this event?" She turned and looked around the store. "And where should we have it? I've never had something like this in the store before but I've done lots of demonstrations . . . Resolve, frozen tacos, and the like. You tell me what I need to do."

"Can we set a date first?"

"Sure can, girl. Come right with me back to my office. I'll grab my calendar. I think this should be good for sales in the store, too. Teensy Coldicutt. I can't get over it."

They agreed to hold the signing on the Saturday following the launch, late morning as that was often the busiest time of the day at the store. After a walk around the store, they both agreed that placing Teensy at a table to the right of the entry doorway would work best. The display case at that location could be easily moved.

"And I'll be most pleased to provide a cake and cold drinks for our patrons, at no charge. Make it like a party." She clapped her hands like a little girl and her bleached blonde curls jumped in time. "Now, can you give me the details of how to order the book?" She led the way back to her office.

"Molly Mathews has the books stored at her place," Lizzie explained. "They were published by Riverwell Press, you know."

"Oh my Lordy, that poor Orwell Rivers. Who would have gone and done something like that to such a quiet, retiring fellow? There's no way he could have made any enemies."

"How well did you know him?" Lizzie asked, pleased at the opening.

"I've known him all my life but not really well. You know how it is around here." She straightened the hem of the pale blue cotton vest she wore over a formfitting short-sleeved black T-shirt.

"Did you know or hear anything about his business?"

She chewed the bottom inside of her mouth while she gave it some thought. "Now, I can't really say because I didn't hear it direct from Orwell but there was talk that he had some financial problems a few years back. I know there was worry because him being the only printer around hereabouts, some of the smaller businesses would have to figure out something else for their sales flyers and such. But that all blew over in a few months so I guess there wasn't much to it to begin with. You know how rumors are and all that."

Lizzie nodded. Oh yeah . . . she knew. "Well, thanks so much, Miz Killick. I mean Eugenia. I'll get back to you a couple of days before the signing, just to confirm."

Lizzie felt buoyed by her first success into the promotional world as she drove over to the Piggly Wiggly on Ulysses to line up another signing. The manager, Vernon Unger, was less excited but willing to hold a signing in his store. They settled on the Saturday afternoon a week later than the Winn-Dixie signing.

"Mr. Unger, did you know Orwell Rivers at Riverwell Press?" Lizzie finally asked.

"Yup, yup. We were brothers in the Knights of Columbus, you know." His blue striped bow tie bobbed along with his Adam's apple as he talked. Straight black hair parted on the left side and tucked back behind his ears ended just below them. *Rather lengthy for someone obviously no longer young*, Lizzie thought. His generous mouth looked like it smiled a lot. although his eyes lacked the same warmth. "Can't believe what happened to him. He wouldn't hurt a fly. He didn't even see any action in Nam because of his bum knee so he went upstate and worked in a steel mill that made military supplies. Is he the one who published Miz Coldicutt's book?"

"Yes, he was. I understand he'd had some hard times at the business so it's lucky she was able to get it published there."

"Hard times. Yup, yup." He shook his head, in agreement and distress. "Orwell didn't have much of a business sense but just enough to keep that place ticking by. In fact, I think that he started the publishing end of the business just in time to keep his place afloat. You know how it works, don't you? The writer pays half the costs up front. They split the royalties fifty-fifty is what I think he said. Anyways, it's probably what saved the place." He shook his head again. "Shame about what happened to him."

Lizzie agreed and then set off to the next stop on her list, the main branch of the Ashton Corners Public Library. Tradition had held out and the library was still housed in the original Carnegie Library building, built in the late 1800s opposite the town square.

Lizzie had loved reading for as long as she could remember and would often spend all Saturday afternoon tucked away in a corner of the children's section on an overstuffed chair, rereading *Charlotte's Web* or *Anne of Green Gables*. Those were the times when her mama was seen to by her friends, some of them cleaning the house, another doing the ironing, a couple of them caring for Lizzie's needs like mending her clothes or giving her room a thorough washing down. Then they'd all have tea and sweets together, just like old times, before her mama had become sick. Lizzie loved being a part of the ritual at first but then realized this was a good time to be on her own, doing what she wanted. And what she most wanted those days was to read.

Her good friend Paige would often go with her and they'd read aloud in exaggerated whispers parts of the books they'd chosen. Too often that resulted in giggles that ramped up into laughter and got them stern looks from the librarians.

All those memories flooded through Lizzie's brain as she set foot through the main door. The library was surprisingly full for a Wednesday, but that might have been because of the air-conditioning. The goose bumps on Lizzie's arms attested to it working quite well. She realized immediately that the sound level reflected the number of users. Gone were the days of whispers and moving about stealthily. Fortunately. She walked across the tiled floor to the far corner where a small office had the only closed door in the place and was labeled "Librarian." Lizzie knocked and was asked to enter.

Isabel Fox, the chief librarian who had started her job the day Lizzie started high school, looked up from her desk and smiled. Lizzie had had many dealings with Ms. Fox over the years as she relied on the public library for numerous books the school board couldn't manage with its limited budget. They'd also spent many hours brainstorming ideas on how to get children more interested in reading.

"How wonderful to see you, Lizzie. Would you like a glass of sweet tea?" Fox asked, getting up from her desk and walking over to the nearby countertop with a tray with a pitcher and glasses sitting on it.

"I'd love that. I hadn't realized how sticky it was getting outside until I stepped into the library."

Fox laughed. "I know. It's always a shock at the end of the day when I leave this cooled bubble. Now, what brings you here? Are you into work plans already?"

Lizzie shook her head. "Not as much as I should be. Any

day now. I've got another role this summer. I'm helping a local resident, Teensy Coldicutt, to publicize her new book. Have you heard of her?"

Fox sat back in her chair and considered for a moment before answering. "No, I'm sure I haven't. Would I have met her at something or other?"

"Probably not. She just moved back to Ashton Corners at the beginning of summer after living away for decades. But her book is published by Riverwell Press."

Fox pushed back a stray piece of hair from her face. She still wore her hair in the same style Lizzie remembered, pulled back and wound into a chignon, although it was now gray. She couldn't weigh more than the 120 pounds Lizzie did. And as usual, she wore a dress, this one a floral pink cotton sundress with a white knit cardigan, and white sandals. "Oh, that was such a sad thing about Mr. Rivers. Did they find out who murdered him?"

"Not yet. It was an awful thing to happen here in town. But on the upside, we were able to get hold of copies of Teensy's book and Molly Mathews is determined to get them all sold."

Fox laughed. "I'll just bet she succeeds. What can I do to help?"

"I was hoping you'd ask. How about hosting a reading one evening?"

"Certainly. I'd be really pleased to do that. I think that's an important mandate for any library, to highlight local talent. I think September would be a better time to hold an event than summer, though. How about I email some suggested dates, once I've checked our calendar, and you can let me know what suits best?"

"That sounds excellent."

"Do you think Miz Mathews would sell me some copies for the library?"

Lizzie smiled. "She'd sell you a whole box full if she could. But, would we be able to sell copies of the book at the reading?"

"Sure, I don't see why not. You'll have to handle it totally, though."

"Not a problem."

"What's the title and plot?" Fox took a drink of her tea and leaned back in her chair.

"*The Winds of Desire* and to hear Teensy, I mean Theodora, describe it, it's a contemporary *Gone with the Wind*." She left it at that.

"Aah. I hope she does well with it."

Lizzie finished her tea and stood to go. "I won't take up any more of your time right now. I'll ask Molly to call you and settle the details about the library's copies, shall I?"

"Please do. Will you have a poster or something I can put up on display?"

"For sure. I'll drop it off as soon as it's ready. Thanks again."

Lizzie left feeling pretty pleased with herself. Three for three. Maybe she should consider doing this as a part-time job all year round. Although, it wouldn't take that long for all the venues in Ashton Corners to be exhausted.

Next on her agenda, returning home and getting the guest room ready for Andie to move in to later in the evening, and possibly time to worry about Bob and the counterfeit connection.

The doorbell rang at exactly eight. Andie stood there, weighed down with two backpacks, her laptop in a carry bag, and a small cage with a gerbil in it.

"Uh, hey, Lizzie. Is now okay?"

Lizzie was eyeing the gerbil cage and nodded. "I really could have picked you up, you know."

"Uh, yeah, no problem. My daddy actually dropped me off."

Lizzie looked toward the driveway. He hadn't bothered to stay or come say hi. She tried not to let her face show what she was thinking.

"Let me take some things from you," she said instead.

Andie passed over her laptop and held the cage out a ways. "Uh, I sort of forgot to mention Bieber. He's a gerbil and he's real quiet-like. I'll just keep him in my room with me. You won't even know he's here."

Lizzie grimaced. "You'd better make sure you keep the door closed at all times. I think my cats would be really interested in him. Come on upstairs and we'll get you settled."

Lizzie left Andie to sort out her things and went to fix them each a glass of tea. When Andie joined her about ten minutes later, she held out her glass to toast. "Here's to a comfortable stay."

Andie grinned. "It will be fun. You'll see."

The grin was infectious. Lizzie returned it and crossed her fingers.

Chapter Nineteen

◇◇◇

"Police work wouldn't be possible without coffee," Wallander said. "No work would be possible without coffee."

ONE STEP BEHIND—HENNING MANKELL

Lizzie eyed the ringing telephone on the table beside her bed with alarm. Still groggy, she tried not to jump to the conclusion it was bad news about her mama. The cats leapt out of bed as she rolled over to snatch the receiver.

"Lizzie, I'm so sorry if I woke you, honey." Molly's worried tone got Lizzie's full attention. She glanced at the clock radio at the same moment the radio burst into song. "Spring" from Vivaldi's *Four Seasons*, if she wasn't mistaken.

"No, it's all right, Molly. This is about the time I usually get up. What's wrong?"

"Nothing, everything . . . oh, I'm just being silly I guess, but I can't stop worrying that Bob's in deep trouble here and what's to become of him? I didn't get much sleep last night and I finally just felt I had to talk to someone."

Lizzie let out the breath she'd been holding in. Bob. Hmmm. "Molly, I know it's really hard to just sit by and watch the FBI take over but there's nothing else we can do." She didn't want to get Molly involved in the little bit of extra digging she'd been doing. Who knew where that could lead?

"I know you're right. But there must be something."

"How about if I come by later this morning and we'll talk, see what we can figure out?"

"Oh, would you, honey? I'd so appreciate that. I'll have something tasty waiting for you."

It didn't take Lizzie long to get dressed for her run. No sound from Andie's room, although Lizzie hadn't expected her guest would be up and at 'em real early. After feeding the cats, she peered out the front door and checked both directions carefully, looking for any hint of Special Agent Drew Jackson. Seeing none, she decided to chance it and left the house, continuing at a brisk pace until she was down the street four doors, then notched it up to a jog. By the time she'd done fifty minutes through town and along the river heading back home, she had to admit to a little disappointment in not meeting Jackson.

She'd spent most of the previous evening trying to figure out how the counterfeiting was tied in to the two murders, or at least if it tied in with Cabe Wilson's death. It must have. She was pretty certain that Orwell Rivers had to have been a part of it and that could be the reason he had been killed. How could he not know what was going on right on his own premises? Had Riverwell Press been strictly the distributor for the bogus bills or had they been printed in house? Not that it really mattered when it came down to Bob's involvement, because that was zilch, regardless of where the operation took place. Of that she was certain.

It was entirely possible that Cabe Wilson had been involved in a part of it, though, given his criminal record and the fact that some money had been found on his body. But why was he at Bob's house? Had his body been dumped there in order to implicate Bob, and if so, who had it in for him after all this time to set him up like that?

Had Special Agent Jackson joined her this morning, Lizzie had planned to get some answers from him. Maybe that was still possible, she thought, walking the final block to her house. Maybe she should track him down and just ask.

She glanced up at Nathaniel's door as she passed and it opened at the same time. He waved her over, a mug of coffee in his hand.

"Won't you join me, Lizzie? I've got freshly baked cinnamon buns."

She started salivating at the thought, remembering that Molly had promised her treats today, too, but readily agreed.

"Let's take it out on the patio," he said, leading the way. "It's already up in the low eighties. Going to be a scorcher again today."

"Could I start with a tall glass of water, please?"

"Of course, my dear. Just help yourself." He had set the two mugs and a plate of cinnamon buns on the green wicker table by the time Lizzie joined him.

"Lavenia and I are going for a drive over to Alexander City and then have a picnic on the way back at Highwater Park," Nathaniel said.

"Sounds lovely." Lizzie took a large bite of a bun and slowly chewed it, enjoying every morsel. "I haven't been there in a long time. Is that carousel still in at the amusement park?"

Nathaniel chuckled. "I'll say. I'd have thought it would have fallen apart by now. You know, when I was a small lad, they were just putting it together. Brought it all the way from Germany. That was the biggest attraction in these parts for decades until we got our own smaller version in Ashton Corners. It was a lot less elaborate, too, but it didn't require a long drive to get to it."

"I used to love riding on the one in town when I was younger. That and the Ferris wheel, of course. I remember there used to be long lineups for it every day of the Spring Fair."

"It was always thus," Nathaniel agreed and took another sip. "You know, it was a really popular site when I was growing up, even more so than in your day. We'd be over there every Saturday, a gang of us, spending our allowances on rides. I remember that Theodora and Molly and the rest of them used to really wind us up. Theodora would sidle up and slip something extra to the young lad manning the gate at the Tilt-A-Whirl. Always got the girls in before the rest of us. Huh. I hadn't thought of that in years. Theodora and Orwell Rivers."

"Orwell Rivers. What do you mean?"

"Well, it was his papa who owned most of the rides. Orwell used to work weekends there, doing all manner of jobs. But I suspect he liked being keeper of the gate as it turned into a nice little moneymaking business for him. Always on the lookout for a scheme, he was."

"I didn't realize Teensy knew him back them. And I didn't realize you knew him so well."

Nathaniel chuckled. "I'd plum forgotten but I didn't really know him up close and personal-like. We were older, the lads and I, so we didn't really talk to the kid. Just observed. Now, have another cinnamon bun."

Lizzie shook her head. "I'd love to but have to practice some restraint here." She glanced at the watch on Nathaniel's wrist and managed to read it upside down. "I also need to get a move on. Thank you for the coffee and delicious bun."

"My pleasure. I'll just pack up the rest of these for our picnic."

"By the way, I should mention that you'll probably be seeing Andie Mason coming and going a lot over the next couple of weeks. She's staying with me until her folks return from a vacation."

Nathaniel chuckled. "That should make for an interesting time."

"You're telling me."

Lizzie gave a small wave and headed home for a quick shower. She figured the cinnamon bun had doubled as breakfast, particularly with another calorie-laden stop coming up. Still no sound from Andie's room. She did a quick check of her email, which didn't take long as there was nothing needing a response, wrote a brief note for Andie and left for Molly's.

"I'm so glad you're able to come by and I do apologize again for such an early phone call," Molly said, giving Lizzie a quick hug. "And I'm sorry, I didn't stop to think about your houseguest. I assume Andrea arrived and settled in last night? I hope I didn't wake her."

"I think there's little chance of that," Lizzie said with a smile. She could see the tension in her friend's face. They'd have to figure out some action in order to set Molly's mind at ease.

"I was talking to Nathaniel this morning and he mentioned that Teensy had known Orwell Rivers when you were all younger. In fact, he told me about the lineups at the Tilt-A-Whirl ride at the Spring Fair."

Molly chuckled. "Oh, Teensy was quite notorious there for a while. She'd stoop to any level in order to get what she wanted, and fortunately for the rest of us, it usually included all of the Jitterbugs."

"Is that why she went to Mr. Rivers to have her novel published?"

"It seems reasonable even though I highly doubt she kept in touch with him in all that time away."

There seemed to be a lot of assuming going on, Lizzie thought. Time to replace some of that with facts. She followed Molly into the kitchen and sat at the place set for her at the banquette.

"I've been wondering to what degree Rivers was involved in the counterfeiting ring," she said.

"Yes, that question's been on my mind, too," Molly answered. "I hate to think ill of the poor man but it's the counterfeiting that seems to be at the root of all this business, isn't it?"

Lizzie nodded. "The questions are, was Rivers the mastermind or just a player, did they use his photocopying machine or just his distribution system and was Cabe Wilson part of the scheme?"

"I can't understand why someone as well-known and respected as Orwell would be involved, though."

"Money. They always say, follow the money."

"You're so right. It's similar to Agatha Christie's *The Secret of Chimneys*."

"How so?"

"Well, she has Superintendent Battle of Scotland Yard investigate what turns out to be two murders, a case of blackmail and some missing jewels. Different events but all tied in together at the end." Molly paused as she passed a plate of almond peach muffins to Lizzie. "And money, at the root of it all."

"I think it wouldn't hurt to find out something about Rivers's financial circumstances but unfortunately, I can't just access his bank statements. I wonder if Mark's done so? Of course, he wouldn't tell me. Or would he?"

"Knowing our police chief, I think it's better you didn't make him aware of our interest."

Lizzie smiled. "Why, Molly. You have a sneaky side, too."

"Of course I do, honey. I think a good place to start is with Teensy herself. Maybe she does know a bit more than she's willing to share."

"You think she'd hide something from you?" Lizzie asked, somewhat surprised.

"Honey, I know so."

Lizzie eased her car into the driveway at the side of Teensy's rental home on Lee Road. As Molly joined her at the front steps, they could see the front curtain move. Molly waved and a minute later Teensy opened the front door.

"My goodness, what are y'all doing out and about so early?" Teensy asked, glancing down at her orange floral dressing gown and yellow marabou slippers.

"Early? Why it's almost noon, Teensy. But that is early for you, isn't it? I'm sorry if we're disturbing you but this is important," Molly said, giving her a kiss on the cheek then walking right past toward the kitchen.

"You go right ahead and mock me, Mopsy Mathews. These broad shoulders can take it."

Lizzie gave a shrug and a smile and followed Molly. Teensy caught up to them, her heels clacking along the slate floor in the hallway. She slipped in front of them as they stood just inside the door of the kitchen that was a circa 1970's U-shaped design trying to look updated. The dark maple cupboards and green laminate counters stood out against the white walls; the stainless steel appliances shined in the morning brightness. A glassed-in sunroom was off the kitchen and the door into it stood open. Lizzie spotted a mug and bowl of cereal on the round country table off to the right of the room.

"I'm sorry if we've interrupted your breakfast," Lizzie began, "but we just had some things we wanted to talk to you about."

Teensy smiled. "Of course, sugar. Come join me for some coffee. Y'all have things about the launch to discuss?"

Molly shook her head but Lizzie added, "Not the launch but I do have news about three book signings I've lined up for you."

Teensy clapped her hands and probably would have done a small jig if it hadn't been for the tricky-looking slippers. "Oh, you're simply wonderful, sugar. I'm so looking forward to getting out there to the readers with my book. Come along, y'all, and have a seat."

Lizzie and Molly sat in two of the remaining chairs at the table and waited while Teensy brought them out mugs of coffee. "Or would y'all rather have something cool? Tea, perhaps?"

"I'm still in need of caffeine," Lizzie said and gratefully took the mug.

"This is fine," Molly said. "Now, Teensy. I just got to reminiscing with Lizzie this morning about the Tilt-A-Whirl at the Spring Fair and I remember how you used to get us up to the front of the waiting line each and every time Orwell Rivers was taking tickets. Do you remember?"

Teensy glanced outside to her right and smiled. "Yes, I did have a knack for getting us special treatment now and then. Was it Orwell, though? I can't rightly remember."

Molly frowned. "Of course you remember, Teensy. You've got one of the best memories in the county. Was that why you went to Orwell to get your book published?"

Teensy looked at Molly. "Why no, Mopsy. I went to him because he's the only printer here in the region that does this co-publishing I was telling you about. Why does it matter anyway? And I'd already decided it was time to move back to Ashton Corners."

Lizzie jumped in. "We were just trying to figure out how and why Orwell Rivers was involved in the counterfeiting ring. Do you think he needed the money?" She wrapped a lock of her hair around her finger and played with it.

"Don't we all?" Teensy said with a laugh, then sobered. "I really have no idea what his financial status was. I only met with him a few times. But he always was on the lookout for ways to make money, as I recall. Remember in high school, Mopsy, he used to sell old test papers?"

Molly started to shake her head then paused. "Oh my gosh. You're right. I'd forgotten about that. It was Orwell and Junior Logan. They used to search through the garbage cans at the back of the school at key times of the year. That was in the days before shredders, of course." She started laughing and Teensy joined in.

Molly wiped her eyes. "For all of his shyness—I guess

we'd have called it nerdiness if we had that word in those days—Orwell really garnered the admiration of the entire sophomore class that year."

Teensy looked pointedly at their cups. "Would y'all like some more coffee?"

Lizzie and Molly shook their heads in unison.

"So, Lizzie, tell me all about the signings."

Back at Molly's place, Lizzie asked what was troubling her. She'd been awfully quiet during the drive home.

Molly sighed. "I'm not really certain but I think Teensy's either hiding something or she's worried and not willing to trust me."

"How can you tell?"

"She was twirling a piece of her hair when talking about Orwell. I haven't seen her do that since we were real young and she was trying to cover something up. Often, something she didn't want the rest of us to know about and that used to make me so mad. Here we were sisters of a sort, and we were supposed to share all our deepest secrets. Well, I think she's at it again."

Lizzie wondered if Molly was reading too much into it. She'd not noticed anything. Of course, she hadn't known Teensy all that long.

"What should we do about it?"

"I don't know." Molly shook her head. "She's stubborn and won't tell us a thing until she's ready to, that I do know."

"She did that when she said she'd not seen Orwell in years, didn't she?"

"Uh-huh."

"I wonder if the office gal from Riverwell Press might

be able to help with that?" Lizzie was thinking out loud. "I noticed her in the back room when Teensy and I picked up the books."

Molly tilted her head, a big smile on her face. "That's my girl."

Chapter Twenty

<<>>

Serendipity. Look for something, find something else,
and realize that what you've found is more suited
to your needs than what you thought you were looking for.

LAWRENCE BLOCK

Lizzie had just walked into the front office at Riverwell
Press, the door still open behind her, when she heard a
car pull into the parking lot. She glanced outside and cringed
when she saw the car with the two FBI agents come to a
stop beside her car. She quickly shut the door and looked at
the girl behind the desk. The nameplate beside the phone
read Dana-Lynn Norton.

"Hey, Dana-Lynn. I'm Lizzie Turner. I was here the other
day picking up the Coldicutt books."

The girl smiled hesitantly, showing off the tips of her
braces. Her short blonde hair looked like she'd used a lot of
product to tame it. A dark green sleeveless blouse topped a
pair of brown-striped Bermuda shorts.

"Oh yeah, I saw you along with Mr. Rivers's lawyer." She
smiled.

Lizzie glanced out the window to check the location of the two special agents. "I was hoping to talk to you in private but I see we're about to be joined by the FBI."

The door opened and Jackson walked into the room followed by Ormes. "I thought it looked like your car, Ms. Turner," Jackson said. He looked over and smiled at Dana-Lynn. "We meet again, Ms. Norton."

Dana-Lynn giggled and her face turned beet red. "So we do." She lowered her lashes then slowly looked back up at the agent. "Can I get y'all both something? Some iced tea? I brought a thermos since it gets so hot in here without the air-conditioning on. I think Mr. Rivers would have been mighty unhappy about that. The humidity is not good for the books in the warehouse."

"Why is it off?" Lizzie asked, curious.

"That's Mr. Emerson's doing. He's trying to keep the bills down and he said there's not much of value left in the warehouse anyway."

Lizzie thought Teensy would take issue with that, since there were a few cartons of her book still warehoused there.

Jackson smiled at Dana-Lynn. "I'd love some tea if you're sure you can spare some."

Lizzie groaned inwardly as Dana-Lynn knocked over her in-basket, sending several sheets of paper airborne in her haste to get over to the thermos on the desk. Jackson winked at Lizzie. *Poor girl. She has a crush on the special agent and he knows it.*

"So tell me, Ms. Turner, what brings you here today?" Jackson asked. He wore a light gray summer suit but had loosened his blue-striped tie to cope with the heat. His dark sunglasses had been pushed up on top of his head.

Lizzie thought quickly. "I've managed to arrange some

book signings for Teensy Coldicutt so I thought I should check on the remaining cartons of her books here." That sounded like a good idea. She'd better do it before leaving. "And what about you, Special Agent?"

"Just doing my job, ma'am," Jackson answered. "Trying to tie up all the loose ends. Following the money, as it were."

Me, too. "And would you care to share what those loose ends might be?"

"Now, I couldn't do that, you being a civilian and all."

Ormes, who had been wandering around the office peering in corners and on top of counters, finally spoke. "Especially with you being a suspect and all."

"What?" Lizzie asked indignantly. "I was the one who found the stash of money, remember?"

"My point exactly. What better way to try to look innocent. Supposedly 'finding the money.'"

Lizzie bristled at that. She could almost see the quotation marks.

Ormes continued, "Turn it in. Walk off scot-free."

Lizzie noticed Dana-Lynn had stopped in midaction of pouring the tea. "What money?" she asked.

Lizzie answered before Ormes could stop her. "You know, the counterfeit money your boss was producing."

Dana-Lynn looked surprised, but of course, she could be a good actress. Lizzie knew nothing about Dana-Lynn Norton. Perhaps she should find someone who did know her and might shed some light on just how wide-eyed and innocent she really was. Lizzie looked from one agent to the other. Ormes glared at his partner. Jackson nodded and opened his mouth to speak.

"All right. I'm leaving." She suddenly remembered her excuse. "I just need to check how many of the Coldicutt books are in the warehouse before I leave." She walked toward the door to the warehouse and Ormes moved in front of her.

"Maybe she should check it out now," Jackson suggested. "Save her having to come back here another time."

Ormes thought a moment before moving. "Okay, but make it snappy."

Make it snappy? "Thank you," Lizzie said and quickly slipped into the warehouse. She walked over to the shelves, trying to ignore the sticky feeling. This humidity couldn't be good for the books. Should she just take them and try to explain to Mark after or phone him for permission? Or should she try to hear what was going on in the outer office?

She tiptoed back to the door and leaned her ear against it. The drone of the fan blocked out the words, although she could hear voices. Drat. The door opened suddenly and Lizzie tried to make it look like she'd been about to open it but had stopped to look back at the shelves.

"Are you ready to leave, Ms. Turner?" Ormes asked.

"I am but I'm taking the books since we do have permission from the DA. It's way too humid in there for them. If you and Special Agent Jackson would be so kind as to carry them out to the car for me, then I'll be out of your hair." *So to speak.* She couldn't resist looking at the thin strands of hair that had been combed across his scalp. "There are six boxes," she continued as she walked to the front door. "I'll just back up my car to the loading dock." She left quickly before Ormes could respond.

She was actually surprised to see the two men with all six boxes stacked beside them when she backed in. They loaded them into the trunk, stopping to wipe the perspiration off their foreheads.

"I don't think you'll need to come back and trouble Ms. Norton again, will you?" Jackson asked as she started to thank them.

Lizzie closed the trunk. "I shouldn't think so," Lizzie agreed. *But you never know.*

"Thank you, gentlemen." She slid into the front seat and turned the air-conditioning on full blast before leaving the parking lot.

She let out the breath it felt like she'd been holding since the agents had first entered the room. First, she'd drop the books at Molly's, adding them to the other boxes in the garage, giving thanks that Molly had installed air-conditioning in order to protect the Corvette. She'd then go see if Amanda at Scissors 'n Snips had time to give her a shampoo and trim. It was getting close to her four-week visit and she felt the need to do it now, while Dana-Lynn was still fresh in her mind. Amanda not only gave the best cut Lizzie had in town, she also gave the best gossip. If anyone knew anything about Dana-Lynn Norton, it would be Amanda Atkins.

"Why, Dana-Lynn was in my younger sister Tracy's year at AC High," Amanda said, warming Lizzie's heart. "She was always a bit ditzy as I recall. She could be talked into just about anything, and my sweet little sis, Tracy, was just the one to do it."

"So, a fairly straightforward kind of person? Do you think she'd be involved in anything shady?"

"Only if she didn't know it was shady. I seem to remember you could sell her a bill of goods and she'd be at the counter paying for it before you finished your spiel." Amanda had quickly trimmed Lizzie's hair but was playing around with the front, draping strands across the forehead, as she usually did in a bid to get Lizzie to change her hairstyle. "Ready for bangs yet, sugar?"

Lizzie started to shake her head then remembered the scissors in Amanda's hand, right close to her left ear. "No. Nothing different, thanks anyway. Have you heard anything about Dana-Lynn lately?"

"I hadn't heard nor thought about her in years, not until the owner of that printing press was killed. The paper said she worked for him. The poor thing must have been in total shock."

"For sure." Lizzie only semi-listened as Amanda went on to fill her in on what Tracy had been up to over the years. Her mind stayed on Dana-Lynn. Could she have been persuaded that the counterfeit money was a legit enterprise or something? Lizzie still couldn't believe Dana-Lynn would not have known something about it.

"Is Dana-Lynn a customer of yours by any chance?" Lizzie asked as soon as Amanda had turned the hair dryer off.

"No. I don't know where she goes, remember . . . I haven't heard or seen her in years. What's this all about anyway?" Amanda caught a stray curl and tucked it into the upsweep she'd done with her own bright auburn naturally curly locks, about the only way she could tame them.

"I'd just like to talk to her in neutral territory, without the FBI swooping in on us. I'm sort of interested in trying to find out who killed Orwell Rivers."

Amanda raised her eyebrows. "Really? I can think of nothing more distasteful. Of course, you were involved in that murder just a few months ago, weren't you?" Her eyes cut to the front of the shop and did a quick sweep around.

Lizzie wondered if she thought murder might be following her around.

"I had a cousin, well I still do, Billy Bob Keller over in Wetumpka, who collected handcuffs. Now, that was a class-A weird interest." She gave Lizzie's hair a final comb-through then pulled a hand mirror out off the shelf and aimed it so the back of Lizzie's head was visible in the large front mirrors. "Like it?"

Her dark brown hair gleamed in the flattering lighting. It fell in straight clean lines about two inches below her shoulders. She knew that would last until she stepped outside into the humidity. *Gotta love summer.*

Lizzie nodded. "That's great. Thanks, Amanda." She slipped a tip in the top drawer as she stood up.

"Thank you. Just wait a sec." She turned to the stylist at the station two chairs over. "Holly, do you ever see Dana-Lynn Norton these days?" She said in an aside to Lizzie, "She's the same age as that group."

Holly, tall and skinny as a rail with her bold blonde hair done in dreadlocks, finished putting her combs in a jar filled with blue liquid and sauntered over. "I don't but if you're looking for her I'll bet you can find Dana-Lynn hanging out at the Fassbender. She's got the hots for one of the bartenders. I think his name is Jason or something like that. Why you asking?"

Amanda shrugged. "Her name just came up in conversation and I was saying my sister hadn't seen her in a long time. Thanks."

Holly looked from one to the other and shrugged as she walked away. "Whatever."

Amanda waited until Holly was at the back. "She's got

a real big mouth," she said sotto voce. "I didn't think you'd want her blabbing your interest in this."

"Thanks. And thanks for the tip."

"Right back at you," Amanda said and started blowing stray hairs off the chair with the hair dryer.

Lizzie wondered where Mark was and whether she should call him about the books, then decided to leave it until later that night.

Chapter Twenty-one

◇◇◇

I was smart enough to know exactly what I was
going to do next. And smart enough to keep my
mouth shut about it, too.

BUTTON HOLED—KYLIE LOGAN

Lizzie was having trouble relaxing enough to enjoy her
Shiraz. She sat perched on the edge of a stool at the bar,
nursing the wine that had to do her until Jason came back
from his dinner break. She'd been waiting for thirty-five
minutes, hoping the woman she'd been told he'd left with
was Dana-Lynn. The perky blonde bartender was new and
didn't know Dana-Lynn by name.

This whole scene made Lizzie feel old. Most of the kids
must be just above the legal drinking age and the music
blasting from the sound system left her nerve endings jan-
gling. A couple of times she'd wondered if this was such a
clever idea after all. Even if she did find Dana-Lynn, they
wouldn't be able to carry on a conversation. She was seriously considering leaving the rest of the drink and exiting

when Dana-Lynn walked through the front door, hanging on to the hand of a short, dark-haired guy with lots of tattoos on his arms. They shared a mushy kiss before he walked into the kitchen at the back.

Lizzie watched as Dana-Lynn looked around the room, possibly searching for friends. She'd better nab her first. Lizzie waved, which caught her attention.

The initial look of surprise had been replaced by a friendly smile by the time Dana-Lynn perched on the empty barstool next to Lizzie. "Why, what are you doing here, Ms. Turner? I don't think I've ever seen you here before."

Lizzie smiled and leaned toward her so as to not shout. "It's Lizzie, please. And I'm actually here looking for you."

Dana-Lynn went back to looking surprised. "Why?"

"Can I buy you a drink?" Lizzie asked and then paid for the margarita she ordered. She waited until Dana-Lynn had her first sip then said, "I wanted to talk to you some more but those two agents sort of took over." She smiled to make light of it.

Dana-Lynn gave a small laugh. "Oh, that younger FBI guy, he's so sexy. Oops, I shouldn't say that with Jason here. But he is, don't you think?"

Lizzie tried not to think about it but had to agree. "I keep wondering how the counterfeiting operation worked and how Mr. Rivers was able to keep it a secret from you. Do you have any ideas?" Lizzie pushed the small dish of pretzels toward Dana-Lynn.

"No, ma'am. I truly don't. I know Orwell—he wanted me to call him that, you know—asked me to stay in the front at all times. If I needed him, I was to use the intercom. He said it was in case a customer came in off the street. He said there's nothing more upsetting than having an empty reception area greet you. I didn't think there was anything funny about that." She'd slid into a whiny voice.

Lizzie was quick to placate her. "Of course not. It makes a lot of sense. But did you hear him talking to anybody, maybe about money problems? I'm trying to understand why a good guy like Orwell Rivers would turn to something criminal."

Dana-Lynn shuddered. "Oh, don't talk about him like that. He was truly a very nice man. I don't know anything bad about him. He was always good to me. He often suggested I just take extra time off for lunch when it was slow. And sometimes, just leave early. I wish you wouldn't ask me to bad-mouth him."

"I don't want you to bad-mouth him. I just would like to find out what's behind his murder. I'd think you'd want the killer to be brought to justice, too, wouldn't you?"

"Uh-huh. But, I'm scared. What if this killer also thinks I know something? Could I be next?" She shuddered.

Lizzie hadn't thought of that. She doubted it but felt bad about having planted that scare in Dana-Lynn's mind. She reached out and touched her arm. "I'm pretty sure you're not in any danger, otherwise the police would have done something about it. Believe me, they are good at their job and they wouldn't let anything happen to you."

"That's very kind of you to say that, Ms. Turner."

Lizzie jumped at the sound of Mark's voice behind her. She turned around quickly enough to see the scowl on his face. "Hi, Chief. Won't you join us? Dana-Lynn and I were just having a drink."

"And a talk," he said, still obviously displeased.

Dana-Lynn stood abruptly. "Hey, Chief Dreyfus. I think

I'd better get going on home. Thanks for the drink, Lizzie. Bye now."

Lizzie watched, dismayed, as Dana-Lynn hurried out the front door. Mark sat on the vacated stool.

"Just what do you think you're doing?" he asked. The cute young bartender arrived immediately, Lizzie noticed, even though it had taken her ten minutes to get her drink. Mark ordered a beer and then gave Lizzie a piercing look.

"I was just asking her a few questions, that's all."

"Picking up where you left off this morning?"

"How did you know about that?" One or both of the special agents, of course.

Mark cocked an eyebrow at her.

"No need to answer. But what are you doing here?"

"I thought it was time I got into the act with everyone else having grilled my witness before I got to her."

"How did you know she was here?"

"Her roommate," Mark answered and leaned closer.

"And why did it take you until now to get to her?" Lizzie asked, bouncing between chagrin and indignation.

"Let's just say, after my initial questioning of Ms. Norton, I didn't think she'd have much additional to add. I just wanted to be sure I'd been right."

"You had been," Lizzie confirmed. Not wanting a lecture, she said, "Well, at least we can have a pleasant drink together." She tilted her glass to him.

He snorted. "You call this pleasant? I can hardly hear myself think. Come on, let's take that table in the far corner. It might be a bit quieter there." He steered her between the tables crowding the small floor space. "Have you had anything to eat?" he asked when they were seated.

"I grabbed a snack at home but that was it."

"What say we finish our drinks and go over to my place? Grab some takeout on the way?"

Lizzie nodded.

"And then I can lecture you without any distractions around," he added.

Chapter Twenty-two

◇◇◇

"Do you find it easy to get drunk on words?" "So easy that, to tell you the truth, I am seldom perfectly sober."

GAUDY NIGHT—DOROTHY L. SAYERS

I know what you said, Mark, but I thought maybe Dana-Lynn would tell me something she might be afraid to tell you male police authority figures. It makes sense that she would know something, don't you think?" Lizzie asked as Mark handed her an iced tea.

They were sitting out on his patio with Patchett wandering around the backyard, enjoying the sights and smells of the mid August evening.

"I do have female officers on staff and I do ask them to take over if I ever sense some reluctance like that. We're paid to do that, Lizzie. You're not and it could be dangerous."

Mark leaned back, clasped his hands behind his head and stretched his long legs in front of him. His black T-shirt hugged his chest; his jeans fit comfortably. Lizzie watched him from the corner of her eye, not wanting to turn and face him in what would be an obvious exercise in ogling. But she was enjoying the view. She could smell the fragrant crimson honeysuckle growing at the side of the house, and the stars dancing in the twilight provided a good view as well.

"You surely don't think I was in any danger from Dana-Lynn?"

"It's unlikely. But if someone, namely the killer, is feeling threatened seeing you running around town asking questions, he might just make you stop. Now I, on the other hand, may be able to coerce you into backing off." He leaned toward her from his Adirondack chair and kissed her.

Her whole body felt tingly but she wasn't going to be that easy. He'd have to give her a few answers along with the kisses, in order for her to stop sleuthing.

"That was nice," she murmured, "but I do have a question for you."

Mark pulled away and groaned. "I guess you might as well ask it or we'll just sit here and look at the stars all night."

Lizzie smiled in the dark. "Well, I was wondering if it's possible all that counterfeiting could have been going on at Riverwell Press without Orwell Rivers knowing about it?"

Mark didn't answer right away. "No, it's not likely that would happen. Rivers would have been involved to some degree, probably totally."

"And, would it be just as likely that Bob was not a part of this ring?"

"Yes, that's also highly likely, and before you ask, I am working hard at finding evidence that proves that. I do not believe he was part of the counterfeiting scheme. However, there's still the matter of murder."

"Why is the FBI so keen to pin it on him?"

"I shouldn't even be talking to you about this, Lizzie. But, I know you won't leave it alone until we have this discussion. Bob had motive and that's what they're focusing on."

"What motive? Not that bit about paying his sister's mortgage loan?"

"How do you know about that? I guess I shouldn't be surprised. That does count as a motive, Lizzie, whether you like it or not. He said he'd take care of it yet he doesn't, or didn't, have the money. Counterfeit money is found in his house. A tidy deposit of real, non-counterfeit money was made into his account. And, let's not forget, there was a dead man with counterfeit money found on his property."

"A deposit?"

"Uh-huh. Bob says he has no idea where the money came from. And it could have been deposited by someone else, but he'd have to know the account number."

"But Bob's being framed, don't you see?"

"Oh, Lizzie, Lizzie. What am I going to do with you?" Mark turned so he was facing her. "I think you're probably right but it doesn't matter what you or I think. It's what the proof says that counts with the FBI."

"But you're not going to let them do something stupid like arrest him?"

"I'm working hard to find me a murderer and maybe that person will unravel the rest of it."

Lizzie leaned forward and gave Mark a big kiss. "I'm so glad to hear that."

Mark smiled. "Maybe we should move inside?"

"I think that would be an excellent idea."

Patchett came running over as Mark stood. "Uh, after his walk, that is."

Mark stretched and yawned.

"Why don't I take him around the block and you can go inside? Put on something comfortable," she added in a suggestive voice.

He chuckled. "You're on." He squeezed her shoulder as he went to get the leash.

"By the way, how's it going with your new roommate and all?" Mark asked, stifling a yawn.

Lizzie shrugged. "Fine. Although now that you mention it, I'm not sure where she is tonight. I haven't really come to grips with how nosy I should be about her movements. I hope she's left me a message somewhere." *If not, then what?*

Lizzie hooked Patchett up and coaxed him to follow her. The dog stood for a couple of minutes watching the door after Mark went inside and then finally decided to go along with Lizzie. She kept coaxing him the entire time. "Go now, Patchett. Here's a good spot, boy. Pee, Patchett, pee. That's it, give it a good sniff. Good spot, right?"

Finally, the dog cooperated and they headed back to Mark's. Inside the kitchen, she added a handful of treats to his dish, replenished the water bowl then walked to the bedroom. Just before switching on the overhead light, she heard the soft snoring and saw Mark illuminated by the light of the moon shining through the window. He was in bed, under the covers, propped up against the two pillows. She tiptoed over and gave him a kiss on the forehead then left.

This case was really taking its toll.

Lizzie spent the next morning in her office at home sorting through a box of files she'd brought home at the end of the school year. As usual, she'd put off sorting and filing, something she'd meant to do right away at the start of the summer vacation, and now that there were just two weeks until school started again, she knew she had to get serious about it. She planned to sort them into a pile for filing, a pile for discarding, and the final stack would be material she'd need again this school term.

She heard Andie eventually get up and make sounds like her day was in gear. Lizzie yelled out what she was doing as she pulled open a drawer in the three-drawer file cabinet. She realized right away she'd have to sort through and possibly discard the oldest files. That or buy another file cabinet. Maybe a better suggestion would be boxing the oldest year or two of files, after giving them a quick read through and pulling anything that might still be relevant or recyclable, and then stash the others in filing boxes.

She looked around the room and envisioned her new decorating scheme—boxes in every corner. Maybe she could stack them, stick a tablecloth on them and use them as end tables. Too bad she didn't have a basement or a garage. Although Paige and Brad did have both. Maybe with some room to spare. She reached for the phone and stopped herself before dialing. A phone call would lead to something else, maybe a visit or at the very least a long call. That would be great work avoidance. Not now. She'd sort first, then phone.

Lizzie sighed as she sat in the middle of the floor and opened the box closest to her. She'd need to empty it first before clearing out the drawers. Andie popped her head in the room after grabbing a quick breakfast and said she'd be out on the patio with her computer.

Shortly after, the phone brought Lizzie out of her stupor. She reached for it, groaning as she knocked over one stack of books.

It was Sally-Jo wanting to get together with her and Molly to finalize some details of the book launch. Lizzie looked around at the mess on the floor. She did need a break and later that afternoon she could tackle it afresh.

"It's okay by me. Is Molly free?" she asked.

"She is and she's expecting us for lunch. Does that work for you?"

"It's a reprieve from getting organized for back-to-you-know-what."

"Don't remind me," Sally-Jo said in mock despair. "I have to have my year's work plan in to the principal by Monday. I can't believe the summer's over already. Where did it go?"

"I think, for you, it went into renovating your living room. It's just too bad you didn't take any time to get away."

"If I admitted to a vacation, my folks would have demanded why I had no time to visit them for a week. This has been a good cover for me. I wouldn't mind sneaking away to a spa weekend, though, before we get too immersed."

"You and Jacob?"

Sally-Jo let out an unladylike snort. "Hardly the spa type. No, I meant you and me. Think you could swing it?"

It sounded like a great idea. Lizzie hadn't been to even a day spa in quite some time and she did love to be pampered. "I'm in. Any suggestions?"

"Not yet but I'll come up with some. So, see you at noon?"

"For sure."

Lizzie gave Molly a quick call to say she might have Andie along and then looked at the clock on the wall after they'd hung up. That gave her less than an hour. She boxed the stack of old files she'd been going through, wrote out sticky notes tagging the various piles and closed the door behind her. No way she'd let the cats loose in there. Piles of accidents just waiting to happen.

Lizzie swallowed the last mouthful of gazpacho and sat back with a sigh. "That was totally delicious, Molly."

"Well, it was easy to whip up. I'm so glad you girls came over today. We have so much to talk about. I'm getting fairly excited about the launch. I can imagine how Teensy's feeling. In fact, I suggested she might like to join us. She's at the hairdresser right now but will be over later. I hope that's all right."

"Of course," Sally-Jo said. "We should get her input since it's her event. I should have thought of that." She leaned over and helped herself to another piece of cornbread and swatted at a bee that had been heading for the same piece.

"I think we'll go ahead and finish off the planning. I'm not sure when Teensy will arrive." Molly suggested. "I'll just take these dishes inside. Are y'all finished?"

The three of them nodded and Andie jumped up out of the garden chair to help her. Andie came back outside with a fresh pitcher of iced tea and Molly held another plate of pecan chocolate chip cookies.

"Now, what about the menu, Sally-Jo?" Molly asked.

"I have it here. I went through the menu from Herbs, Spice & Everything that you gave me, Molly. I hope you'll like what I'm suggesting. It's all finger foods: tuna-apple mini melts, stuffed mushrooms with pecans, endive with scallops and curry, crab cakes with creole mustard and for a light dessert, fresh fruit skewers. What do y'all think?"

Just thinking about it made Lizzie's mouth water and she'd only just finished eating. "Sounds perfect to me," she said.

"Did you have some chocolate in there for treats?" Andie asked hopefully.

"Of course," Sally-Jo said, laughing. "How about chocolate-coated cake balls?

"Super cool!"

"I think it's a good idea to have it catered, Molly, and then you'll be able to enjoy the launch rather than worry about the food," Lizzie agreed.

"I couldn't agree more." Molly stood and started moving around the patio. "I thought the food tables could go along here and the bar at that end, much like the setup for that garden party I had for the literacy students last fall." She looked at each of them and they nodded.

"Good," she said and walked toward the large willow tree at the right of the stone patio. "And right here, framed by these lovely branches, we'll place the signing table for Teensy to bask in the attention."

"I sure do like the sound of that," squealed Teensy as she rounded the corner of the house. "Hi, y'all. Sorry I'm late. Do y'all like my new coif?"

She did a slow twirl so they all were able to have a good look. The turquoise background of her midlength Grecian-style Lycra dress emphasized the large yellow butterflies as well as her many natural curves. In fact, many of the butterflies looked ready to take flight as she moved across the patio.

"My goodness, Teensy. Did you walk through a butterfly conservatory?" Molly asked and smiled to soften the words.

"Looks like it, doesn't it? I plan to make a statement now that I'm back here in Ashton Corners."

"And what would that be?" Molly asked.

"I'm back in town, folks . . . Take cover!"

They all burst out laughing as Teensy paraded around

the edge of the patio. She stopped in front of Sally-Jo. "Sally-Jo. It's a pleasure to meet you, sugar. Now aren't you just the cutest little thing—that short red hair and you being so petite." Sally-Jo's cheeks matched the color of her hair. "Now, just call me Teensy. That's been all I've been answering to for too many years."

"And you are?" She reached out to touch Andie's arm.

"I'm Andie Mason, ma'am."

"Ah, yes, Andrea. I've heard all about you. So nice to meet you, child."

Before Andie could answer, Teensy went on. "Now y'all may wonder at my name. It's really Theodora Kathleen, but the girls started calling me Teensy way back in grade school and it stuck with me. See, even then I was more full-bodied than the others. They were all jealous of me. Why even back then, the boys were all hankering after me. I mean, just take a gander at Molly here."

Molly grimaced.

"She was always thin as a reed in a swamp. Hasn't filled out much over the years. Tall. No boobs." Teensy chuckled. "It's a good thing she's such a wonderful-hearted person or she'd have nothing to attract the men."

Lizzie tried to hide her smile, so Molly wouldn't notice. Andie's mouth hung open. Sally-Jo looked from one to the other of the women.

"Huh," said Molly. "That's one version of the story."

Teensy burst out laughing. "Mopsy always did get a bit huffy when I'd tease her. Anyway," Teensy went on, "Sally-Jo, I do thank y'all for helping out with all this."

Sally-Jo smiled. "It's my pleasure."

"So tell me all about the layout here," Teensy said, back to walking around. "I'm thinking this is my launchpad?"

Molly shook her head and then went through it again, adding the bookselling table to the left of the signing table.

"That's where Steph and I will be?" Andie asked.

"Yes, honey. We'll sit y'all back here where all the action will be taking place. I expect you two will be kept busy selling a lot of books."

Molly went on to point out that the small round bistro tables she planned to rent would be scattered around the back lawn but all with a good view of the main patio, where Teensy would give her speech.

"A speech! I hadn't even thought about that," she squeaked.

Lizzie couldn't tell if she was pleased or upset. "I think people will want to hear where the idea came from and how you got started writing, things like that," she said.

Teensy brightened. "Yes, of course. You are so right, sugar. I can dress that up all nice and exciting-like. I am a writer, after all." Teensy walked over to the table and poured herself a glass of tea, then sat in Molly's chair.

Molly continued walking around the lawn, picturing the placement of tables.

"I've been meaning to ask you, Teensy, if you're working on a sequel," Lizzie asked.

"I'm thinking about it but I've been so busy since moving here. I'm still trying to find a house, you know. The rental's fine but it needs updating and I do so want a place of my own." She took a long sip. "And it's been hard to concentrate what with Orwell's murder and all."

"Are you having second thoughts about holding the launch right now, before everything gets cleared up?" Lizzie asked.

"Certainly not. It's just . . . it's not what I'd thought I'd be coming back to."

"I'd imagine not," Sally-Jo said, sounding solicitous. She slid the proposed menu over to Teensy. "What do you think about these foods?"

"Looks like a taste-tempting feast, sugar," Teensy said then looked at Lizzie. "I'll just bet my eyeteeth that you've been poking around, trying to come up with some information on the murder, haven't you? Found anything?"

Lizzie took her time in answering. She didn't really want to go into any details about her visits to Urliss Langdorf and Dana-Lynn, not until she had something to share. She remembered the books. "Not really, but I did stop by River-well Press yesterday and the air conditioner had been turned off. It seems Mr. Emerson is penny-pinching. I didn't think that would be good for the books so I picked up all the remaining ones and moved them into Molly's garage." *And still haven't told Mark.*

"Why, you're a smart one. Thank you for doing that, sugar."

"Speaking of which," Molly said, pulling another chair over to the table, "I got a call from the manager at the Winn-Dixie asking about ordering the book. Now that we have the books here, why don't I set up an account for each of these places where Lizzie has you booked for signings, and then take their orders. I'll get Bob to deliver the books and then I'll send them all statements at the end of the month. I understand the vendor gets forty percent of the price, is that correct?"

"Why, aren't you the businessperson, Mopsy? Well, that would be great if you'd take over all the financial parts. I'm no good at that but I did do some investigating of publishers when I was deciding which way to go with the book, and that's certainly a standard rate." Teensy leaned over and squeezed Molly's hand. "I don't know what I'd do without you."

Molly beamed. "I'm just so happy to be helping, Teensy. And you know, it's really a lot of fun putting this all together. Now, I think we'll be taking books to the library with us, is that right, Lizzie?"

"Uh-huh. I'm hoping Andie or Stephanie will want to come and sell there, too. It won't be until September." She looked over at Andie, who nodded. "I understand the library will want to order copies for their shelves and we can bring in some to sell."

They spent the next hour talking about the plans and then Teensy left. As Molly walked her out to her car, Sally-Jo leaned over to Lizzie and said, "What a character. I love her. Is she always like that or is this her author persona?"

"That's the Teensy Coldicutt I always get. I bet she was larger than life in her day."

Sally-Jo grinned. "Well I'm glad we have something more than a couple of murders to liven things up here in Ashton Corners."

Chapter Twenty-three

◇◇◇

"Watch out for O'Mara," he whispered. "He's a bit
of a cad. Not quite trustworthy."

HER ROYAL SPYNESS—RHYS BOWEN

Lizzie stepped out of her car and looked at her house. The
afternoon sun made it look even more welcoming. She'd
read recently that good feng shui was a front door facing
west; it made the house brighter and welcoming. She glanced
around. West facing it was. And that car pulling into the
driveway had none other than Special Agent Jackson at the
wheel. She took a deep breath and resigned herself to
some more questions. She was glad she'd dropped Andie at
the Ashton Center Mall after leaving Molly's.

"I'm happy I caught you," Jackson said as he approached her.

"What, you need my help with the case?"

"Not with the case but I'd sure be grateful if you'd suggest
a good spot to eat dinner tonight."

Lizzie narrowed her eyes and looked at him. Was he for

real? Was it a trap? "What kind of food did you have in mind?"

"Well, what do you like?"

Lizzie heard warning bells. "What does that have to do with anything?"

"I'd like to choose someplace you'd enjoy since I'm hoping you'll join me." He gave her a big smile that reached his eyes. He looked as far removed from a federal agent as possible, with a black short-sleeved cotton shirt and beige chinos. The black emphasized his black hair and swarthy coloring. She wondered if there were some Latino roots in his family tree.

Lizzie's breath caught as he grabbed her left hand and looked at her ring finger. "I didn't think so. Are you worried he'll be upset? I could check with the chief to make sure it's okay with him if you'd like."

Now she knew he was joking; still she felt her face turn red. "You do not have to ask Mark's permission."

"Good. Then it's settled?"

"It is not. That's not what I meant. It's just that I make my own decisions and I still think it's not a good idea." She was glad she'd worn her sleeveless red dress today. She knew it made her look more determined. It certainly gave her self-confidence a boost.

Jackson leaned against her car, arms folded across his chest, a Cheshire grin on his face. "What about if I said I need your help on the case and having dinner would be a much more pleasant way than in the police station."

"Police station? What, am I a suspect? Of what?"

"I didn't say that. It's just that Ormes could be in on it, too, if we went to the station. He's checking some things there as we speak. That might work out better after all."

Entrapment. He must know I'm not too enamored with his partner. What's his game anyway? Is this a come-on or is he being up front? She thought the latter was highly unlikely but still . . . she might just learn something useful. But what would Mark say? She'd been that "dinner-with-another-male" route before and didn't want to travel it again. She'd accept but she'd also tell Mark about it.

"Fine. Dinner sounds good. When and where?"

Jackson grinned. "I'll pick you up, say about six tonight? You decide where we should go."

She thought about it a moment. The Broward Street Brew Pub would be nice and public. Mark couldn't mistake this for a romantic dinner, although a very small part of her wondered what that would be like as Jackson drove off. She pulled her cell out and punched in Mark's number.

"Where are you?" she asked when he'd answered.

"I'm heading back to the station. What's up?"

"I need to talk to you. It won't take long."

"This doesn't sound good." She heard his police radio in the background. "How about a quick Patchett walk?"

"Great. I'll see you shortly."

She hopped in her car and drove the few short blocks to Mark's house, arriving at the same time as he did. She parked on the street and met him as he exited the cruiser. He gave her a quick kiss and an inquiring look.

"Just let me harness up Patchett and we'll talk as we walk," Mark said and went to get the dog. Patchett strained at the leash and started barking excitedly at the sight of Lizzie. "I know how he feels," Mark said with a grin.

Lizzie felt a flutter of apprehension. "You're going to be working late tonight?" she asked, looking at Patchett.

Mark groaned. "Again. Now, what did you want to talk

to me about?" he asked as they headed down the block toward the school.

"Umm, I wanted to tell you that I'm having dinner out tonight." Mark looked over at her, eyebrows raised. Might as well just get it out and over with. "With Special Agent Jackson."

Mark's look of surprise quickly turned to a frown. "And the reason you're telling me this?"

"Because I didn't want you to hear about it and get the wrong idea." She told Mark how it had come about. "Am I a suspect?"

Mark stopped when they got to the back field of the school and let Patchett off his leash. He threw an old green tennis ball for him then put his hands on Lizzie's shoulders.

"You're certainly not a suspect in either of the murders. And I can't imagine how the FBI would tie you in to the counterfeiting. I made Officer Vicker our FBI liaison just so I wouldn't have to be drawn into every conversation and he hasn't said anything about you even being on their radar." His face hardened. "Either Jackson's playing it close to his chest, not sharing information with us, or there's something else he wants close to his chest."

Lizzie smiled. "You know there's only one chest I want to be close to." She wound her arms around his neck and kissed him. He pulled her closer and she lost all sense of time and place until Patchett came running back and jumped up on them.

"Down," Mark commanded and Patchett sat looking from one to the other. Mark looked at his watch. "I'm sorry, I've got to get back to the station. This will have to make do for a walk."

"Why don't I keep him out a bit longer?" Lizzie suggested.

"Great. He does need it. You don't happen to have a little plot hatching about trying to get information out of Special Agent Jackson, do you?"

"Now, why would you think that?" Lizzie tried for an innocent look.

"Because I've gotten to know you pretty well."

Lizzie gave her image the once-over in the tall hallway mirror. The cream ruffled tank, oatmeal woven cardigan and darker embellished polyester skirt she'd chosen to wear to dinner hit the right note. Flattering but nothing that gave out the wrong signals. She would treat this like a business dinner, no matter how cute the agent was. She was not interested in him other than for the information she might get, something to help clear Bob, she hoped, or to clear herself if need be. She couldn't believe she'd be on their suspect list. In fact, Mark had called her shortly after she got home to say he'd met with Officer Vicker and Lizzie had not been mentioned as a person of interest by the FBI.

That was good news but a part of her mind had wondered if they would share that information with Vicker knowing that Mark and Lizzie were friends. As the liaison between the police and the FBI, Vicker would certainly report everything to Mark. She smiled as she remembered Mark's parting words to watch herself.

The doorbell rang precisely at six and Jackson stood there, bouquet of flowers in his hand.

"Do you give flowers to all your suspects?" Lizzie asked,

relief giving way to a slight apprehension that another game was afoot.

"You got me. We'll skip the questions for now. Just enjoy the evening."

Lizzie quickly put the flowers into a vase filled with water and grabbed her handbag. She decided there was no need for a sweater as the temperature hovered around seventy-eight degrees and she didn't plan to extend the evening too long.

Jackson talked about his impression of Ashton Corners as he drove to the restaurant. By the time they were seated at their table, he had switched to telling her about why he'd become an FBI agent.

"So tell me, what does a reading specialist do and why did you choose to do that?" he asked after they'd ordered drinks—a glass of Pinot Gris for Lizzie and a scotch on the rocks for Jackson.

Lizzie began to relax as she described the challenges and successes that made up her days. "I can't believe summer is over in another week, for me anyway. The teaching staff heads back before the kids do."

"You like what you do, obviously."

"I do."

They then took their time in perusing the menus with Lizzie finally settling on shrimp creole while Jackson went with porterhouse steak.

Lizzie took care with wording her next question. "How did a small town and a small press become involved in counterfeiting?"

Jackson looked at her a moment before answering. "It's the perfect cover. Who would suspect it in a nice, small Middle America town like Ashton Corners? And who in town would ever suspect someone like Orwell Rivers, who's lived here all his life and run a small business that many people used at one time or another?"

Lizzie shrugged. "There's got to be more to it than that. How did he get involved? Surely it wasn't his idea?"

"Not likely. It's a very well-organized, well-oiled operation. It takes more than a commercial photocopier. There's the distribution network to set up and that takes someone with a bit more resources and power than Orwell Rivers would have had. Now, are you going to grill me all evening about this or can we just enjoy ourselves?"

Lizzie smiled. "I just find it fascinating, that's all. It is my town, after all."

"And Bob Miller is your friend," Jackson added. "You're not trying to find out a way to clear him, are you?"

"How could I even start to do that?" Lizzie asked innocently. "You've said yourself that it's a big operation, or at least you intimated that," she added as he opened his mouth to speak. "And besides I'm sure you already realize Bob Miller does not fit that description." She pressed on. "I find it fascinating. Your job, too. I've never dated an FBI agent before."

"Ah, we're dating now. That's what I like to hear," Jackson teased.

Lizzie felt her face turning pink. Best to ignore that comment. "Is Bob still the primary suspect?"

Jackson stopped smiling. "He is and I can't talk about the case any further."

"So am I really a suspect?"

Jackson looked as if he were giving that some thought. "I think you can rest assured that I've ruled you out . . . in that, anyway."

Lizzie realized where he was heading with that statement. She'd found out as much as she probably would, even though it wasn't what she'd hoped for. It was time to plead fatigue.

Jackson saw her home and walked her to her door. Before she knew what he had in mind, he pulled her into his arms and kissed her. She knew a serious kiss when she felt one.

She gently pulled out of his arms and said, "I'm so sorry if I did or said anything that misled you, Drew. I've only been dating Mark a short while but I've known him a long time and we're trying to figure out what it's all about. I don't want to jeopardize that or even open the door to other possibilities."

Jackson didn't look surprised. "I guessed as much but you can't blame a guy for trying, as they say. The fact that you even mention other possibilities is something. I won't bother you but I will keep my eyes open in case it could happen. After all, Birmingham is not all that far away." He gave her a buss on the cheek and left.

Lizzie let herself into the house and stood in the dark for a few minutes, thinking. Sure, it was flattering to have someone as dynamic and dashing—okay and sexy, too—as Drew Jackson make a play, but she realized her heart had already made its choice. And unless she was totally wrong about Mark, that was how it would play out.

She phoned Mark to share what she hadn't found out at dinner, hoping he'd get the message about what she'd realized about her feelings.

"I'm glad you called," he said. "I've been sitting here wondering if I should tip my hand as the worried lover or just play it cool."

Lizzie laughed. "No worries. It turns out I'm not on the suspect list and he's not on any of my lists."

She could hear the smile in Mark's voice as he said, "I'm happy to hear that. I won't ask any questions."

"That's good because a lady never tells tales."

Chapter Twenty-four

◇◇◇

I'd like to be able to say that something awesome,
significant, or even scary happened, and that I
singlehandedly solved the case while I stood there,
paintbrush in hand, but alas, no such luck.

FLIPPED OUT—JENNIE BENTLEY

By late Saturday morning Lizzie was already behind on
her day's "to do" list. She'd managed to get some vacuuming and her grocery shopping done for the week. Of
course, still being on vacation she could do that at any time
but she stuck to the routines of her workweek without giving
it much thought. Since tomorrow was the launch, she
planned to visit her mama this afternoon. She didn't know
what the evening held. She'd learned over the past several
months that when Mark was enmeshed in a murder investigation, he took little time for himself, at least at the beginning of the investigation. Had it only been a little less than
two weeks since this all started? Now with two murders,
who knew when she'd spend an evening, much less a night
with him?

She realized they'd been dating for almost a year now.

That seemed like such a short time, but on the other hand, it felt like Mark had always been in her life. Maybe that was because she'd admired him from afar in high school. School friends seemed like forever friends, no matter how old or how long ago it had been. No wonder Molly had been so excited about reconnecting with Teensy.

After finishing a green salad for lunch, Lizzie changed into a pale pink cotton sundress and checked on the cats, who were curled up and sleeping back-to-side, even in the heat. She'd bought her mama a gardenia-scented sachet the day before and stashed it in her handbag before leaving the house. Nathaniel was sitting on his porch out of the direct sunlight. He raised his glass to her and she waved back, then drove out to Magnolia Manor.

The parking lot at the long-term assisted living residence was unusually busy. Lizzie managed to find a space at the far end of the lot and felt herself melt as she walked across the asphalt toward the front door. She gave a small sigh as she entered the air-conditioned grand entry hall that had been opened up into a waiting area. The building had originally been a family home, reminiscent of a plantation mansion from bygone days. The renovations had included two new single-story wings branching off at angles toward the back. Evelyn Turner's room was on the right-hand side, a few doors away from the large sunroom that joined the two wings together. A courtyard complete with water feature, padded lounge chairs and palms filled in the center portion.

Lizzie greeted by name the staff members whom she passed in the hall. She tapped lightly on her mama's door and was surprised to hear a welcome called out. Her mama never did that. In fact, she often thought her mama didn't even know she was there, visiting. Lizzie pushed the door open and saw Evelyn sitting in her usual chair by the window with Beulah Truman, her next-door neighbor at the Manor, sitting on the edge of the bed.

"How nice to see you, Miz Beulah," Lizzie said as she walked over and kissed the woman on her cheek.

Beulah smiled and patted Lizzie's cheek in return. "And, you, too, sweet pea. I was just wondering if Evelyn wanted to go for tea but now that you are here, I'll just get along."

"Why don't you join us?" Lizzie asked.

"I'd be delighted," Beulah said, pushing herself up from the bed. Her bulky body made for slow movement. The short-sleeved floral cotton shirtwaist dress reminded Lizzie of styles worn by housewives decades ago. It looked comfortable on Beulah.

The three of them walked unhurriedly down the hall, across the foyer and into the large main room where an aide was busily filling glasses and passing them out to the residents. They chose two facing love seats close to the door as all the seating with the view of the wonderful gardens was taken. After settling Evelyn with her tea and a small plate of cookies, Lizzie asked Beulah how she was doing.

"Oh, I'm perfectly dandy. Just the usual aches and pains and I don't talk about them much because everyone here has the same thing." She gave a hearty laugh, which was just perfect for her size. "We did have a resident pass earlier this week, though. I don't know if you knew her, Velda Franks. She was in her nineties so she'd had a good life and I guess that's all one can expect."

Lizzie nodded, but before she could say anything, Beulah

continued. "Not like poor Orwell Rivers. That man was far too young to die. And in such a horrid manner, too. Poor man."

"Did you know him?" Lizzie asked, surprised he'd been mentioned.

"Of course I did. I know most of the older generation around town. I even babysat him once or twice when he was just a young one. Always so serious, especially after his mama died. He was only six at the time. She had a heart condition and didn't make it much past thirty. Very sad. His daddy took it real hard and didn't have too much time for the boy. He used to be so eager when I'd get there. He wanted me to read to him and play pick-up sticks and the like." She shook her head. "So sad."

"He never married?"

"No, although it wasn't too surprising. He kept too much to himself."

Lizzie noticed her mama had finished the two cookies so got up to get her another one. She passed the plate around to those close by, then sat back and asked, "Did you ever talk to him or hear anything about him after he opened his business?"

"A printing press, wasn't it? No, our paths never crossed. But hold on, yes, I believe I did hear something more, come to think of it. My son is a banker in town and I remember once he told me Orwell had asked for a loan. Seems he was worried about losing his business."

"Did he get that loan?"

"I don't think so or Yancy, my son, would have mentioned it when he was telling the story. It couldn't have been easy for Orwell. I think he was paying off some of his daddy's debts for several years. He, the older Rivers, never had a head for business, I recall people saying. It's a good thing Orwell never married or had a family to support." Beulah leaned over to Evelyn. "Do you remember him, Evelyn? Of course, I'm not sure she even knew him," Beulah said to Lizzie. "She's quite a bit younger."

Two residents, a couple who were still able to live together, paused in their walk around the room and had a short chat with Beulah. Lizzie noticed her mama was starting to nod off. Maybe she'd read to her back in the room until she dropped off for a nap.

"I think I'd better get Mama back to her room before she naps in the chair," Lizzie said.

Beulah nodded. "Yes, dear. That's a good idea. I think I'll just sit here awhile longer. It was so good to see you again."

Lizzie kissed her cheek. "And you."

She tucked her arm under her mama's and was steering her away from the love seat when Beulah spoke again. "I just remembered. Yancy must have gotten that loan for Orwell. It wasn't too long after that he started publishing books. My dear friend Carolina was his first customer, and he published a book of her poetry."

Lizzie nodded and thought about it as they walked back down the hall. So, Orwell needed money, then got some money. Was it indeed a loan or did his business branch out in another direction?

Andie arrived home just after Lizzie had finished talking to Mark on the phone. Lizzie glanced at the clock. Ten P.M. Another exciting Saturday night.

"Hey, Andie. Did you have fun tonight?"

"It was okay. A bunch of us hung out at the Dixie Doodle then went over to Serena's house to play Xbox Backyard Sports. Have you ever tried their fitness games?"

Lizzie pretended to be offended. "Are you suggesting I need to?"

Andie looked mortified then noticed Lizzie was grinning. She laughed. "Never. They're just way cool."

"Nope. Never tried it although I might like to someday. Did you have supper?"

"Yeah. I thought you might be out, tonight being Saturday and all."

Lizzie sighed. "I thought so, too. Anyway, I'm going to head to bed."

"I think I'll watch a movie on my computer. Or do you want me to do some more Internet searches?"

"I'm not really sure where to go with the Orwell Rivers angle at the moment." She filled Andie in on what Beulah Truman had told her.

Andie shrugged. "It sounds like stuff you already knew, sort of." Andie helped herself to a banana from the ceramic tray on the kitchen counter. "You know, I think you're kinda looking at the wrong murder."

Lizzie looked thoughtful. "What do you mean?"

"Well, it's like, you want to help Chief Bob, right? Well, the other guy's the one they tagged him for to start with, isn't it? And this Orwell Rivers, he's kinda more mixed in with the phony money. Isn't that what the FBI is here for?"

Lizzie shook her head. "You are so right. I've really gotten sidetracked. How could that happen?"

"You're following the money, I s'pose. Just like you said."

Lizzie huffed. "Yeah, but that's not good enough.

Tomorrow's the launch, but on Monday, I'll try to find out a lot more about Cabe Wilson."

"That dude was nowhere on the Net."

"Okay, then it will have to be the good old-fashioned type of sleuthing."

Chapter Twenty-five

◇◇◇

Old friends were the best kind, it's been said; they
know all the old jokes and where the bodies are
buried.

A DEADLY GRIND—VICTORIA HAMILTON

When Lizzie and Andie arrived at Molly's late the next
morning, the tables had already been set up on the
back lawn. The food tables sported white tablecloths and
were awaiting the arrival of the caterer with the food; the
portable bar was being stocked; and the area set aside for
the Cajun trio was ready. It reminded Lizzie of the garden
party Molly had held for the literacy students who took their
classes at the mansion. Everything was laid out much the
same, except for there being a lot more tables.

That had been a tense time in Molly's life, and also for
Lizzie and Sally-Jo, who had been hoping none of
their students had been involved in some thefts from the
mansion.

Lizzie wandered over to the bookselling table. Andie

had actually worn a long black with white polka dots sundress. She looked down at it and grimaced. "I shouldn't have worn this. I really don't feel right in it. My mama bought it for me."

"I think you look just fine and it adds the right touch to the afternoon. I also like your hair." Totally black. No neon patches. And lying flat, not in spikes, and tucked behind her ears.

Andie shrugged. "I couldn't think of what color to add this time. It's also getting a bit too long for spikes. I'm not sure what I'll do. But for now, I'd better get this table looking right and ready to go for when Stephanie gets here. I can hardly wait to see baby Wendy." She clapped her hands together and smiled.

Bob called over to them from the corner of the house. "I'm just waiting for Jacob to arrive and then we'll load those there boxes onto the dolly and bring them over to the table. Is that how y'all plan to have it? No cloth over it or anything?"

Andie looked at the table and then at Lizzie, who shrugged. "Better ask Molly. She'll have something ready to go if that's not how she wants it."

Molly wasn't to be seen, so Andie went inside to find her. Lizzie wandered over to Bob. "How are you doing?"

Bob didn't look at her but continued scanning the backyard. "Oh, fair to middling. As well as can be expected, I guess."

"Have the police found anything new?"

"Not that they're telling me."

"What about Cabe Wilson?"

Bob shrugged. "I guess they're doing what they can but I'd sure like to jump in and do some of my own asking around, just a few questions. I've had a couple of more chats with the feds but they're pretty tight-lipped." He snorted. "I don't think they're anywhere near tracking down who's in charge of the whole counterfeit operation. I'm pretty sure I'm under surveillance, though. Just not sure who's doing it."

"Well, I'm not being watched. Tell me who you'd be talking to and what questions I should ask."

Bob looked at her then. "I won't do that, Lizzie. It's far too dangerous. There are two bodies already. I don't plan for you to be the third."

Lizzie thought a moment. "If you think that's best, but you know, I'm going to do it anyway. It seems it would be a lot safer and faster if I'm asking the right people the right things."

Bob shook his head. "I know you well enough to know that's just what you'll do." He sighed. "So help me, I'll never forgive myself if anything happens to you. Neither will the chief. So I want you to promise me you'll always have someone with you when you're out detecting. It'd take a lot more effort and gumption to try to do away with two of you." A look of doubt crossed his face and Lizzie knew that he, too, was remembering when a murderer had tried to run Lizzie and Sally-Jo off the road last fall.

"I promise," she said quickly before he could change his mind.

He looked around and spotted Molly walking toward them. "Let's talk about this either later today or tomorrow morning, at my place."

Lizzie nodded her agreement as Molly reached them.

"Y'all look deep into serious conversation," Molly greeted them. "This is supposed to be a fun affair. What are y'all talking about anyway?"

"My fault," Lizzie jumped in. "I was asking Bob if he'd heard anything more about the murder investigations."

Molly shook her head. "That's it. No more talk about it today. I'm giving you fair warning. You are to relax and enjoy yourself, Bob Miller, and you, honey"—she reached out and touched Lizzie's arm—"are going to be too hard at work making sure this whole thing runs smoothly to have time for talk of murder."

"And you will be?" Bob left the question hanging.

"Well I'll be playing the ever-so-charming Southern hostess, all the while trying to ensure our guests leave with lots of purchased books."

"You're taking to this bookselling way too seriously, girl."

"Don't you 'girl' me, sir. Besides, I've taken on this task and I plan to do it to the best of my abilities. Now here comes Andrea with the special tablecloth I found on the Internet." She took it out of Andie's hands and opened it to reveal a black background almost totally covered with books of all sizes, shapes and colors; some open, some stacked.

"Wow, that's so appropriate. Good for you, Molly," Lizzie said.

Molly beamed. "Yes, I'm quite pleased with it. Let's get it spread out on this here table and when the books arrive— where are the books, Bob?"

"Just waiting for Jacob to arrive to give me a hand. And, speak of the devil . . ."

The three of them turned to look at the back door and Sally-Jo stepped through followed by Jacob. And he was followed by Teensy.

"Yoo-hoo, y'all. The author has arrived!" Teensy waved a small red and orange scarf in her right hand and used her left hand to gather up the large amounts of material in her long orange, red, pink and yellow gauzy sundress.

Bob said, "huh," under his breath. Andie stood eyes agog. Lizzie couldn't think of what to say but Molly rushed over to her friend and gave her a hug.

"You look ready to light up the entire Alabama horizon, Teensy."

"Well that's just what I intend to do, thank you very much." She gave Molly another quick squeeze and looked around. "This is amazing. Thank you, my dear friend. I am so excited I can hardly contain myself."

Molly glared at Bob as he opened his mouth. He quickly shut it and signaled Jacob to follow him. Sally-Jo scooted around the two older women and gave Lizzie and Andie a quick hug each.

"I think this will be quite an entertaining afternoon," she said softly and continued her walk around the yard, inspecting each table.

Andie snorted and turned quickly to the table, pretending to smooth out the tablecloth.

"She certainly does have a flair for clothes," Lizzie said.

"And hair," Andie said, her back still turned to them.

Lizzie looked at Teensy's hairdo. It had been caught up and hidden under a wide-brimmed orange straw hat with a yellow organza band around it. A few tendrils of red hair dramatically framed her face. She certainly wasn't afraid to be true to herself. Lizzie admired that.

A baby's crying signaled that Stephanie had arrived with Wendy. "I'm sorry, y'all. She's just woken from a nap and is never in a good mood when that happens."

Andie rushed over. "Here, let me take her while you put your things down."

Molly and Teensy joined in admiring the baby, who suddenly quieted down with all the attention.

Bob and Jacob arrived back with the trolley and set about unpacking the books while Andie arranged them in stacks on the table. Teensy swooped over, pulling a pen with a large white quill on the end out of the handbag.

"Before we get involved in anything else this afternoon, I want to give you each a signed copy of my novel," Teensy said. "It's just a small token of how much I appreciate all your help."

Lizzie glanced at Molly, who gave a slight shake of her head. Lizzie had guessed right. They wouldn't tell her they'd all bought a copy already. When it came to Lizzie's turn, Teensy said, "Now I know you and Molly have already read the book but a signed copy may be worth something in the future."

Lizzie smiled and thanked her for the book. The others could return their purchased books and get their money back if they'd not already started reading them.

By the time all the invited guests had arrived, the noise level on the patio was drowning out the music supplied by three graying, elderly men dressed in wildly patterned sports shirts, white cargo pants and sandals. The music they were playing was just as hot as the weather.

The two bartenders were kept hopping as were the catering staff, who kept a watchful eye on the various plates of appetizers, refilling them as soon as too many spaces showed. Lizzie stood to the side, keeping track of who was doing what just in case she needed to step in and help out. She was pleased the lineup for book purchases wound around the yard. The readers would then move over to the autographing line, a more casual formation. Teensy's identifiable laugh would float above the din every now and then.

Lizzie had a moment's unease as she look around the scene, wondering, hoping that it was safe. She noticed that Andie stepped back to do something to the baby, so Lizzie slipped in behind the table to help with the bagging of books. Stephanie looked from the lineup in front of her to her baby. When she saw that Andie had everything under control, she continued taking people's money. Eventually the crowd tapered off.

Teensy's high-pitched laugh rang out and Lizzie glanced toward the back door in time to see Mayor Harold Hutchins step through it and give Teensy a two-sided air-kiss.

Very politic of him, she thought. His white suit, shirt and tie along with the white straw hat gave him the air of a Southern gentleman. Or Colonel Sanders. He looked right at home with the attention he'd attracted, as he tucked Teensy's hand through the crook of his arm and steered her over to the bar. Lizzie noticed he ordered the hard stuff, Bourbon, probably, from the color of it. They really were a well-suited couple.

By that time, most people were sitting and enjoying their drinks or wandering and talking, taking in the gardens. Teensy nodded at Lizzie, who found Molly in conversation in the far corner of the yard. Lizzie excused herself as she broke into the talk and asked Molly to accompany her.

Molly then asked for everyone's attention, thanked them for coming and spending, to which everyone laughed, and then introduced Teensy. The guests cheered and clapped as Teensy walked over to the patio stairs and pulled out her speech.

"I hope y'all will bear with me. I know I can talk up a

blue streak and y'all can hardly shut me up—that's not changed over the years—but I wanted to make sure I got this all right and didn't leave out anyone, so being a writer, I wrote it down."

Ten minutes later, after thanking Molly and the book club members, the mayor and everyone for coming, Teensy opened her book and read from the beginning. After fifteen minutes, she closed the book.

"Now, if y'all haven't bought *The Winds of Desire*, how will you ever know what happens? And I promise, things heat up"—she fluttered her eyebrows—"and it's worth every steamy penny." With that, she curtsied as best she could and headed to the bar for another drink as some whistles mixed in with the clapping.

By the time everyone had left, three hours after it all started, Molly sank gratefully into a chair and nursed a glass of Chardonnay. Bob finished putting the remaining unsold books back in the boxes while Jacob piled them on the trolley.

"You go and relax," Jacob said. "I can handle this. Only three boxes going back into the garage. Looks like sales were good."

Stephanie looked up from where she was counting money. "Y'all can be sure of that," she said with a grin.

Andie finished totaling up the numbers. "We sold one hundred thirty books," she announced.

Teensy let out a loud whoop as she sat in a chair across from Molly. "That is what I'd call a successful debut. And I have y'all to thank for it." She waved her arm around in a circle above her head.

"You've already done that," Lizzie said as she joined them.

The caterers and bartenders were finishing loading up. Molly stood. "I'll be back in moment. Just a bit of business to attend to."

Teensy grinned at Lizzie. "I think that I am probably the bestselling author for this day in all of Ashton Corners, possibly even the entire county."

Lizzie returned the grin. "I'd say that's a sure bet. I'm glad it went so well, but it was certain to be a success. Everyone wants to see your book do well, Teensy."

Teensy's eyes misted over. "John would have been so proud of me. I wish he were here to see it. I wish he were here to see just how good everything in my life is turning out to be." She dabbed at her eyes. "Now, what else should I be doing?"

Lizzie stopped to think. "Nothing. Just show up next Saturday, ten thirty A.M. at the Winn-Dixie on Broward, with your signing pen of course. I think Molly said the books have already gone out to them. You were interviewed for the *Colonist* the other day, weren't you?" Teensy nodded. "Good. That will be in Thursday's paper, along with the photos their guy took today, so that should get some excitement going about the signings, too."

Teensy visibly brightened as she looked over to the edge of the patio where Harold Hutchins stood talking to one of the caterers. He glanced at Teensy and nodded. She gave him a small wave. "Well then, I've got me another dinner date with the mayor so we'll just be leaving now." She bussed Lizzie's cheek. "Thanks again, sugar." She sashayed over to Hutchins and crooked her arm through his. He leaned toward her and said something that made her laugh as they walked into the house.

Bob and Jacob came wandering back about the same time

as Molly. They all looked at one another and let out one big sigh. Wendy started crying, startling them.

Stephanie walked over with her. "The money's there in the cashbox. I think it's time I took this little one home. She's getting hungry and cranky."

"We'll give you a lift," Jacob said and looked at Sally-Jo, who nodded and grabbed her purse.

"Gee, thanks, but I've got to talk to Lizzie first, real quick." She looked at Lizzie.

"Sure, I'll help you get all your gear together." Lizzie walked over to where Stephanie had propped the diaper bag.

"I'm getting real worried again about work tomorrow night," Stephanie whispered.

"Would you rather I picked you up and gave you a ride home?"

"No," Stephanie said louder than she'd meant to. She lowered her voice again. "No, I'd really like it if you'd park outside my place like we planned, see if you notice him and make sure that I'm not going out of my mind."

"I'm all set. I'll be there. Don't you worry," Lizzie assured her and gave her a hug.

Stephanie's smile looked small and sad. She called out to Jacob that she was ready and met them at the gate.

Bob pulled out a chair for Molly and she gratefully sank into it. "I don't trust Mayor Hutchins as far as I can throw him. I'd watch it, if I were Teensy. I've come to loggerheads with him a few times over the years. But he did outlast me, I'll give him that. Teensy better watch her virtue . . . but I think she's gone done lost it already." He chuckled. He pulled out a chair for Lizzie.

She shook her head. "Thanks, but Andie and I had better get on our way. I'll talk to you tomorrow, Molly."

"How cool was that," Andie said as they got in the hot car. "My first book launch." She gave Lizzie a mischievous look. "Maybe that's another day shaved off the tutoring in the fall."

Chapter Twenty-six

◇◇◇

To say that man is a reasoning animal is a very different thing than to say that most of man's decisions are based on his rational process. That I don't believe at all.

REX STOUT

Lizzie made sure she was at Bob's early the next morning. She wanted to catch him before his day began, and since they hadn't set a time to meet, she figured earlier was better.

He greeted her at his front door, mug of coffee in hand. "Hey, Lizzie. I just happen to have a mug with your name on it, if you'd like."

"Am I that easy to read?" She laughed and followed him down the short hall to the kitchen. The sun streamed through the window, giving the room a bright, cozy feel even though all the windows and doors stood wide open.

"Just trying to get some real air in here before it heats up too badly. Let's go sit outside. You might just be able to see some of the pike jumping."

Lizzie followed him out and took the Adirondack chair

farthest from the door. Bob remained standing and scoured the river for a few minutes before joining her.

"You know," he started, then paused. "If ever I was to lose my freedom—now I'm not saying that's about to happen—but this is what I'd miss the most."

Lizzie felt a jolt shoot through her body. She sat up straighter and tried to cover her anxiety. "Do you have any idea at all who could be behind all this?"

"I've wracked my brain, tried to remember every incident in my time as chief, trying to look for some clue as to who might have it in for me. Because that's what this amounts to. The counterfeiting ring is one thing. It's obviously been established for a while, even while I was in office. But to try to pin Wilson's murder on me and also tie me in to the phony bills, that's a separate agenda item. I might just be the most expedient way of deflecting police attention but there's got to be something personal in all this, too."

Lizzie thought what he said made sense but it sure didn't get them anywhere.

"I talked to his fiancée. Her name's Urliss Langdorf." She shifted a little in her chair as Bob didn't comment, just stared at her. "She thought Wilson might be going to see you to get help dealing with whatever he'd gotten into."

"You went to see her? I guess I shouldn't be surprised. Did she have any idea what this thing was that he was mixed up in?"

"No, but she thought it was something illegal. Do you think it could have been the counterfeiting?"

"It's possible. It might have seemed like the kind of get-rich-easy scheme he liked. Well, I wonder if Wilson might have wanted out and needed my help, maybe to make a deal with the law. I wonder why he decided to go straight?"

"Love. She said she wouldn't marry him until he did just that."

"Hmm. Rivers, on the other hand, might have wanted a bigger cut. Or he, too, may have been having second thoughts. I'd like to think it's the second one. Orwell Rivers might have been a bit of a loner but he'd never struck me as deep down bad."

"What if Rivers was the head of the scheme and somebody wanted to take over?"

Bob thought a few moments. "That's possible, I guess. But it doesn't account for what happened to Wilson." Bob shook his head. "I can't get over the fact that this was operating right under my nose."

"And here you thought you were perfect," Lizzie said playfully.

Bob glanced at her and chortled. "Well said, little lady."

"So, what's the next move?"

Bob stared out at the river again. "Like I've said before, this is a dangerous game and you're definitely not one of the players. You need to stay out of it. Don't go chasing suspects or asking any more questions. I appreciate the opportunity to sit and talk this through but that's the extent of your involvement. Go it?"

Lizzie knew better than to argue. "I hear you."

Bob harrumphed. "Yeah, but will you listen?"

Lizzie pulled into Urliss Langdorf's driveway, got out of the car and scanned the street looking for any sign of a big black sedan. Not this time. She breathed a sigh of relief and walked up to the front door.

Urliss answered on the first buzz of the doorbell. She

stood dressed in a shapeless long beige T-shirt that stopped midthigh. Brown shorts peeked out at the bottom of it. Her blonde hair was even more in need of a dye job and looked like it hadn't been washed in days. Her eyes looked dully at Lizzie. It took her a few seconds to realize who was at her door.

"Oh, it's you. Do you know who killed Cabe?"

"Uh, no, I'm sorry, I don't. Not yet. Do you mind if I ask you a few more questions, though?"

"We've talked before. I don't know anything else," she said in a monotone.

"I'll only take a few minutes. It might just jog your memory, remind you of something you didn't realize you know."

Urliss shifted from one foot to the other. "All right, I guess so." She stood aside and opened the screen door.

Lizzie followed her into the living room, which was already hot and stuffy. Urliss dropped into an old armchair; Lizzie perched on the edge of its twin, right across from her.

"First of all, how are you holding up?"

Urliss shrugged. "Some days are better than others, ya know?" She turned her head to the left, away from Lizzie. "It's just, I miss him a lot," she said, almost a whisper.

"I can't begin to imagine what it's like. I'll try not to upset you with the questions." Lizzie waited until Urliss was once again looking at her. "I'm wondering if you saw any of Cabe's acquaintances, someone who wasn't a close friend but came over to talk to him?"

Urliss gave it some thought before shaking her head. "No one came over when I was here. I'd only moved in about five months ago, though. I wonder what will happen to the house now?" She glanced around the room in disinterest.

"You said he got a phone call the night before he, uh, died. Had there been others? Maybe one that upset him?"

"No. He didn't have many visitors or phone calls. I guess you could say he didn't have many friends at all. Just other guys like him who tried to avoid getting caught. In fact, that's one thing he did say to me. He said he had to be careful to stay on the right side of the law." She started crying. "That was just a line to keep me happy. He was mixed up in some illegal things, wasn't he? We were never going to be married at that rate." She stood abruptly and clenched her fists. "Damn you, Cabe. Why couldn't you go straight?"

Lizzie wondered if maybe Urliss had killed Cabe in a fit of rage. He kept lying to her and that wedding moved further and further away. She could be a suspect. She knew where he was going; she could have followed him or even gone another route, then killed him at Bob's. Except, Lizzie reminded herself, there was no indication Cabe had been killed at Bob's. And what about the money? Urliss may have been in on the scheme but that would mean she was an excellent liar. *Or maybe I'm entirely too gullible.* She focused herself to get back to her original line of thought.

"Did Cabe have a lot of extra money all of a sudden?" Lizzie asked.

Urliss sat back down. "He had enough. We never wanted for anything. But the police did tell me they found a speedboat registered in his name." She sniffed. "I would have loved to have a boat of any kind. And he never told me. What was that all about?"

Lizzie knew a rhetorical question when she heard one. She also knew this was a dead end. Urliss didn't know anything, and if she did, the FBI would already know about it. She wondered if they'd shared with Mark any details of their interview with Urliss.

Dusk was sliding into darker shades of night as Lizzie pulled alongside the curb on Fader Street, half a block away from Stephanie's apartment building. She'd just hunker down and watch for an hour or so, and if no car showed up, she'd leave. She'd already been in place when Stephanie had arrived home from work. No car on her tail, at least.

Lizzie's mind played with what she'd learned about Cabe Wilson while she waited. He sounded like a likely candidate for the counterfeiting ring. Maybe he got worried when Rivers died and wanted out. Maybe the bad guys couldn't chance he'd talk. But would they resort to murder? If they'd already killed Rivers, then one more victim wouldn't bother them. But what if something else Rivers had done had resulted in his death? There were far too many what-ifs with no answers. How did the police ever solve anything?

She'd been so engrossed in her mental games that she jumped at the knock on her driver's window. Lizzie took a few seconds to absorb what or rather who she saw, then rolled down the window.

"Officer Craig, you almost gave me heart failure."

"That's similar to what you're doing to the people who live over there." She signaled with her head toward the house to the right side of Lizzie's car. "They've seen a vehicle several times over the past couple of weeks parked outside here with the driver never getting out, then just driving away. What are you up to anyway?"

"I'm sorry if I scared them. I was just trying to keep an

eye out for the pickup they must be referring to. It's my first night parked here. Honest." Lizzie took a deep breath to calm her heart rate.

Craig straightened her back and rolled her head from side to side, stretching. "So who or what are you looking for?"

Lizzie sighed. "I don't know. It's just that Stephanie Lowe thinks she has seen the same truck following her home from the diner for the past few Mondays and then it stays parked here awhile. She's scared it's someone keeping an eye on her. I just wanted to check it out for her."

Craig stiffened. "Why would someone keep tabs on her?"

"She's been afraid her ex-boyfriend, the father of her baby, might try something."

"Does he have any custody rights? Are there lawyers involved?"

"Not on her side and she hasn't heard from him since last fall. But she was very scared of him back then."

Craig looked around. "Well, if he were coming tonight you can bet seeing my cruiser here kept him driving on. What's your plan?"

"I just thought I'd park here for about an hour and see if he showed up. I hadn't really thought beyond that." She realized the sun had finished setting. House lights shone in the windows along one side of the street while lights in the apartment building across the street twinkled back.

"Why don't I take a turn next Monday night?"

"As a police officer?"

"No, in my spare time. If there's no complaint, I can't do it on the tab."

Lizzie smiled. "Thanks. I know Stephanie will appreciate it."

Craig waved the thanks away. "I'll just go have a talk

with our antsy homeowners, set their minds at ease. You do have to promise me you won't do anything crazy like try to approach him if he shows up when you're here. Just call the station or me. Okay?"

Chapter Twenty-seven

◇◇◇

I almost wondered what else could go wrong today,
but I stopped myself just in time. I was afraid I'd get
an answer.

CAKE ON A HOT TIN ROOF—JACKLYN BRADY

Sally-Jo caught Lizzie Thursday morning right out of the shower after her run. Lizzie opened the door, totally surprised to see her there that early, and invited her in for a coffee.

The day had started out sweltering, but this was the coolest part of it, so they took their mugs out to the patio and sat on the two chaise lounges. Lizzie blew on her coffee and waited for Sally-Jo to share her reason for the surprise visit, which she seemed in no rush to do.

"How are this week's renos coming along?" Lizzie asked at last.

Sally-Jo shrugged. "Pretty much on schedule."

"Remember to let me know if you need some more laborers. Mark's more than happy to help out again, if he can manage the time."

"Not too likely with these murders, is it?"

Lizzie's turn to shrug. "Probably not but I'm still here."

Sally-Jo smiled. "Thanks. Jacob's been doing the bulk of the extra work lately." She chewed her bottom lip a few seconds then said, "Last night Jacob asked me to marry him."

Lizzie's initial reaction was to whoop it up but she took her cue from Sally-Jo's low-key behavior. "And you said?"

"I told him I'd think about it. It just took me totally by surprise. I couldn't think straight. I told him as much." Sally-Jo pushed her short, wispy red bangs to the side.

"How did he take that?"

"He wasn't too happy. I guess he thought it was a sure thing. We've been getting closer for some time now but it's still awfully early in a relationship to get engaged, don't you think?"

Lizzie thought she'd be better off not giving advice. "What about his marriage?"

"He's filed for a divorce. We'd wait, of course, but then he'd like to get married." She let out a whimper.

Lizzie glanced at her sharply. "What's wrong?"

Sally-Jo gave a deep sigh. "I know I love him but I guess I'm not totally sure it's the right thing to do. Yet. What if I say yes, we get married and then decide it was a totally stupid thing to do? What then?"

You get divorced. Not the right answer, she knew. "I'm not the one to give advice. I've never even been engaged. But I'd like to think your heart will know when it's the right person and you won't be looking for reasons not to get married. Like being worried about a divorce. Might this not have more to do with what happened last time you were engaged?"

Sally-Jo turned to face Lizzie, her eyes wide. "Do you think so? I hadn't thought of that. In fact, I've spent the last couple of years trying *not* to think about it. But if I still have issues about it, I'll just have to figure it out and deal with them. I won't let that jerk who two-timed me ruin my whole life." She pushed herself off the lounge.

"You're right, Lizzie. Thanks so much for the advice." Sally-Jo smiled. "I feel so much better now that I have a plan of action. I've got to dash. The building inspector is due any minute to check the fixtures in the powder room." She gave Lizzie a hug and left her there musing about advice not given.

They seemed to be the perfect couple but who really knew. Lizzie hoped they could work it out because she'd really like to see her friend happy and settled. Both of her friends. Jacob had turned out to be that, too. She started humming as she went back inside with the empty mugs.

Andie slogged her way into the kitchen as Lizzie was finishing her breakfast of granola.

"Did I hear Sally-Jo a little while ago?" Andie asked, helping herself to a glass of orange juice from the fridge.

Lizzie nodded, her mouth full. When she'd swallowed she said, "She stopped by briefly. Had to run back for another stage in her renovation. How did you sleep?"

"Okay." Andie stared at Lizzie's empty plate.

"There are plenty of eggs in the fridge, if you'd like," Lizzie said. She'd already told Andie to feel at home enough to make her own meals, especially if Lizzie wasn't there. Dinners were a different matter. Hopefully, they could enjoy those together. Lizzie had never had a sister and seldom did anyone stay overnight. Few sleepovers at her house when she was a kid. Evelyn Turner just couldn't handle it. She'd never felt she'd missed out on much before, but having Andie at her place, even for just the past few days, made Lizzie realize how much she enjoyed the company.

Andie took a side plate out of the cupboard and placed a banana and apple on it before joining Lizzie at the table. It looked like there was something else on her mind today. Lizzie waited until the banana had been devoured.

"What are your plans for the day?" she asked.

Andie shrugged. "I might go shopping with some friends. There's a big sale on over at Walgreens in the mall. Might as well get school supplies while they're on sale. Mama left me a credit card for such things. Or else we'll just hang out." She glanced at Lizzie from under lowered eyelashes.

"I've been wondering." She hesitated long enough to make Lizzie a bit anxious. "Do you think I could keep on living here with you when school starts?"

Lizzie almost choked on the sip of juice she'd taken. "Where did that come from?"

"Well, you know, I kinda like being here, with you. Nobody would miss me at home. I'd keep all the house rules and help you around here and things like that. I wouldn't be any trouble, I promise. I could even get a part-time job and pay you some rent, although it wouldn't be a lot," she tapered off. "Things have been okay so far, haven't they?"

Lizzie nodded and then took a minute to compose herself. She didn't want to put Andie off, but if this was a plea for help, she needed to know that, too. Her immediate reaction was to say, "No way." But that would be too harsh.

"What do you think your parents would say about that?"

Andie shrugged. "Like I said, they wouldn't even know

I was gone. They're never around. They don't care what I do. I just get in the way when they have parties and things. Besides, you could really keep track of my reading," she threw in with a hopeful grin.

Lizzie couldn't help smiling back. "It's not a decision I can make right now, Andie. I'd have to think about it and we'd have to talk it over with your folks." She held up her hand as Andie opened her mouth. "I will give it serious thought. I promise."

Andie shut her mouth and nodded.

Lizzie kept coming back to the question all morning, long after Andie had gone out with her friends. What would she do with a teenager living with her? It was fine short-term. But to have that much responsibility every day? No way. Besides, she was certain the Masons would object. You didn't let your sixteen-year-old just move in with a virtual stranger. She wondered what Molly would say when she told her.

The phone rang and Lizzie glanced at the call display . . . speaking of Molly.

"Hey, Molly," she said, shifting out of her reverie.

"Lizzie, the most awful thing has happened." Molly sounded totally beside herself.

"What happened? Are you all right?" Lizzie's heart was pounding in her chest.

"Yes, honey, I'm fine. But Teensy's had a break-in at her house."

"Is she all right?"

"Oh yes. It happened while she was out to dinner last night again with Mayor Hutchins and when he brought her home, they found her house had been ransacked. She was in some state. The mayor brought her over here after the police had finished up and she stayed the night. Can you come over?"

"Of course. I'll be right over." She hung up, her mind already thinking about what she needed. Shoes and handbag. That was it.

She checked on the cats and found them each curled up, heads touching, on her bed. She quietly exited and grabbed her car keys from the hall table on her way past. The heat assailed her as she opened the front door. She gratefully switched on the car's air-conditioning as she backed out of the driveway, leaving the windows open for about half a block. She loved her add-on to the eighty-year-old house and yard that her landlord, Nathaniel Creely, so painstakingly kept in appealing shape but she sure missed not having a garage on days like this. It was like getting into a sauna when she first sat in the car.

By the end of the block the air-conditioning was doing its magic. She waved to the Finsteads, an elderly couple at the corner house, sitting out on their covered wraparound porch, drinking glasses in hand. Traffic moved at a crawl for another couple of blocks until she'd passed the large moving van parked in her lane. She wondered who'd finally bought the 1970's bungalow that had sat empty since last Christmas. She'd have to take a run past one morning and scope it out a bit better. As she turned onto Molly's street, her mind played over different scenarios for what had happened at Teensy's place. It obviously had something to do with what had been happening but they'd all believed her manuscript wasn't part of it. So, had they been wrong? Or what else had been sought?

Molly was waiting at the door when Lizzie arrived. "I've

got some nice freshly made iced tea out back. The sun's not come around there yet so it's not too bad."

Lizzie followed Molly through the house, noting that a small purple piece of luggage sat at the bottom of the stairs. Teensy must be getting ready to go home.

Teensy opened her arms to Lizzie for a hug, without getting up from her spot on a chaise lounge. Lizzie obliged her then slowly untangled herself.

"How scary for you, Teensy. You're sure you're all right?" Lizzie asked.

"Oh my, yes, sugar. We could see right away that the front door stood open a bit so Harold just told me to stand back and he'd investigate. He's such a brave soul." Teensy sighed. "He called 911 while he went through the house. It's such a mess, I couldn't tell if anything had been taken. The police want me to make a note today if I realize something's missing."

"Oh my God. That's terrible. Did you have many valuables there?"

"Not really. I brought lots and lots of colorful, cheap jewelry but only a very small selection of the good pieces, thank goodness. The jewelry was strewn across my bed. Even my underwear had been tossed around the bedroom." She shuddered. "I can't bear to think that some man was pawing through my lingerie."

Molly leaned across the arms of both their lounges. "It's a good thing you weren't at home or you could have been hurt."

Teensy gave a small smile. "I've thought about that."

"I wonder if it was random. Maybe someone saw you go out for the evening or could have been ringing doorbells looking for empty houses," Lizzie suggested.

"Or?" Molly asked.

"Or, did it have something to do with all that's been going on around here?"

"Oh, surely, sugar, you don't think that? What's the connection? We've gotten the books sorted out and the FBI is handling the counterfeiting thing. Just because the money was mixed up with my book boxes doesn't mean there's any left there. Does it?" She looked from one to the other. "Maybe we should look through those boxes again."

Lizzie nodded. "And maybe we should move them out of Molly's garage. I don't like the idea that either of you could be in danger."

"But where would we put them? They're so handy in the garage," Molly protested.

"We'll rent storage someplace," Teensy answered. "Y'all must have one of those big storage rental places in town."

They could hear the front doorbell ringing. Lizzie jumped up. "I'll get it."

She hurried through the cool house and took a moment to peek through the peephole. *Oh, not them again.*

She pulled the door open. "Special Agents Jackson and Ormes. What can I do for you?"

Jackson's initial look of surprise turned into a broad smile. "I didn't expect to see you here, Ms. Turner."

Lizzie looked from him to Ormes, who stood, arms crossed in front of his chest, frowning. "I'm often here visiting my friend, Special Agent Jackson. Did you want to see Molly?"

Ormes cleared his throat. "No, ma'am. We're here to talk to Miz Coldicutt. I understand she's here, too." He started walking forward.

Lizzie hesitated a moment then opened the door wide for them. "I'll take you to them."

Molly and Teensy looked up in surprise as the agents followed Lizzie out to the patio. "You have visitors, Teensy," she said.

"Yes, ma'am," Jackson said and pulled a patio chair over next to Teensy. "May I?" he asked Molly and sat when she nodded. Ormes stood standing, watching.

"We'd like to ask you a few questions about what happened at your place last night, ma'am." Jackson pulled out a small black notebook.

Teensy sighed. "As I told the police, I'd been out to dinner with the mayor and when we arrived home, the place had been tossed. What's it to the FBI anyway?"

Lizzie bit back a smile as she sat back in her chair. *Go get 'em, Teensy.*

"And you haven't had a chance yet to see if anything was missing?"

"Not yet. That's what I plan to do as soon as we've had lunch, gentlemen. Do you think it has anything to do with the counterfeit money? Obviously you do or you wouldn't be here."

Ormes cleared his throat. "It is mighty strange all that's happened since your book was published." He looked at Molly. "We'd like to take a look at all those boxes of books in your garage, ma'am. Something may have been overlooked the first time around."

"And you think they thought the books must be at my place?" Teensy asked.

Ormes nodded.

Molly stood. "Of course. I'll show you where they're kept."

Jackson winked at Lizzie as he followed his partner and Molly around the corner of the house.

"It seems we're on the right track," Lizzie said to Teensy.

* * *

Mark stopped by Lizzie's on his way home from the station. "I have some unhappy news for you, Lizzie. I thought I'd best tell you in person."

She sat down hard on the chair in the kitchen. She went through a mental checklist as he sat down across from her. If it were about her mama, the residence would have phoned. She'd just finished talking to Molly so she was fine. One of her friends?

"The FBI has taken Bob Miller into custody. They left for Birmingham with him a couple of hours ago."

Lizzie felt stricken. "No, they can't arrest him. He's innocent."

"I know you believe that, Lizzie, but they seem to think they have enough proof." Mark sat down and ran his right hand over his smooth scalp.

"What did they find out? It must be something new. And bad."

"Well, it seems that they've had him under surveillance for the past week."

Lizzie opened her mouth but Mark shook his head. He knew she wondered if he'd been in on it. He hadn't.

"And?" she asked instead.

"He managed to give them the slip last night and didn't show up back home until around midnight. And, he refuses to tell them where he was."

"Last night? They think he broke into Teensy's house? And that ties him into the counterfeit ring? How? What was he . . . or rather, the real thief, looking for?"

Mark shrugged. "Miz Coldicutt says nothing important

is missing, as far as she can tell. She thinks it has to do with the remaining books."

"That's it. It couldn't have been Bob. He knew the books were at Molly's. He wouldn't have been looking for them at Teensy's."

"There's nothing to say that's what this person was after. The FBI had a couple of my men searching through those boxes of books but nothing was in them, either." Mark reached across the table and squeezed Lizzie's hand. "I know you're upset by this but maybe that's a good place for Bob right now. If this counterfeit scenario is still taking place, he's safer in custody."

Lizzie didn't feel convinced.

"And if what Bob thinks is true," Mark continued, "that he's being framed, the real bad guys might think they've succeeded and get just a bit too complacent. That's when they're bound to slip up. The FBI will continue the investigation until they find all who've been involved."

Lizzie sighed. "Wow," she said dejectedly. "Does Molly know?"

Mark shook his head. "I thought you might like to be the one to tell her." Lizzie nodded.

"'Like.' That is not the word I'd use."

Chapter Twenty-eight

◇◇◇

There was no backing out now.

THE CHRISTIE CURSE—VICTORIA ABBOTT

Lizzie was on the phone first thing in the morning, calling the book club together for a meeting that night. After she explained about Bob, all were happy to change whatever plans they'd already arranged.

They met at Molly's outside on the patio. A light sprinkling of rain in late afternoon had left the air more comfortable than it had been in days but still warm enough so that the chairs had dried quickly.

"I can't believe they've put Bob in jail," Sally-Jo exclaimed as she came through the back door carrying a tray with a pitcher of sweet tea and glasses. Molly was right behind her with a plate of molasses cookies.

Jacob had held the door open for them and hurried around to take the tray from Sally-Jo. Lizzie had been lighting the hurricane lamp candles set out on the large patio table and also the smaller ones beside each chair. Andie finished putting the cushions on each chair and sat in the one closest to the table with the food.

"It's just not the same without Chief Bob here at our meeting," she moaned.

Molly heaved a heavy sigh. "I'm with you there, Andrea. Which is why we have to do some serious thinking and try to come up with some way of helping him. Lizzie, why don't you just sort of recap all that's been happening lately."

Lizzie had been about to take a sip of her tea but she put the glass down and gathered her thoughts. "Well, it all started with Molly being beaten and Teensy's books stolen." She squeezed Molly's arm then continued.

"Then Orwell Rivers was murdered and his place ransacked. It wasn't long before Cabe Wilson turned up dead in Bob's yard, along with some counterfeit twenty-dollar bills. The FBI arrived on scene. Bob's house was searched and more counterfeit money found in it, along with an unexplained hefty deposit in his bank account. Bob has been taken in for questioning by the FBI. And Teeny's house was broken into. I think that's everything."

"I'd say the only thing that we know for sure," Jacob interjected, "is that Bob was more than likely framed."

"That's a certainty," Molly said, her hands clutching the arms of the wicker chair.

"For sure," Sally-Jo added quickly. "By the way, no Stephanie tonight?"

Lizzie answered. "She's just so tired after her shift ends at seven. All she wants to do is get home to Wendy and not have to do any more talking for the day. She felt bad but I assured her we'd keep her updated and not to worry."

Sally-Jo nodded.

"So what are we going to do?" Andie asked, tugging at a long dangly skull earring in her right earlobe. She sported a skull and crossbones stud in the left side. "What would Agatha Christie say, Molly?"

Molly chuckled. "Well, let me see. I think Agatha Christie would remind us to take a closer look at motives. Sometimes the motive for a murder is to prevent an earlier crime from being revealed, like in *Hickory Dickory Dock*. Of course, we know the first crime here is counterfeiting. But what if there's an even earlier motive?"

"Cool. So, we keep digging?"

Molly nodded. "Precisely."

"In the meantime," Jacob jumped in, "I'll continue working with my friend, Ken Stokes, on getting Bob released. They haven't charged him as yet, which probably means they're not totally confident they can make it stick. That's a good thing. But they can't hold him much longer, so I'm betting they're out beating the bushes right about now."

"We should be, too," Sally-Jo suggested.

"Any ideas?" Jacob shot right back, sounding a bit testy.

Lizzie stepped in. "Andie and I have been on the Internet looking for more information on the victims and any connections. Nothing suspicious, though. Wilson's fiancée, Urliss Langdorf, did say she thought he was going to see if Bob could help him but she didn't know any specifics. Except that she thinks he was into something illegal."

"That would be a good guess, since he's dead," Molly said dryly. "What about his bank account? Any large deposits in it?"

"We have no way of knowing," Lizzie admitted. "Urliss did say he'd recently bought a big speedboat but there'd been no spending sprees or anything, that she knew of anyway."

"He could have stashed it in his account." Sally-Jo was staring at Lizzie.

She sighed. "I'll try asking Mark but he's told me to stay out of it."

"When has that stopped you?"

Lizzie gave her a thumbs-up. "Now, Orwell Rivers was in need of money at one point but he managed to get it and save his business. Maybe it was a bank loan. Maybe not."

"Maybe he found a lucrative sideline for his machines," Jacob offered.

Lizzie nodded.

"So, let's say Rivers and Wilson were in it together. There had to be more people, because this seems like a fairly intricate operation, and for some reason that person or persons ordered some thugs to retrieve the books that were delivered to Molly's. They then got rid of Rivers. Maybe he got cold feet or wanted more of a cut. Same thing for Cabe Wilson. That leaves any number of conspirators still around calling the shots."

"Like searching Teensy's house," Sally-Jo said.

"Exactly. We need to figure out who they are but I don't have any useful suggestions as to how to go about it," Jacob admitted.

Molly stood and blew out one of the candles that flickered wildly. She offered refills of tea and then sat back down again. Lizzie hadn't seen her looking that dejected in a long time. If ever.

"I'll go back on the Internet and try again," Andie offered. Molly smiled at her and nodded.

"I think I'll stop by Teensy's tomorrow and ask her about Orwell Rivers. He might have let something slip when they were discussing printing her book," Lizzie said and shrugged. "I know it's unlikely but I, too, am out of suggestions."

"What we all probably need is a good night's sleep," Molly suggested. "Maybe after our discussion tonight, something might occur to one of us tomorrow."

The others left, with Andie hitching a ride to a friend's house after assuring Lizzie she'd be home at a reasonable hour.

"I'm mighty impressed, honey," Molly said as Lizzie helped with the cleanup. "Andie seems quite responsible these days and agreeable to your setting the rules."

Lizzie nodded. "Yeah, it's working out quite well, actually. Much to my relief."

The phone rang and Molly answered, listened for a couple of minutes and then gasped. "I'll be right over," she said, her hand shaking as she tried to return the handset to its cradle.

Lizzie watched her expectantly.

"It's Teensy," Molly said, a small sob escaping. "She was attacked in her home and is in the hospital. They wouldn't tell me how badly injured she is. We have to go there." She looked at Lizzie, desperation in her eyes.

"Of course. I'll drive. You gather your things and I'll lock up."

They quickly left the house and drove to the Mercy General Hospital. Lizzie was fortunate to find a parking spot at the end nearest the hospital. They hurried into the emergency room where Lizzie spotted Officer Craig leaning against the wall, writing in her notepad. They rushed over to her.

"Please, Officer Craig, can you tell me how Teensy is? She's still . . ." Molly faltered.

Craig pushed off the wall and put her hand on Molly's arm. "She's alive but she has been badly beaten. I don't know anything else at the moment. The doctors are with her now. Why don't we just go over there and sit while we wait?"

Molly nodded. "Thank you so much for phoning me."

Craig nodded. They sat facing the hallway to the examining rooms.

Craig flipped her notepad open again. "Did you talk to Miz Coldicutt this evening at all?" She was looking at Molly.

"No. Not since this afternoon. You know about what happened at her house the night before last?"

Craig nodded.

"Well, she stayed at my place and we went over there and did some straightening of things. I asked her to come stay at my place again, at least until everything had been put in order, but she said she wanted to keep working at it." She looked at Craig. "We didn't even stop to think she might be in any danger."

"Neither did the police," Lizzie muttered.

Craig looked at her. "The chief had us driving past her house on a regular schedule. In fact, I'd gone by maybe twenty minutes before and slowed down, took a look, but nothing seemed amiss." Craig looked stricken by the fact.

Lizzie said more gently, "How did you find out what had happened?"

"I was still driving around but decided to go back down Lee Road from the other direction. Like I said, it was maybe twenty minutes or so later. From that angle, it looked like the drapery was missing from a side window. I was sure it had been closed earlier in the evening. She was asked to keep her drapes closed. So I stopped and checked."

"Lucky for Teensy you were so astute," Molly said. "Who knows how long it would have been till she was found."

"I gather the place was empty?" Lizzie asked.

Craig nodded. "Empty and, once again, a few things had been thrown around. Mainly from the desk in the corner of the living room. And it looked like she'd grabbed the drapes and pulled them down when she fell." She paused. "I really shouldn't be telling y'all this but I feel so bad."

Molly gave her hand a quick squeeze just as a young man in green scrubs walked over to them. He nodded at them.

"Officer, I'm Dr. Barnes." He looked over at Molly and Lizzie. "Are you friends of Miz Coldicutt?"

They both nodded.

The doctor crossed his arms over his chest. "We'll need to keep her in the hospital a few days to make certain we know the full extent of her injuries."

Lizzie could hear Molly loudly exhaling.

"What injuries are evident?" Craig asked.

"She's suffered a concussion, broken right collarbone and her face"—he glanced at Molly a moment—"is badly bruised. There might even be some damage to her right eye. We'll have to wait for the swelling to go down before we can do any further testing."

Molly let out a little sob. Lizzie put her arm around Molly's shoulders.

"Can I see her?" Molly asked.

"I'm afraid not, ma'am. She's heavily sedated anyway and wouldn't know you're there. It's probably best you wait before seeing her."

"Tomorrow?" Molly persisted.

The doctor looked at her. "Yes, probably tomorrow will be all right."

"Let's go home, Molly," Lizzie said. They were both thanking Officer Craig when Mark strode into the waiting area.

"Hey, Lizzie, Miz Mathews. I'm very sorry to hear about your friend. I want you to know I'm posting an officer at her door and I really won't stop until we find who did this."

Molly nodded. "Thanks, Mark."

"I'm going to take Molly home and stay at her place tonight," Lizzie said. Mark nodded and gave her arm a quick squeeze.

They left and drove to Molly's in silence. Once in the house, Molly turned on the hall light and went into the library and straight to the side cabinet. She brought out a full bottle of Bourbon. "I thought it best to stock up with Teensy in town. I hadn't realized I'd be into it so soon."

She poured the drinks while Lizzie phoned home, quickly explained to Andie what had happened and asked her to feed the cats in the morning.

They sat and sipped quietly for a few minutes. Molly was the first to break the silence. "I can't believe all that's happened in just two short days. Bob gets hauled off to jail and Teensy ends up in the hospital." She chewed on her bottom lip. "I don't think I can bear thinking about it. I'm going to bed. Do you mind if I let you take care of yourself? You know where the linens are. Just take any old bedroom."

She stopped at the doorway. "It means a lot to me that you're here with me tonight, Lizzie. Thank you."

Lizzie nodded, thinking how old Molly suddenly looked. She finished her drink and was hit by another thought. Teensy had been attacked while Bob was in custody. Surely, they'd release him now.

* * *

Lizzie dropped Molly at the hospital early the next morning while she drove over to the police station to see Mark. She was told he was at Teensy's house, so that's where she headed next.

A police identification van had parked on the roadway in front of the house behind a police cruiser. Mark's Jeep bookended the driveway and Lizzie parked behind him. She was stopped, once again by Officer Vicker, as she tried to go along the pathway.

"I'm sorry, ma'am, but this is off-limits until the investigation is completed," he said, not bothering with a smile.

"Would you mind telling the chief that I'm here and would like to talk to him if he has a few minutes?"

"He's busy," Vicker said. "I'll pass the message on. Why don't you just run along now?"

Lizzie was not in the mood to be mollified. "Would you mind letting the chief decide if he has time to see me or not?"

Vicker hooked his thumbs over the top of the utility belt he wore. Lizzie prepared to do verbal battle when Mark walked out the front door.

"Hey, Lizzie. It's all right, Vicker. I need to ask Ms. Turner some questions anyway." He walked past the officer, put his hand on Lizzie's arm and steered her back to her car.

"Why are you always at odds with my staff?" he asked, half joking. He was once again minus his hat, and his forehead glistened with sweat. His gray uniform looked fairly fresh for this time of day. He took a long drink from the water bottle he carried in one hand then offered it to Lizzie, who shook her head.

"Only when they try to bulldoze over me. I don't think Officer Vicker likes me, anyway."

"Officer Vicker is immune to his feelings when he's on the job."

"Huh—like you?" she asked coyly.

Mark gave her chin a playful tug. "Exactly. Now what did you want to see me about?"

"Oh, I just wanted to look at your handsome face"—she grinned—"and find out if you know anything about what happened here yet?"

"Flattery would ordinarily get you everywhere but I don't have any clues to share."

"You don't or won't?"

"Don't. This guy was a professional. He wore gloves. I'm presuming he took a careful look around before leaving and anything that might have been evidence is now gone. I'm wondering if Miz Coldicutt has been entirely forthcoming with us."

"Teensy? What would she know?" *Just what I was thinking.*

"I plan on asking her that question as soon as I'm allowed. For the perp to return a second night and gain entry when she was at home makes me believe she was the target. He'd already searched the house and come up empty. He wanted to make her talk this time."

"That's only supposition, isn't it? How do you know it's the same guy both nights?"

Mark gave her a "get real" look. "It's just too much of a coincidence otherwise. No, someone is searching for something. First at Molly's, then at Riverwell Press, and now here. The question is, did he find it last night?"

"Aha. I think there's another question, too. If it is the same guy, then it's obviously not Bob because he's in custody. Therefore, they have to let him go. Right?"

Mark shook his head, ever so slightly. "That's what you'd assume but doesn't mean it will automatically happen. They still have other evidence against him."

"That doesn't make sense. What you really mean is they're not about to admit he's the wrong guy until they have someone to take his place."

"Don't go putting words in my mouth, especially within hearing distance of the FBI. I'll push that fact with them but I really don't think they're listening much to me at the moment."

Lizzie nodded, feeling all her earlier elation deflated. "I dropped Molly off at the hospital on my way over here. I'm not sure how Teensy is doing this morning. I sure hope she's able to tell you something."

"You're not the only one. I want to put a stop to this before anyone else gets hurt. Or murdered." He ran his hand across his forehead where perspiration glistened.

Lizzie willed herself not to reach out and touch one of the large damp spots on the front of his uniform shirt. "A day like this, too bad you can't wear shorts," she offered, managing a small smile.

Mark grinned. "You wouldn't believe how many officers volunteer for bicycle duty just to get to wear shorts."

"I can think of one or two officers I'd rather not imagine in that situation. I'm going over to the hospital now. Will I see you tonight?"

"You are the only name on my agenda for this evening. Do you want to go out?"

"No. I'll make something and then we can just relax.

That's if you promise not to fall asleep on me," she added with a smile.

"Believe me, only a fool would do so intentionally."

Lizzie waited for the elevator to the fifth floor at Mercy General Hospital. She jostled for a spot in the crowded car, wondering what she'd find in Teensy's room. Officer Yost sat in a chair next to the door of room 514. He nodded at Lizzie, who gave him a quick smile. She then attempted to quietly push the door open but it squeaked and Molly peeked around the half-closed curtain and watched her tiptoe past Teensy's roommate, who appeared to be asleep.

Lizzie managed to hold in a gasp when she saw Teensy. Her face looked like someone had added colorful putty at random. A gauze had been wrapped around her head but her red hair stuck up on top. The right eye was swollen half shut. She had a sling holding her right arm and shoulder in place.

Lizzie leaned over and gave her a light kiss on her left cheek. Then she grabbed Molly's hand and squeezed it.

"I feel so bad for you, Teensy. Is there anything I can do?" Lizzie asked.

Teensy closed her eyes. Molly said, "She can't talk or shake her head without it hurting. Closed eyes mean 'no.' If I could get her to wink, I'd say we'd have a definitive 'yes.'" Lizzie could see how difficult it was for Molly to joke about what had happened to Teensy.

"Well, I won't bother you then. I just wanted to see how you're doing, Teensy. Molly, do you want a lift home?"

"No, honey. I'm going to stay here awhile or until they kick me out. I'll just call a taxi when I decide to go. You run along and tend to all your chores. And, thanks again for staying over last night."

"I was happy to do it. You call if you'd rather I picked you up, you hear?" She left as Molly was settling back into the one very worn burgundy leather chair by the bedside.

The realization that Teensy was scheduled to do a book signing at the Winn-Dixie in just over an hour jolted Lizzie. She drove over to the store to explain what had happened. A few customers had already started lining up at the table set up with stacks of Teensy's books.

Eugenia Killick came bustling over to Lizzie as she looked around. "Why, Ms. Turner. You're here early. That's a good sign."

"I'm afraid it's not," Lizzie said and went on to explain why Teensy wouldn't be at the event.

"Oh my goodness, Lordy no. How is Teensy? Will she be okay?"

"Yes, she will. But I doubt she'll be able to do any events for a while. And you've got this so beautifully set up, too."

Eugenia beamed. "I like doing special events and displays. We'll just be sure to have her in as soon as she's able." She glanced at the line that had now grown to six. "I'll have to tell them. They were all so excited that a real live local author would be signing today. I can't believe something like that's happening right here in Ashton Corners. It's just horrible, that's what it is."

Lizzie left her in a huddle with the eager book buyers. Word would spread fast through town now.

Chapter Twenty-nine

◇◇◇

The truth of anything at all doesn't lie in someone's account of it. It lies in all the small facts of the time. An advertisement in a paper. The sale of a house. The price of a ring.

THE DAUGHTER OF TIME—JOSEPHINE TEY

The next morning, Lizzie tried to work up some enthusiasm for her run. She'd had a late night with Mark over and thought he might stay. But between yawns, he begged off and headed home for a short but necessary sleep. Lizzie knew that some of his reluctance to stay also stemmed from the fact that she had a housemate. They'd drawn away from each other and sat, knees touching, when Andie arrived home from dinner out with her friends.

Andie looked at them both and grinned, then told them she'd say good night right then and there and watch a movie on her computer in her room until bedtime. *Smart girl.*

Lizzie planned to visit her mama and have lunch with her. She'd try to stay available later in the afternoon in case Molly needed her for anything.

She finally decided on a two-piece blue and green jersey tank and short-sleeved top with cream-colored roll cuff pants and dressed, pleased that she'd finally been able to get her brain working enough to make a decision. It must be emotional fatigue. She spent several minutes doing tension-release exercises for her neck and shoulders, then left a note for Andie, who was still asleep, and drove out to Magnolia Manor.

She found Evelyn Turner in the sunroom, eyes closed, face bathed in the beams of the rising sun. She wondered if her mama was asleep or just contented. Someone laughed farther down the hall and Evelyn opened her eyes. She looked at Lizzie a few minutes and then smiled.

Lizzie felt her heart do a flip-flop. She felt sure her mama knew who she was today. She saw it in her eyes. She reached for Evelyn's hand.

"Mama, it looks like you're enjoying some sunbathing."

Evelyn turned her face back to the sun and closed her eyes but said in a quiet voice, "Yes."

Lizzie almost danced around the room. Instead she opted to tell her mama about the events of the week, with some major editing out of the nasty parts. The lunch bell rang and Lizzie took Evelyn by the arm and led her to the smaller dining room where guests dined with the residents. She enjoyed the baked pike on the menu and noticed her mama had a healthy appetite for a change.

After a dessert of lemon meringue pie, they walked back to Evelyn's room and Lizzie read a few more chapters from *Emma* by Jane Austen. When Evelyn's eyes started slowly closing, Lizzie helped her lie down on her bed and covered her with a light afghan. She tiptoed out of the room and left the building feeling much happier than she had for several visits.

Lizzie's cell phone rang as she pulled into her driveway. She turned off the ignition and pressed the talk key. It was Jacob.

"Lizzie, I'm going up to Birmingham to see Bob shortly and I wondered if you'd heard an update on Teensy. I couldn't reach Molly and I would like to tell Bob about what's happened. Maybe he'll have some ideas."

"I'm so glad you'll be visiting him. I can't imagine how he's feeling right now. Teensy seems to be doing as well as can be expected, I guess. She's bruised and sore, and still has pain from the break to her collarbone, but it looks like her concussion wasn't serious, so that's the main thing. Molly's been with her most of the day and said that Teensy should be out of the hospital in a couple of days if she continues to improve. I know Molly will be thrilled you're visiting Bob." She ran her theory by him again about how Bob should be released since Teensy's second attack happened while he was in jail.

"It makes sense to you and me, Lizzie. But his not explaining his whereabouts was only a part of the total picture to them. I'm meeting Ken and we'll see what can be done. If they charge Bob it will probably be possession of counterfeit money but the amount was really minimal so we should be able to get him out on bail. I'll try my best, Lizzie."

"I know you will. Please tell him we're all thinking about him."

"Will do. I'll phone when I know something."

"Thanks," Lizzie said and sat holding her cell phone a few minutes before putting it away and going into the house.

Andie had left a note that she went home to get a change of clothes but would be back for dinner, which gave Lizzie plenty of time to focus on what still needed to get done before school started. Too bad her mind kept returning to Teensy and Bob. Just what was going on? Who else was involved? How close was the FBI to finding them?

L izzie had arranged with Molly that she would spend a few hours the next afternoon sitting with Teensy. They met outside her door in the hospital corridor as Molly prepared to go home. She looked tired and disheveled. Lizzie wondered if she'd spent the night at the hospital.

"Mark was here this morning and questioned her some," Molly said. "She wasn't able to remember much of what happened, unfortunately. He was good with her. She's still a bit hard to understand, her cheek's so swollen. I think she's enjoying the painkillers, though," Molly added with a chuckle. "She doesn't always make a whole lot of sense but doesn't care, either."

Lizzie smiled. "That sounds promising."

"Did you hear from Jacob last night?"

"Yes. He said he's staying on in Birmingham at least another day. He's trying hard to get them to formally charge Bob so he can attempt to get him out on bail. Seems they have to decide today."

"Poor Bob." Molly sighed.

"Jacob will take good care of him and I will take care of Teensy, so you go home now and just relax."

"I'll try to do just that. The mayor stopped by to see how she's doing. He said they had a date for tonight."

"That's an awful lot of dates in a short time span," Lizzie commented.

"Uh-huh. I think our good mayor may be smitten. Then

again, I believe that Teensy is also." Molly smiled. "She always was one to rush into things. I'll come by after supper again and see how she's doing."

"By the way, I cancelled this past Saturday's book signing. The manager of Winn-Dixie was shocked to hear what had happened and asked that we let her know when Teensy's able to come in."

"That's very nice of her," Molly said then gave Lizzie a quick kiss on the cheek and left.

Lizzie sat reading a magazine while Teensy slept. Finally, after about an hour she heard Teensy stir.

"It's Lizzie, Teensy. Can I get you anything? Some water, maybe?" She spied the drinking glass and straw on the bed-side table.

"Yes, thank you, sugar," Teensy mumbled.

Lizzie held the straw to her lips and waited while Teensy took a small drink.

"You're looking much better," Lizzie lied. *What else do you say?* "I hear you'll be home in another day or two."

Teensy closed her eyes and Lizzie wondered if she'd gone back to sleep but she whispered, "I can't wait to blow this joint."

Lizzie laughed softly even though the next bed over was empty. She wondered if the woman had been released or moved to another room. They sat quietly for a few minutes. Teensy eventually looked as if she were wide-awake. Lizzie hoped it would be a good time to ask her some questions. She had a feeling that Teensy was the crux of the matter, even if she didn't know it herself.

She leaned closer to the bed. "Teensy, do you mind if I ask you a few questions?"

"No, sugar, but you know the police chief tried that this morning. I couldn't remember much of anything to tell him."

"I'm not thinking about what happened on Saturday. I'm trying more to figure out why this is all happening. Why your house, then you? Teensy"—she leaned even closer and grabbed her hand—"do you know anything at all about the counterfeiting or the murders?"

Teensy smiled. "I know those last painkillers I took seem to be settling in now." She sighed and closed her eyes.

"Teensy," Lizzie whispered. "Do you know anything? Please think. Your life could be in danger. Bob's, too. Maybe even Molly's."

It took several minutes but finally Teensy said in a soft voice, "I'm real scared, Lizzie. I don't want to die." She opened her eyes and tried to focus on Lizzie. "I might know of a motive, why I got beat up. But you've got to promise not to tell Molly."

"Molly needs to know, Teensy. She's worried about you also and wants to help protect you."

"I don't know who it was. I was attacked from behind. I've already told the police that, and Molly, too. But Molly's not to know the rest of it. Swear. On pinky fingers."

Lizzie had no choice but to do so. She was pleased, though, that Teensy had said nothing about not telling the police.

"What's been happening, Teensy?" she asked.

"My deceased husband, John, God rest him, was a kind and generous man. He truly was. Anything I wanted, I got. And he'd give the shirt off his back to a friend in need." She paused, almost as if dropping off for a nap, and then roused herself. "But, and it pains me to say this, he had a tendency to get mixed up in big schemes. That's how he made all his money . . . and he had a pile of it."

Lizzie found it difficult to hear her clearly so leaned in closer.

Teensy sighed then continued, "Unfortunately, quite a bit of it came from somewhat shady activities. Gambling and money laundering being the main ones." She paused and looked at Lizzie, who tried to maintain a blank face.

Teensy sighed. "I sort of introduced Big John—that's what they all called him—to Orwell Rivers when John wanted to expand his money laundering business. Orwell was working in the bank at that time. He agreed to be part of it, for a tidy sum. Eventually, Orwell had enough set aside to open his own printing shop." Teensy burped. "Oops, excuse me."

Teensy tried to sit up a bit straighter but she groaned and grimaced as she slid back down.

"Do you want me to get a nurse to help you?"

"No, don't bother, sugar. I'll be okay. Now where was I?" She seemed a bit more alert. "Oh yes, Orwell. A few years back Big John got involved in a counterfeiting scheme. When his business partner told him they'd need a new printing location, John went to Orwell. He threatened to expose his earlier dealings if he didn't cooperate. And they of course enticed him with a real good paycheck.

"I knew and I didn't do anything to try to talk John out of all this." Teensy was quiet a few minutes. "Do you totally think I'm a horrid old woman?"

"No, I don't, Teensy. I'm just a bit shocked. Quite a bit, actually." She thought through what Teensy had just told her. "I can't help feeling if you'd told the police all this to start with, you might not be in here right now."

Teensy agreed. "But I couldn't just turn on Big John. He may have been a crook but I loved him very much."

Lizzie nodded. "So, John's partner is still out there. I wonder if he's responsible for all of this. But why?"

"Search me, sugar." She tried to take a deep breath but couldn't manage it. "I don't even know what he's looking for, if it is indeed him." Her eyelids fluttered shut and a few minutes later, Lizzie could hear her lightly snoring.

She walked softly out of the room into the hallway and pulled out her cell phone. When Mark answered she told him she had some vital information for him and would be right over. She nodded at the officer sitting beside Teensy's door and left.

On the drive to the police station, Lizzie tried to sort through all the information she'd just heard. Big John Coldicutt had been a gangster and Teensy had known about it. What did that make her? Hopefully, not an accessory. *Oh boy.*

The officer at the front desk sent her right into Mark's office. She sat across from him in the only comfortable visitor's chair and wondered where to begin. When she'd finished telling him what Teensy had told her, Mark just shook his head.

"Does she realize that she probably wouldn't be injured and in the hospital if she'd told me all that at the beginning?"

"She does and she regrets it. I asked if she knew who his partner was and she says she doesn't know. He's behind all this, isn't he?"

"Could very well be. Maybe Rivers did want out after all and our Mr. X wasn't about to let that happen. But what does Cabe Wilson have to do with it?" Mark mused, more to himself than to Lizzie.

"And Bob? I guess you'll have to tell the FBI?"

"When I'm ready to. I have two murders to solve first and I don't want them using this information in any way that will damage my investigation." Mark sighed. "Thanks for telling me, Lizzie. I've got a meeting with the mayor right now so I'll have to run."

"What will happen to Teensy?"

"You mean, will there be any charges? I doubt it. She had knowledge but wasn't part of it. I'm inclined to believe her. What good would it do charging a widow in her seventies with anything? No. Her reputation might be a bit tarnished when this all gets out but that's about it."

Lizzie thought about it a moment. "I think she's most worried about how Molly will take it."

Chapter Thirty

✧✧✧

When I glanced back just as I rounded the corner
onto Main Street, he was standing there watching
me, a puzzled look on his face, as if he had no idea
what he had said that bothered me.

FLIPPED OUT—JENNIE BENTLEY

By Monday evening, Lizzie was mentally prepared for
stalker duty. She'd been thinking about it on and off all
day. Who could it be? The unnamed father of baby Wendy,
the man—still a boy, really—who'd treated Stephanie so
badly and made threats in the fall? Or some unknown
stalker?

Officer Craig had called earlier and had to cancel as she
had to work a real police stakeout, so Lizzie was it. She took
along a bottle of water and a book that she hoped to read as
long as the light held out. She once again parked several
doors down from where Stephanie's apartment faced the
street. At seven ten P.M., Stephanie came walking along the
street and glanced over in the direction of Lizzie's car before
going into the building. Lizzie resisted the urge to give her

a wave. A few minutes later, the light went on in her apartment and the drapes were closed.

She'd been there about fifteen minutes when the headlights of a vehicle coming from behind flashed in her rearview mirror. Lizzie wasn't concerned about being seen from behind; the headrest took care of that. But in case he happened to look at her car as he drove by, she slid slowly down sideways onto the seat. After a minute or so, she sat up.

By this time, the shadows from the setting sun and overhanging trees made it difficult to read the license plate. But she knew it was the same vehicle Stephanie had described. A black pickup. Parked with a good view of Stephanie's apartment. She decided to wait half an hour before doing anything, just to be certain this wasn't someone who was waiting for a passenger from another house.

At the half-hour mark, Lizzie turned off her interior overhead light so it wouldn't flick on when she opened the door, and she got out of the car, careful not to slam the door shut. She moved over to the sidewalk and walked casually toward the truck. She'd brought along a small flashlight that she slid into the pocket of her lightweight black hoodie. Her car keys, palmed in her other hand with keys poking through her fingers, were at the ready. She just prayed the door to the passenger seat wasn't locked.

She gave it a try. The door opened with a creak. Both surprised and pleased, she hesitated a moment then leapt into the seat. She had just enough time before the door shut and the roof light went out to see the driver was an elderly man. *He could still be dangerous.*

"Who are you and what are you doing here?" Lizzie

demanded. She pointed her hand with the keys at him, hoping he couldn't see what really was in it.

The man raised his hands above his head. "Don't hurt me. I don't have much money on me. But you can take the truck if you want." His voice sounded croaky and shaky.

"Do you have an interior light you can switch on?" Lizzie asked.

He did as he was told, quick to put his hand back up in the air.

Lizzie quickly slid her hand with the keys into her pocket. She didn't want him to know quite yet that she was unarmed. "You can lower your hands but don't try anything funny."

He let out the breath he'd been holding and lowered his shaking hands, placing them on the steering wheel. "What do you want?" he rasped.

"That was my question, remember? Who are you and what are you doing here, spying on Stephanie?"

The man gasped at the mention of her name. "You know my Stephanie?"

Lizzie stared at him. He certainly looked too old to be the father of the baby. Her mind clicked. "Are you her granddaddy?"

He slowly nodded. "Yes. Ezekiel Dobson's the name. Are you a friend of Steph-girl's?"

Lizzie nodded and loosened her grip on her keys. "I am and I want to know why you've been following Stephanie. She's been scared out of her mind."

"I didn't realize she'd seen me. I borrowed this pickup truck so she wouldn't know it was me, if she did see it, but I hadn't stopped to think it would scare her. I'm sorry. Can't seem to get any of this right."

"What are you doing here? I thought you'd kicked Stephanie out."

He took a few minutes before answering. "I did. I've got to own up to that. I'm as much at fault as her grandmamma in doing that. But I realize that was wrong. Stephanie is family, our only grandchild, and that's our only great-grandbaby. I just wanted to make sure she was okay."

"But why not just go up to her door and talk to her?"

"Because I wasn't sure she'd want to see me. And who can blame her. Her grandmamma don't know I'm here, either. She hasn't changed her mind. I need peace at home but I needed to make sure for myself that everything's okay here."

Lizzie sighed. How sad all around. "Well, Stephanie knows someone's out here. Do you want to give it a try? I'll go with you. I think you owe her that."

He nodded and they both got out of the car. He hesitated before following Lizzie but then caught up at the door. Stephanie answered before the knock. She gasped when she saw who it was.

"What are you doing here? And following me like that? I can't believe you'd want to scare me so much." Her whole body shook.

"I know, l'il girl. I didn't mean to scare you. Your friend here explained it to me. I just needed to see how you are, make sure everything's okay."

"Everything is not okay. I'm a single mother with a baby. I have to work and take care of my baby on my own. It's hard. But I can do it. And it will get better. So, now that your conscience is eased, you can just leave." She made to close the door but Ezekiel quickly jammed his foot in between.

"I'm so sorry, Stephanie, for what we did. What I didn't

do. It was wrong to turn you out like that and there isn't a day I don't feel bad about it."

Tears were running down Stephanie's face but she said nothing.

"Can I please see my little great-grandbaby?" Dobson had tears in his own eyes.

Stephanie looked from him to Lizzie. "Maybe I should go and let you two sort this out," Lizzie said.

It took Stephanie a few minutes to answer. She stepped back and pulled the door open. "Thanks, Lizzie. You're probably right. We have a lot to talk about."

Lizzie gave her a quick hug and nodded at Dobson before he walked inside and the door closed.

Lizzie had just gotten off the phone the next morning after canceling Teensy's upcoming signing at the Piggly Wiggly. By now, the news had spread around Ashton Corners, and Vernon Unger, the manager, had been waiting for her call. He was eager to reschedule whenever Teensy was ready. Lizzie didn't think she'd have to call the librarian just yet. That gig was several weeks off. Maybe by then Teensy would be eager to be out promoting again. It was her call, really.

She next tried Jacob, hoping he'd have some news about Bob. After several rings, his cell went to the message feature. Discouraged, Lizzie was trying to decide if she'd do some grocery shopping or wait until Andie got up and maybe suggest an outing for the two of them. It might be a bad idea, considering Andie was already eager to move in on a longer-term basis, but it might also give Lizzie a bit more leverage when the discussion arose again.

The phone ringing cut into her internal debate.

"Teensy's being released from the hospital early this afternoon," Molly announced. "I'm bringing her to my house for a few days. It'll give me a chance to keep an eye on her in case someone's still out to get her."

"That's good news that she's well enough to get out. I understand there'll also be a police guard outside the house."

"Yes, the chief said he was assigning someone but that it was okay for her to stay with me. I also thought you and I could go over to her house maybe tomorrow and tidy it up for when she's ready to move back in."

"Sure, I'm happy to help. Just let me know if there's anything else I can do."

"Well, actually there is, honey. I have a hair appointment this afternoon but I could cancel it." Molly sounded tentative.

"No, don't do that. I don't have anything planned. I'll stay with Teensy while you're out, if that's what you're asking."

Molly chuckled. "Thanks, Lizzie. I appreciate it. I should leave about two fifteen."

"Right. I'll be there. Do you want me to pick you both up at the hospital, too?"

"No, that's okay. The chief is doing it himself. He said it will give him a chance to just take a look around and make sure everything's secure at my place."

Nice of Mark. Lizzie smiled at the thought of him. "Okay. See you at two fifteen."

Lizzie was pleased to get the opportunity to talk to Teensy alone again. She'd felt Teensy wasn't telling her quite the whole story, possibly because of the medication or maybe she'd been holding back. Anyway, she was hoping that in the new surroundings, Teensy would relax and fill in the gaps.

Lizzie arrived at Molly's at two. Teensy looked worn-out but said she was happy to be sprung from the hospital. Her face showed the yellows and purples of slowly fading bruises but much of the swelling had gone down although not totally disappeared. Her bloodshot right eye was surrounded by the same hues.

"That's so nice of y'all to come stay with me while Molly goes and tends to things, sugar, but you didn't really have to trouble yourself."

"I'm happy to do it, Teensy."

As soon as Molly had left, Lizzie carried a tray with some iced tea and a plate of Molly's molasses cookies into the sunroom. She passed a glass and the plate to Teensy, who was settled on a chaise lounge.

"Thanks, sugar."

"My pleasure. Now, Teensy. I had the feeling there was more you wanted to tell me when we spoke the other day." Lizzie watched while Teensy's face registered bewilderment, then something more like fear.

"There's nothing to be afraid of, Teensy. The police will catch whoever did this."

"Did you tell that police chief of yours what we'd talked about?" Teensy sounded miserable.

"I did. He had to know in order to help, Teensy. You know that."

Teensy nodded. "It's so complicated. I wonder if they'll be able to sort it out."

Lizzie waited patiently while Teensy finished eating a cookie and then washed it down with most of the iced tea. Rushing her wouldn't do anyone any good.

Finally, Teensy placed the plate on the side table, wincing as she leaned over, and brushed some crumbs off her orange and beige flowered housecoat. She looked furtively around the yard before speaking.

"You know that Big John wasn't from around here?"

Lizzie nodded.

"I met him when he came to town to visit with some relatives. I never met them and he never spoke about them. Some big family feud or something. Anyway, the only time he made mention of them was when this counterfeit ring was expanding. He needed someone in town to keep an eye on things for him and also to organize some of the logistics."

Lizzie raised her eyebrows in a question.

Teensy waved her hand. "Things like shipments and such. I don't know what all was involved."

"Are you saying he contacted these relatives?"

"He did."

"Why would John trust a relative if there was a feud going on?"

"It was his nephew once removed that he picked. He said the kid was too young to know all that had gone on and he was blood, so he could be trusted."

Lizzie thought about that for a few minutes. Who knew what families did with and to one another? She hadn't seen much of her extended family since her mama's illness became evident. So much for trusting relatives. "Is there anything else, Teensy?"

"Not that I can think of. I've been trying to remember if Big John ever did let it slip who the main man was, but I'm certain he did not."

"What about this nephew? Do you know his name?"

"No. I don't even know the family name. I think the falling-out came when John's father's sister married against her family's wishes." Teensy chuckled but it didn't sound like fun. "Sort of like my story. There must have been something else involved, too. But anyway, that's all I know."

"Thanks for telling me, Teensy. Now don't you worry. Everything's under control and this will be settled pretty soon."

"I surely hope so."

I do, too.

Chapter Thirty-one

◇◇◇

Every time we start thinking we're the center of the universe, the universe turns around and says with a slightly distracted air, "I'm sorry. What'd you say your name was again?"

BOOTLEGGER'S DAUGHTER—MARGARET MARON

The next day, Andie wanted to do something to help so Lizzie told her what she'd found out from Teensy. She needed someone to talk it all over with. It couldn't be Molly for obvious reasons; Sally-Jo was going through some fairly serious talking of her own with Jacob these days; and Mark hadn't even phoned the night before after his evening meeting with the mayor.

Lizzie knew Andie could be trusted to keep the latest information to herself and maybe she could help, once again with an Internet search for John Coldicutt's once-removed nephew.

"Yeah, cool. I can do that," Andie said, stuffing the remaining piece of her breakfast burrito into her mouth. "This is getting like, so complicated. Does any of this help get Chief Bob off the hook?"

Lizzie hoped so. She hadn't heard anything about Bob's predicament at all yesterday and she'd been hoping to ask Mark what was going on with the FBI investigation.

Andie broke into Lizzie's thoughts. "If we can get into those family tree sites, I could probably track him. I'd need some information about Mr. Coldicutt first."

"I'll give Teensy a call," Lizzie said.

"And I'll boot up the computer." Andie took the stairs two at a time, sending both cats scattering.

Lizzie caught Molly on the third ring, just as she was about to leave for a doctor's appointment. "I'll pass the phone along to Teensy," Molly said, "and then I have to be scurrying along. The police officer said he'd keep an eye on Teensy, otherwise I would have asked you to come over."

"He's probably better protection than I am." Lizzie laughed. "I'll talk to you later. Thanks, Molly."

She heard some shuffling and mumbled sounds then Teensy was on the line. "What can I do for you, sugar?"

"I'm just looking into a few things and I was hoping you'd give me some information on your husband's family."

If Teensy thought that was an odd request, she didn't let on, Lizzie thought thankfully.

"Why sure, sugar. He was mighty proud of his family tree. His daddy was born in Olds, Georgia, not far from where John was born and raised. His mama was an Alabama belle, from Mobile. John always did say those Coldicutt men had to go to Alabama to find themselves a bride." She chuckled.

She then went on to fill in names, dates and assorted limbs to the family tree, all from memory. Lizzie marveled, thinking she'd not be able to do the same. It was probably about time she got around to tracing her own roots, maybe even try reaching out to those long-withered branches. When Lizzie felt she must have enough information to track something down, she thanked Teensy and said she'd drop by soon to see her.

Andie was ready to go when Lizzie passed her all the information she'd gathered. She watched, fascinated, as Andie hopped around between various sites until she found one that was both free and had the kind of information they needed. She did wonder when Andie asked her to leave the room a couple of times, once to bring a glass of water, the next to find a box of tissue. She hoped Andie wasn't into hacking but wasn't sure what she'd do if she asked Andie right out and the answer was yes.

She was just coming back with the tissue when Andie let out a whoop. Lizzie rushed in.

"I did it!" Andie shrieked. "Here's what you want. Maybe it will make sense to you. It's just a bunch of names to me." Andie ignored the tissue box that Lizzie placed in front of her and ran to answer her cell phone.

Lizzie sat and read the contents of the site. The Coldicutt family tree outlined several generations of births and marriages. But what Lizzie wanted was more recent. She checked for John's sister and found he'd had two. She couldn't be sure which lived in Ashton Corners, although the married name of his sister June sounded familiar. She grabbed the phone book and looked for a listing for Henderson Vicker, her husband, and found it. Only two other Vickers were noted.

She looked back at the Internet site. June and Henderson had three sons: Jefferson, Warren and Thomas. She knew what she was looking at but didn't want to believe it. Thomas and Jefferson were listed in the phone book but not Warren. He wouldn't be since he was a police officer. And he was John

Coldicutt's nephew. Just maybe he wasn't the one John had pulled into the scheme, but she had no way of knowing.

She tried calling Mark but he didn't answer his cell phone. She next tried calling him at the station but was told he was interviewing someone and couldn't be disturbed. She again called his cell and left him a message about Officer Vicker's family ties and also that she was heading over to Molly's house to stay with Teensy.

She dropped Andie at a friend's house on the way. The girls were planning a sleepover. It wasn't so bad having a teenager around after all, Lizzie thought as she pulled away from the house. Not that she planned on letting her move in permanently. But maybe she could be a haven every now and then. Even Mark couldn't object to that. She nodded to herself as she turned onto Teensy's street.

An empty police cruiser was parked on the street right in front of Molly's house. Lizzie parked in the circular driveway up close to the house, wondering who was on duty. Whoever it was, should she mention anything about her suspicions about Officer Vicker or just stick close to Teensy? Nothing was proven as yet and the guy might not even have any idea what his brother was up to.

She knocked on the front door and waited, wondering why it was taking Teensy so long to open the door, when it opened and Officer Vicker stood blocking her way in.

Lizzie let out a small exclamation and tried to cover it up. "Oh, Officer Vicker, you startled me. I'm here to stay with Miz Coldicutt until Miz Mathews returns." *Play it cool. He could have nothing to do with all this.*

Vicker didn't move. "It would be better if you came back later. I'll keep an eye on her."

Uh-oh. "That's okay. I promised Molly I'd do it." She

caught a glimpse of bright lime green material floating behind Vicker.

"Why Officer Vicker," Teensy said with a coquettish laugh, "you just move on over out of the way and let my friend Lizzie in." She gave him a small shove to the side.

Lizzie took advantage of the opening and ducked inside. "Hi, Teensy. I'm sorry I didn't get here before Molly left."

Teensy looked puzzled but said, "That's just fine, sugar. Officer Vicker here, being such an eagle-eyed police officer and all, saw someone in the backyard so he's just going through the house to make sure they didn't get in. Now that he's checked that the kitchen is okay, you come right back with me and we'll have us some tea. I'll get a glass for the officer, too."

Vicker didn't look too pleased. "I don't think Ms. Turner should stay. It could be dangerous."

"Well then, I'd better take Teensy with me," Lizzie said, grabbing her hand and starting toward the door.

"No. She'll be safer with me." He stood in front of them both once again blocking the door.

Teensy had winced when Lizzie pulled her but stood smiling, looking from one to the other and seeming concerned. Vicker hadn't done anything threatening. He just wanted Lizzie to leave, alone. She wasn't about to. Something told her he shouldn't be trying to get rid of her so hard. Why shouldn't she stay with Teensy? Unless she was a threat to Vicker?

"Why don't I go and sit with Teensy in the kitchen while you check the upstairs? Nobody would try anything with two of us there," Lizzie said, hoping he'd believe she didn't have a clue as to his intentions.

She noticed the left side of his mouth twitch into a grimace, and while his eyes looked menacing, he agreed, managing to sound pleasant. That really got Lizzie worried. She turned toward the kitchen, looping her arm through Teensy's good one. She hoped Vicker would believe her and continue his search, if he really was doing one, or else continue pretending in order to keep them in the dark. Then, she'd make a dash out the back door with Teensy in tow. Better to play it safe and apologize later for suspecting him.

Vicker made no attempt to follow them, but Lizzie heard the front door being locked behind them. She was determined not to look behind even when she heard him hurrying up behind them.

"Just stand back a minute," he gruffed, pulling his gun out of the holster. Teensy gasped. He shoved the door to the kitchen open. "I'll just check a second time in here before you enter."

Teensy seemed to be picking up on some vibes because she grabbed Vicker by the arm and attempted to turn him back toward the hall. "That's all right, Officer. You just go do your thing upstairs. We'll be perfectly safe here."

She was almost pushing him through the door when he turned back on her abruptly.

"No, I can't do that, ma'am." He backed up and pointed the gun at her. "Now you just move on over there beside Ms. Turner."

Teensy opened her mouth to say something.

"And for bloody sake, stop talking. Just keep quiet, the two of you," he barked.

Teensy scurried over to stand beside Lizzie, who put her hand out to reassure her. They watched as Vicker went to the back door to make certain it was locked. He looked over at them and told them to sit at the table.

"What's happening?" Teensy asked in a soft voice.

Lizzie shook her head, trying to stop Teensy from talking. Vicker stood over Teensy and pointed the gun at her.

"This isn't the way it should play out." He looked over at Lizzie and took a few steps back. "You, sticking your nose in every place."

"What are you going to do with us?" Lizzie asked, trying to keep the wobble out of her voice. Maybe she could reason with him. But he was a cop. Surely he'd be onto her tactics.

"I don't know. Just let me think. Whatever happens, it's your fault. I could have staged it so Miz Coldicutt here didn't know it was me. But if you're found dead, she'll talk."

"Staged what? I can't believe you were planning to just tie her up or something. Maybe you planned on beating her again?"

Teensy gasped. Vicker looked like he wasn't even listening to her. His eyes darted around the room.

"Are you the boss of this whole thing, Officer? Or are you another flunky?" Lizzie tensed, hoping he wouldn't hit her with the gun or even shoot her.

"You know what, you still don't get it. You're supposed to shut up and stop messing around in this. Now sit down, both of you." He motioned to the kitchen table and banquette behind them and paced in front of them for a few minutes.

Lizzie wondered if she could grab her purse off the counter while he was distracted and make a dash out into the hall. If she could get to the powder room in the library, she could lock the door and use her cell phone to call Mark. Had he even gotten her earlier message? But maybe Vicker would just shoot and not bother with chasing her.

Or maybe grab something and hit him over the head. It would have to be within easy reach or he'd still have time to shoot her. She turned her head slightly to the left to see if anything heavy was on the counter.

Vicker stopped abruptly and stared at her. "What are you doing? Planning something?"

Lizzie started shaking her head. In two steps he stood in front of her and hit her across the side of her head with the gun butt. She slumped back against the banquette with Teensy's screaming reverberating through her head.

"Shut up!" She could hear Vicker yell but the pain in her head made it sound like the other two were at the end of a tunnel.

She thought she heard Mark's voice. She struggled to open her eyes and saw Mark standing behind Vicker, his gun in his hand. "It's over Warren. Just drop your weapon. Don't make this any worse than it is."

Vicker spun around. "What are you talking about, boss? I'm sure I saw a prowler. I'm just trying to protect these here women."

Mark glanced at Lizzie and started easing around Vicker toward her. "I know all about your connection to John Coldicutt and his connection to the counterfeiting ring."

Teensy gasped and Lizzie tried to smile.

Vicker looked over at the women and then back at Mark. "This isn't the way it was supposed to play out. I swear. It just got out of hand."

"I know. Put your weapon on the ground, Warren. Slowly." Mark kept his eyes on Vicker but reached out to Lizzie, gripping her shoulder.

Lizzie tested her voice. "It's not bad, Mark. I'm fine." It sounded faint to her. Hopefully he heard.

Slowly, Vicker raised both hands in the air and crouched down, resting his gun on the floor.

"You know the drill. Slide it over to me. Then turn around, hands linked behind your head. Teensy, my cell phone is in my back right pocket. Use it to call for an ambulance."

Vicker did as he was told. "I didn't mean any harm to anyone. I wouldn't have killed Miz Coldicutt. She's kin."

"And Lizzie?"

Vicker shrugged. "She had no business getting involved."

Mark had stuck his gun back in its holster and grabbed Vicker's hands, cuffing him at the same time. "What were you planning to do with Miz Coldicutt?"

"I had my orders to find out what she knew." Vicker tried to turn to face Mark, who instead pushed him down to his knees. "I'm not the brains behind this ring. The boss is worried that she knows his identity. That's all I'm to find out."

"Who is the boss?" Mark glanced back at Lizzie. Teensy was holding a serviette against the cut at the side of Lizzie's head and speaking into the cell phone at the same time.

"I don't know. Honest. He would phone me whenever he needed something done. I'm never to call him."

"What would you have done with her if she wouldn't talk?"

"I was to take her out to Riverwell Press and tie her up and leave her in the warehouse."

Mark shook his head and read Vicker his rights just as Officers Craig and Verge rushed through the door. "Take care of this scum," he told them and went to Lizzie.

"How bad is it?" He gently removed Teensy's hand and pulled the serviette away.

Lizzie flinched. "I'm not as clobbered as Molly and Teensy had been. You got my message?"

"I did. I just wish I could have gotten here sooner."

Lizzie smiled cautiously. "You got here in time to get him." She could hear the sirens in the driveway. *Here we go again.*

Mark guided Teensy to the side while the paramedics checked Lizzie's wound. "I'd like you to come to the station and tell me all about what happened." Teensy started to object. "After we go to the hospital with Lizzie," he added.

Chapter Thirty-two

◇◇◇

He knew that the cruelest of blows too often came with a smile.

ICE COLD—TESS GERRITSEN

Lizzie remained in the hospital for observation for several hours. Molly had joined them and stayed until Lizzie was released then drove her back to Molly's house.

"You sure you're all right, honey?" Molly asked once they'd settled in with glasses of sweet tea out on the patio.

"I am, truly, Molly. It looks much worse than it is. I'll bet my headache is gone by tomorrow then we need to get back to figuring out who the main boss is."

"I'm so grateful to Mark for posting a police officer at Teensy's house. I wish she'd come back here but she can be stubborn. Do you think she's still in danger?"

"It looks like that boss is out to get her. He's tried a couple of times now so I doubt he'll give up." Lizzie hated to be so blunt but it had to be said.

"I know. That's exactly what I was thinking." Molly

pulled an empty wicker chair toward her and rested her feet on it. "I truly hope this will all be over soon. My nerves are getting shattered. And what's to become of Bob? Surely he'll be released now." The intensity in her voice startled Lizzie.

"I hope so, Molly." Maybe they would release him. Maybe they wouldn't. Just because Officer Vicker was under arrest didn't necessarily let Bob off the hook, she hated to admit, even to herself. Vicker said he didn't know who the boss was. Certainly it wasn't Bob. But the FBI might be not so inclined to agree. They could even suggest that since Vicker didn't know the identity of the boss, it could possibly be Bob. So close but so frustrating!

"Maybe you could ask Mark what's happening when he calls you? See if maybe Bob will be released now? Please?"

Lizzie hated it when Molly pleaded. It rarely happened but she knew better than to ignore such a request. "I'll ask him. In fact, I think I'll visit him at the station right now but don't get your hopes up too high. There's only so much he can tell me."

"You will not." Molly's voice rose in concern. "You're not fit to do anything but sit and relax."

Lizzie thought about it a few minutes. She had a headache but she could still function. She wasn't dizzy or anything like that. But she had taken a painkiller so maybe Molly was right. No driving.

"You could drive me but I'd need to go into his office alone."

She could tell Molly was torn between wanting to take her there and demanding she stay put and rest.

"I'm okay, really I am." Lizzie tried to reassure her. "Don't I sound fine? Not slurring, babbling or anything?"

Molly thought a few more minutes then nodded. "All right. I drive and we don't stay more than ten minutes."

"Fine."

"Fine," Molly echoed and reached across to give Lizzie's hand a squeeze.

Molly found a parking space in front of the *Colonist*'s office and Lizzie debated about going in first and seeing if George Havers had heard anything. She noticed a big black sedan pull into the police parking lot. Uh-oh. The feds were back in town. She'd have to scoot in quickly in order to grab Mark's attention before they demanded it. Molly followed her in but took a seat in the outer office.

Fortunately, Mark sat in his office at his desk when Lizzie rushed past Officer Yost and through the inner door. Mark looked up in surprise, which turned to concern.

"I'm okay, really I am," Lizzie assured him. "I had Molly drive me down here because I just had to know what Vicker said and if Bob's off the hook."

The two FBI special agents walked in unannounced before she got an answer. Mark looked at them, obviously annoyed.

"I'm busy at the moment, gentlemen," he said.

Drew Jackson looked at Lizzie and looked surprised. "What happened to you?"

"The chief can fill you in. I'm fine, though, really I am." She was getting tired of asserting that.

Jackson nodded but kept his eyes on her as he said, "We won't take up any of your time, Chief. We'd just like access to your new prisoner."

"How did you know about him?"

"Good news travels fast," Ormes threw in. He'd glanced at Lizzie but appeared unbothered by her bandage.

Mark frowned. "I haven't finished questioning him as yet. I'm just letting him cool his heels for a while. Y'all are welcome to sit in when I resume."

The two men looked at each other and shrugged. "Fine. Can we sit in on this interview, too?" Jackson asked.

Mark leaned back in his chair and interlocked his fingers behind his head. "This here's not an interview." He smiled. "It's of a personal nature."

Jackson's jaw tightened. He looked at Ormes who said, "That'll do us just fine, Chief. We have someone else we need to talk to. We'll be back shortly." He nodded his head in the direction of the door and Jackson, after winking again at Lizzie, followed him out.

Mark's smile turned into a scowl. "I'll be happy to have their fricking hands out of my case." He looked at Lizzie. "Are you sure you should be here? I'd planned to come over tonight."

"I know and just so you know, I'm really getting tired of assuring everyone I'm okay." Lizzie smiled so it wouldn't sound like she'd gotten cranky. "Now, about Officer Vicker?"

Mark visibly relaxed and leaned forward, his arms crossed on the desk. Lizzie noticed his shirt collar didn't look quite so crisp and there were dark circles under his eyes. Another good reason to get this case wrapped up.

"He's admitted to being Coldicutt's man here in town. You were right. He's the nephew, once removed, but he'd never even met the man before getting a phone call out of the blue. It wasn't all familial duty that made him agree to the scheme. There were big bucks in it for him, and Warren Vicker has expensive tastes."

"Didn't anyone in the office notice his spending habits, if that was the case?"

Mark shrugged. "We'd heard there was family money. Which was true, in a manner of speaking."

"So what all did he do in this management role?"

"For starters, he hired the drivers who moved the counterfeit bills out of town. I have people on the way to pick them both up now. He didn't authorize the attack on Molly, though; he's adamant about that. She just got caught in the middle after they delivered a few of the wrong boxes."

"Some middle." Lizzie sat back and let out a deep sigh. "Does that mean some of the boxes at Molly's had counterfeit money in them?"

"Yeah. They could easily have taken just those boxes but I guess the boys were none too bright. They grabbed all of them and sorted through them later. But it was the attack on Molly that led to Orwell Rivers wanting to pull out of the scheme. The boss ordered Vicker to kill him. They couldn't take a chance on his talking at some point."

Lizzie shuddered. "Poor guy. He was just greedy. He didn't deserve to die."

"Not many people do, Lizzie. Cabe Wilson certainly didn't, either. He was part of the ring but also wanted out at that point. Vicker followed him over to Bob's place. It looks like Wilson wanted Miller to help him in some way, maybe by talking to me."

"But why try to implicate Bob?"

"Vicker realized the whole counterfeit ring was compromised and just jumped at the chance to divert suspicion while at the same time get even with Bob Miller for blocking his promotion years ago. Seems Miller had even threatened to fire him at one point."

"So does that mean Bob will be released?"

"It would if it were my decision. I'm hoping the FBI will

see it the same way, which is why I should go and question
Vicker some more before they come back."

"Do you think Officer Vicker used his role as liaison to
attempt to derail the investigation in any way?"

"I've been wondering that myself. We'll have to go over
everything just to be certain."

Mark stood and walked over to the door. He closed it and
turned to Lizzie, pulling her into his arms. In the corner,
away from the windows, he gave her a long, deep kiss. She
was more than a little out of breath when they pulled apart.

"And here I thought you looked tired," she whispered.

He grinned. "That gave me some of my energy back.
Thank you."

She smiled. "My pleasure." She felt much better, too.

Chapter Thirty-three

✧✧✧

Murder is always a mistake. One should never do anything that one cannot talk about after dinner.

THE PICTURE OF DORIAN GRAY—OSCAR WILDE

"Teensy wants to what?"

"Now don't get so excited, Lizzie," Molly said, leaning across the gearshift separating their seats and patting Lizzie on the arm. It was two days later and Lizzie was driving Molly over to Teensy's house. "She wants to get those signings set up again. She's tired of sitting around doing nothing. That girl never had much in the line of patience. Even though it's only a few days since she got out of the hospital and she's still more colorful than a quilt to look at."

Lizzie gave Molly a quick glance. Her own bruises were just faint reminders at this point. "I'm surprised she'd want to have her public see her right now."

Molly chuckled. "She thinks it'll give her a bit of a cachet, her newfound notoriety so to speak, so she's willing to forgo the makeup. Just this once."

Lizzie shifted her eyes off the road back to Molly for a second. "You mean, that's why we're on our way to her place right now?"

"Well, I didn't think you'd mind," Molly stated. "You said you weren't busy."

"No, I don't mind, but I think Mark will. The idea's that she's to keep a low profile until the boss is found. He was the one who ordered Officer Vicker to find out if Teensy knew his identity. And he doesn't have his answer yet."

"Well, Teensy's determined to put that out of her mind, I guess. She never did have a lot of common sense."

Lizzie knew she shouldn't give voice to the thought that just popped into her mind, but she did anyway. "What if Teensy has a lot more than common sense? What if she's in fact very crafty?"

"Whatever are you talking about?"

"Well, just say that maybe Teensy and her husband were running the counterfeit ring and when he died, she took over. That's one of the reasons she moved to town—not the only reason of course," she added quickly at the look on Molly's face. "Maybe she's trying to make us believe there's someone else involved, someone's who's trying to silence her? I know that's hard to even think about but you haven't seen her for so many years, Molly. She may have changed. A lot."

"She'd then be using me." Molly was silent a few moments. "No, I don't buy that. She wouldn't do that to me. And what about her injuries?"

Lizzie glanced at Molly but didn't say anything. "You think she paid someone to do that to her." It wasn't a question.

"It's just speculation, Molly, but if she knows she's not in any real danger she'd be confident about doing events."

They'd driven a couple of blocks in silence when a green sedan approached from the opposite direction. Molly glanced over and gasped as the car passed by. "Teensy was in that car. She was trying to get my attention. I think she was mouthing, 'Help.'"

"What? Are you sure? You can't be sure. The car passed by so quickly. Was she driving?"

"No, she was the passenger. I didn't even glance at the driver I was so busy watching Teensy." Molly's voice had risen by a few decibels.

"But it can't be her. She has a police guard and he wouldn't let her drive off with just anyone."

"Stop this car, Lizzie," Molly demanded.

Lizzie braked hard. "What?"

"Now turn around and follow them. At a discreet distance, of course."

"Molly, you can't be serious." Lizzie was getting a bit exasperated. This was crazy. If it even had been Teensy in the car, she could be on her way someplace with a friend who was police approved. But if she were expecting them, surely she wouldn't just leave?

"Yes, I'm serious and I'm asking you to please do as I say. I don't know what all is happening here but I do know it was Teensy. And I know she's in trouble."

Lizzie searched her friend's face then sighed. "All right, Molly."

She checked for traffic then pulled a U-turn, speeding up until they caught a glimpse of the sedan. Fortunately it had kept going straight along Florida Street but now made a left on Beaufort, heading out of town.

Lizzie waited while another car got between them, and then pulled onto Beaufort. She hoped the car in front would stay there for most of the drive, giving her some anonymity. After about ten minutes, the green sedan they were following turned in to a parking lot and sped up across it, disappearing around the back of the building. Lizzie stopped just inside the lot then drove slowly in that direction. The building, a warehouse of some sort, looked closed for the day. Or abandoned. Lizzie pulled into a loading bay that afforded them some cover, then got out of the car to walk around to the back. She signaled Molly to stay put, which she did.

Lizzie peered around the corner just in time to see a man shut the passenger door of a muddy old pickup truck, dark in color. He then walked around and climbed in the driver's seat. Lizzie hid behind a garbage container as the truck backed up then drove past her. She slipped around the corner and ran to the green sedan. It was empty. She doubled back to her car and took off in the direction the truck had driven, right back onto Beaufort.

"What happened?" Molly asked, out of breath, as if she'd been chasing the car.

"I think they're both in the pickup. They must have made a switch behind the building because the green car is there and it's empty."

"What on earth is going on?" Molly whispered.

Lizzie didn't even want to venture a guess. She sped up until she caught sight of the truck a few blocks ahead, then immediately slowed down. After about a mile, the truck turned right again, into another parking lot, and did the same routine, driving around to behind the building.

"Riverwell Press," Molly said quietly.

"Molly, grab my cell phone out of my purse and call the police. I'll park over beside the building and sneak around back. You wait here until they arrive."

Lizzie left Molly talking on the phone and she hugged the wall with her back, moving to the corner, listening for sounds before glancing around it. The pickup was parked up close to the back entrance but was vacant. Lizzie moved forward cautiously, being careful to crouch underneath the windows as she inched toward the door.

She took a few deep breaths to try to quiet her pounding heart then opened the door and listened again. She could hear voices from deep into the warehouse. She walked softly into the office area and toward the door leading to where the books had been housed. *Thank God I know the layout of this place.*

Before she knew it, Molly was at her side. Lizzie shook her head and pointed to the back door, urging her to leave. Molly shook her head and walked over to the interior door, leaning her ear to it. Lizzie threw her hands in the air and joined her. The words were mumbled but sounded like there was some space between the door and the people. Lizzie quietly eased the door open a fraction and could suddenly hear very clearly.

"I am so sorry, Teensy. I certainly did enjoy your company but you can understand, I am a businessman and I just can't risk the fact that some day you might suddenly remember something John said. Or some deep memory will just wangle its way to the surface and you'll know."

"You're the big boss," Teensy gasped.

The man still had his back to Lizzie but she knew that voice. And she could tell he had something in his hand, pointed at Teensy. Molly pushed Lizzie to the side and peeked through the doorway. She covered her own gasp with her hand. She looked at Lizzie, who frowned. What to do? She couldn't count on the police arriving in time. She looked around for a weapon. Maybe she could creep up on him. Hit him over the head. But with what? She spotted a paper cutter on top of the metal filing cabinet and tapped Molly on the arm, pointing to it. Molly nodded. While Lizzie walked softly over to get it, she heard the door open wider. Her heart stopped until she realized Molly had opened it and was walking noisily across the floor toward Teensy and her captor. *Oh, Molly, you fool.*

"I know what you're up to, Mayor Hutchins, and you're not about to get away with it." Molly's voice was loud but calm. She kept walking toward them.

"You hold it right there, Miz Mathews," Hutchins said as he wheeled around and pointed the gun at her.

Lizzie slowly inched back from the opening.

"Just why did you have to go and poke your pretty little head into this, Miz Mathews?"

"Why, Mayor. You know that Teensy and I are like sisters. I couldn't go letting you hurt her, now could I?" Molly's voice dripped with Southern honey. Lizzie hadn't heard her use such a tone before. But this wasn't the time to admire it.

"You just stop right there. No, move around beside Teensy, where I can keep an eye on you both. Do you expect me to believe you came out here alone?" Hutchins took a quick look around the space behind him. Lizzie remained out of sight.

"I happened to pass you two driving along and I knew the police wouldn't allow her to go driving around without protection, so I just followed you. Good thing, too."

"Not so good for you, I'm afraid. The police, on the other her hand, trust me as the mayor to take good care of the lady. Now, I'll just have to adjust my story when I report to the police that I was car-jacked and they took Teensy along

with them. Or maybe I won't. I could just remove your body
and it could be found later far away from here. It would truly
be a mystery as to why you died." He laughed and Lizzie
felt a chill run down her spine. It's now or never.

She inched toward the door, peeked through and saw the
mayor had his back to the door once again. She took a deep
breath, slipped out of her sandals and hung on tight to the
paper cutter, squeezing through the door opening. She knew
Molly could see her and would keep Hutchins talking. She
concentrated instead on where she placed her feet and doing
so quietly.

"Why did you do it, Harold?" Teensy asked. A tiny sob
escaped her lips.

"For the money, of course. I've dabbled in the odd illegal-
ity for many years but here was my chance to make it big.
And who would question the mayor? I could keep my tabs
on what the police knew and I made sure to keep at arm's
length in case things should go down the drain, which of
course they did. I just hadn't counted on John's dying like
that and then you moving here."

"I hadn't counted on it, either," Teensy said, sarcasm
dripping.

Lizzie had crept up to within striking distance but she
was so afraid he could hear her breathing or the pounding
of her heart. She carefully raised the paper cutter, preparing
to clobber him with it, but found it awkward to get a good
grip.

As she struggled with it, Teensy grasped her chest, moan-
ing and crumbling to the ground. Molly cried out and tried
to catch her. Hutchins lowered the gun as he leaned down
toward her.

Lizzie had been startled too but quickly regained her

sense and smashed Hutchins on the back of the head. He groaned and folded up in a heap on the ground.

Molly was still calling out to Teensy, who opened her eyes, looked at Hutchins then grinned. "Wonderfully done, sugar," she said to Lizzie.

Molly almost let her fall backward on the concrete floor. "Why Teensy Coldicutt, I swear, my heart was in my throat. I thought you'd gone and had yourself a heart attack."

Teensy lay back down again, flat out on the floor, pulling Molly down beside her. "I almost did when I noticed Lizzie creeping up there. I was so worried he'd hear her that it was either have a real heart attack or fake one."

Lizzie leaned over to check on Hutchins. "He's out cold." She picked up his gun and walked over to the two, keeping the paper cutter in her other hand just in case. "Are you certain y'all are okay?"

"Oh yes. I'm just fine," Teensy said as the police sirens whined their way to the back door. "Just be sure to point that thing in another direction please, sugar."

Chapter Thirty-four

◇◇◇

It made her realize that it really was the little things that made life worth living. Okay, that and a hot date.

DUE OR DIE—JENN MCKINLAY

Mark walked over to where Lizzie was standing, next to a display of Bounty paper towels, four feet high. He slipped his arm around her waist and whispered in her ear, "Are you stuck here for the entire signing?"

She pushed his arm away and grabbed his hand. "No, in fact it's getting too crowded. Let's go outside and wait." They nodded at Molly, who stood at Teensy's side opening books and handing them to Teensy for signing as she chatted to the next person in line. Bob Miller had staked out a chair close by and sat enjoying the scene.

"Both ladies seem to be doing fine after their ordeal a couple of days back," Mark said as he led her around to the side of the Winn-Dixie, where a picnic table had been placed on a grassy spot in the shade of the building. The heat had enveloped Lizzie as she left the building. The temperature had sure hit the high point today. She fanned herself with one of Teensy's bookmarks. Her white and black cotton sundress wasn't keeping her as cool as she'd like. She'd removed the lightweight short-sleeved shrug she'd worn while standing in the air-conditioned building.

"They're just fine." Lizzie felt a bit guilty about suggesting Teensy had been the mastermind but Molly hadn't mentioned it again. Nor had she said anything about Teensy's revelation about all that had gone on in the past. "Of course, Teensy's ego is still recovering from the realization that Mayor Hutchins had been using her rather than truly romancing her. In fact, we all thought he was pretty smitten. But Molly's certain Teensy will get past that real soon."

Mark nodded. "Now, it's an entirely different matter as to how long it will take the town to recover."

"I know. Everywhere I go folks are talking about it. They're just so shocked and can't get over the fact that the person they entrusted with the well-being of Ashton Corners was involved in counterfeiting and much worse, murder."

"The next few months should be real interesting, that's for sure. I'm betting Ex-mayor Hutchins's trial will be held in Montgomery. No way they'll find an unbiased jury here in town."

"I'm just glad everything's been sorted out and especially that Bob's a free man," she added.

Mark agreed. "That must have been hard on him but I think Molly will make sure he'll get over it."

Lizzie laughed. "I think you've got that right. Did he ever say what he was doing the night Teensy's house was broken into?"

Mark frowned. "He's a stubborn man when he wants to be. He finally did tell me after the FBI released him but he said I wasn't to tell them. Seems he went to visit Lucille and convinced her to spend some time with a cousin of theirs in Mobile. She left early the next morning. He knew things were only going to get worse for him and he didn't want her being dragged any further into it."

"I can understand that. And what about Officer Vicker?"

"He's facing a lot of jail time. I didn't hire him, he was on the job when I took over, but I never had a moment to doubt him. Now I'm wondering if I should have known something was going on."

"And why would you? I'm sure 'psychic' isn't in your job description."

Mark shook his head but a smile tugged at the corners of his mouth. "Well, it makes me look at the whole job a bit differently these days. We're fairly certain Vicker didn't tamper with any evidence but he committed a break and enter at Bob's house to locate his bank account number. That explains how the cash was deposited without Bob's knowledge."

"I'd forgotten about that. They so totally set him up."

"They were good, which is why I told you to stay out of it right from the start." Lizzie started to protest but Mark held up his hand. "You were very lucky that you and the others didn't get killed in the warehouse, Lizzie. You done good but I sure hope you'll listen next time."

"Next time?"

"I'm honestly and truly hoping there won't be one but I'm realizing you and your book club read far too many mysteries to keep to the sidelines when trouble strikes."

"And I think you've had far too many murders to deal with lately." She smiled.

"By the way, Andie's moving back home tomorrow."

"She is?" Mark wiggled his eyebrows.

Lizzie chuckled. "Yes, her daddy had to come home from the holiday early because of a business concern and she's going home. However, she's asked me if she can move back in for the school term, at least."

Mark stiffened. "What did you say?"

"I asked her to talk to her mama first and try to sort things out. If that didn't work, then we'd talk about what to do." A soft breeze suddenly fanned her face.

Mark nodded. "I guess you can't turn her away."

"No."

He squeezed her hand. "Uh-oh. Looks like we have visitors." He nodded his head to the right. Lizzie glanced over and saw the two special agents exit their car. She looked at Mark, who grimaced and started toward them. She followed him and they reached the two before they entered the store.

"You're on your way out of town?" Mark asked hopefully.

"Just thought we'd stop by and say good-bye, and pick up a copy of the book that caused so much trouble," Drew Jackson said.

"You mean, the book that broke the counterfeit ring," Lizzie piped up.

Jackson grinned at her. "That, too."

They all walked in and over to the signing table at the right. The crowd had thinned but three women still waited in line. Jackson lined up while Ormes wandered over to an aisle. Bob sat watching them, expressionless.

Jackson rejoined Lizzie and Mark, signed book in hand. "Something to remember this town by." Ormes came up behind him. "Time to go."

Ormes nodded at them both then walked out. Jackson

shrugged his shoulders. "G'bye, y'all." He looked at Lizzie. "Be seeing you again."

Mark muttered under his breath, "Not if I can help it," as Jackson left. He gave Lizzie's hand a squeeze. She smiled to herself.

Molly wandered over to them as Sally-Jo and Jacob came through the door.

"I hope we're not too late," Sally-Jo said. Her face was flush but her white satin tank and floral skirt looked fresh.

"Not one bit," Molly answered. "Uh, just in time. In fact, I have an announcement to make." She looked at Teensy, who smiled. "I've really enjoyed working here with Teensy on this book business and I've decided to put things right in Ashton Corners."

Lizzie looked at Mark and shrugged. First she'd heard of anything.

Bob walked over to Molly and stood beside her. "I've bought the Book Bin. I'm going to run it and Bob will do the financials. And I thought I'd ask Stephanie to learn the ropes and then manage it, and Andie to do part-time hours while going to school. Now what do y'all think about that?" She beamed as she looked around at each of them.

"And I plan to stay right here in Ashton Corners and will write the books," Teensy said, with a slight bow of the head.

Lizzie grinned. It looked like another page had just been turned.

Reading Lists

Lizzie Turner

1. Victoria Abbott—*The Christie Curse*
2. Avery Aames—*Clobbered by Camembert*
3. Jacklyn Brady—*Cake on a Hot Tin Roof*
4. Elizabeth Lynn Casey—*Reap What You Sew*
5. Julie Hyzy—*Grace Among Thieves*

Sally-Jo Baker

1. Lucy Burdette—*An Appetite for Murder*
2. Victoria Hamilton—*A Deadly Grind*
3. Janet Bolin—*Threaded for Trouble*
4. Rebecca M. Hale—*Adrift on St. John*
5. Jenn McKinlay—*Buttercream Bump Off*

Molly Mathews

1. Wagstaff & Poole—*Agatha Christie: A Reader's Companion*
2. Ann Granger—*Mud, Muck and Dead Things*
3. Lorna Barrett—*Sentenced to Death*
4. Jacqueline Winspear—*Elegy for Eddie*
5. Alexander McCall Smith—*The Limpopo Academy of Private Detection*

Bob Miller

1. James Lee Burke—*Creole Belle*
2. Jonathan Kellerman—*Mystery*
3. John Connolly—*The Burning Soul*
4. Robert Crais—*The Sentry*
5. Peter Robinson—*Bad Boy*

Jacob Smith

1. Linwood Barclay—*The Accident*
2. Carl Hiaasen—*Star Island*
3. David Rosenfelt—*Dog Tags*
4. David Baldacci—*The Innocent*
5. Harlan Coben—*Live Wire*

Stephanie Lowe

1. Laura DiSilverio—*Die Buying*
2. Janet Evanovich—*Smokin' Seventeen*
3. Dorothy St. James—*The Scarlet Pepper*
4. Miranda James—*File M for Murder*
5. Lila Dare—*Die Job*

Andrea Mason

1. Janet Evanovich—*Plum Spooky*
2. Josie Belle—*50% off Murder*
3. Allison Kingsley—*Mind Over Murder*
4. Charlaine Harris—*Deadlocked*
5. Bailey Cates—*Brownies and Broomsticks*

Turn the page for a preview of Erika Chase's next
Ashton Corners Book Club Mystery . . .

BOOK FAIR AND FOUL

Coming soon from Berkley Prime Crime!

66 I know we're here to celebrate Stephanie's birthday, and I don't want to take any of the shine away from your day, honey, but I was wondering if we could take a few minutes to go over the final plans for this weekend." Molly Mathews looked around the table at the other three women, Lizzie Turner, Sally-Jo Baker and Stephanie Lowe, and they all nodded their agreement.

"Good. But first off, a most happy birthday to you, Stephanie. You've had quite the year and I say this truly: I'm so happy you've become part of our book club. No, it's more than that. I'm happy you're our friend. I hope this coming year will bring you true happiness." Molly lifted her wineglass in a toast. "To Stephanie."

Stephanie's grin covered most of her face. Lizzie hadn't seen her so excited since her baby, Wendy, was born the previous Christmas. Once again she looked so much younger than her now twenty years. Her shoulder-length brown hair was pulled back in a ponytail, showing off her new dangly red earrings, a gift from Lizzie; she'd started wearing more colorful eye makeup after the birth; and her figure had quickly gone back to a size six, as emphasized by the clingy white tunic top and black stretch pants she was wearing.

"To Stephanie," Lizzie repeated. "I can't imagine the Ashton Corners Mystery Readers and Cheese Straws Society without you."

"Nor the Book Nook," Molly added. "You're my star bookseller."

"Oh, stop it all now. Y'all are going to make me start crying. I don't know what I did to deserve such wonderful friends." Stephanie swiped at the corner of her eye before a tear could fall.

Sally-Jo clinked her glass against Stephanie's. "It's all true. However, I'd be cautious if I were you. Never know what extra duties might flow your way this weekend once we have you good and buttered up," she added with a chuckle.

Stephanie waited until the server had placed the three-tier cake stand filled with fancy tea sandwiches and scones in the center of the table. "I've always wanted to come to the High Tea here at the Jefferson Hotel. It's all so elegant and"— she spied the dessert tray at the next table—"fattening."

They all laughed. "But I gotta tell y'all," Stephanie continued, "I'm so excited about the mystery festival that I'm starting to lose sleep. It will be such fun meeting big-name authors and spending the whole day just talking mysteries. I'm sure glad you decided to do it, Molly."

"It was not my decision entirely. I wouldn't have taken it

on if the entire book club hadn't been so enthusiastic. Even with everyone pitching in, I had no idea how much work it would be." She said it with a smile but Lizzie felt concerned that the oldest member was the one doing the most work.

"Is there something else we can be doing, Molly?" Lizzie asked. Not that Molly couldn't handle it. At seventy-three, she could match even Andie Mason, the youngest member of the book club, in the stamina department any day. Of that, Lizzie was certain.

Molly shuffled through the papers on the table next to her place setting. Lizzie could hear the clatter of teacups threaded with the soft din of voices. One didn't want to speak too loudly in the hotel's Echo Lounge.

"I don't think so," Molly finally answered, having found the page she was searching for. "You'll be able to stop by the bed-and-breakfast on Thursday after school? I'll try to get there by about two P.M. I can't imagine that the Farrows will arrive any earlier. They said they'd be leaving Columbus after lunch and just take a leisurely drive over."

"I'll be over. You can just text me when they arrive." She grinned as Molly frowned. Although Molly was resisting learning to text, Lizzie had a feeling that she was also secretly intrigued by the idea. Lizzie would get her on board sooner than later. "When did you say the other authors are arriving?"

"Well, Jackson Pruitt said in the evening, and Lorelie Oliver won't be there until Friday afternoon. I sure hope she's here in plenty of time for the evening dinner I have planned. Ashley Briggs should also be arriving early Friday afternoon. That's the four of them. I can't imagine keeping track of any more authors than that." Molly took a sip of her tea.

Sally-Jo moved the sandwiches closer to Stephanie, and after she'd chosen a smoked salmon pinwheel, helped herself to one of the same before passing the tiered stand over to Lizzie. "I've heard there's often a bit of tension between Lorelie Oliver and Margaret Farrow, or Caroline Cummings as she's known in the mystery world."

"Really?" Molly asked. "I hadn't heard that. Oh dear. Let's hope we don't have a couple of divas on our hands."

"Well they both have series with a Southern belle as protagonist," Lizzie said. "That could put them in competition, don't you think?"

"They do, but Lorelie Oliver has a fashionista and Caroline Cummings writes about a caterer. You'd think that would provide enough distinction between the two," Sally-Jo ventured. "I understand they're pretty much Southern belles themselves."

"Now that could make things mighty interesting," Molly reflected. "Does anyone know anything about Jackson Pruitt?"

"Only that Bob is extremely happy that we've got one writer on the list who has a police procedural. I haven't heard any gossip about him," Sally-Jo added as she tucked a stray strand of auburn hair behind her ears. She'd started growing out her pixie cut but constantly complained about it getting in the way. Lizzie secretly hoped she'd go back to the shorter style, which totally suited her small build and large green eyes and hot-pink glass frames.

"Seems to me, since the three of them have appeared together before, at least that's what their promotional flyer said, then they should be able to cope. I hope Ashley Briggs doesn't get lost in the fray." Lizzie had worried about adding the much younger author to the guest list but it was hard to turn down an enthusiastic writer who made such an earnest appeal to be included.

"Well, we'll all see that doesn't happen. Lizzie, as moderator of their panel on Saturday morning, you'll just have to keep them under control," Molly reminded her.

"Yes'm," Lizzie managed to say, her mouth full of goat cheese and watercress sandwich. She glanced around the room as she ate. She was lucky to have been able to schedule all her appointments for the morning. As the reading specialist with the Ashton Corners public school, her days consisted mainly of meetings with students, parents, and teachers. A far cry from the very chic lounge where they now sat, enjoying the ever-so-special High Tea.

Trust Molly to choose something so beyond Stephanie's usual activities as a birthday treat. In fact, Molly had insisted on treating them all. The room was full even though it was a Monday afternoon and the variety in ages spoke to the fact that gracious rituals still appealed to a wide range of women. The crisp white linen tablecloths, edged in a taupe trim, the plush taupe chairs, the crystal chandeliers and the expanse of window overlooking the back gardens made the setting idyllic. Lizzie realized how happy she felt to be in this place, at this time, and with her close friends.

"The food arrangements are all confirmed, Sally-Jo?" Molly asked, pulling Lizzie out of her reverie.

"They are. The Ladies' Guild of St. John's will prepare a salad and cold cuts buffet for lunch for the participants and the Baptist Women's Group at Bethany Church has a yummy hot menu set for supper.

"Now, try to visualize it," she continued. "You're in the Picton Hall at the Eagles Center. We'll have the authors sitting on stage and the audience seated theatre-style facing

them. That should take up about half the floor space. At the
opposite end of the room, we'll set up the tables for lunch.
It's really spacious so nobody should be crowded."

"That's excellent. And both groups will attend to clean up?"

"They will. And they'll supply all the dishes and linens.
I think we really lucked out here."

Lizzie snagged another sandwich before the serving plate
was removed and a bone china tray filled with squares,
cookies and cakes put in its place. "I confirmed with George
Havers at the *Colonist* that he'll have both a reporter and a
photographer at the hall first thing on Saturday morning.
We'll do a photo op with the authors to start and then he'll
wander around and take pictures of the attendees for a
couple of hours. If there's space, George will devote about
half a page to the event in the following Thursday's
newspaper."

"The authors should be very pleased," Molly said, adding, "not to mention that it's great publicity for the bookstore." Since Molly had bought the closed store several
months before, she and Lizzie had been working on rebrand-
ing the store away from the former owner and her misdeeds.
It even had a new name, The Book Nook. The fact that
almost everyone in Ashton Corners knew Molly and thought
well of her for her many philanthropic ventures, made the
task easier than it might otherwise have been.

Stephanie let out a low moan. "Oops, I'm so sorry," she
whispered, looking sheepishly at them. "It's this chocolate
thingy. It's just the most delicious treat I've ever tasted. I
had no idea. What's it called?"

Lizzie looked at the menu. "That must be the Viennese
Chocolate Sable. I'll have to try some, too."

Molly reached over and snagged the final mini vanilla

meringue and placed it on Stephanie's plate. "Enjoy this, too, my dear. In fact, all of you enjoy today because come Thursday, we're headed for a weekend of mystery and mayhem."

Amateur sleuth and bookstore owner Tricia Miles gets caught up in a local election that turns lethal…

FROM *NEW YORK TIMES* BESTSELLING AUTHOR

LORNA BARRETT

NOT THE KILLING TYPE

➤+ A BOOKTOWN MYSTERY +◄

It's November in Stoneham, New Hampshire, and that means it's time for the Chamber of Commerce elections. The race is already a bit heated, as the long-standing Chamber president is being challenged by a former lover—Tricia's own sister, Angelica. Then local small business owner Stan Berry throws his hat in the ring.

Unfortunately, it's not there for long when he's found murdered in the Brookview Inn. The murder weapon is a brass letter opener belonging to the inn's receptionist. Tricia knows there's no way the receptionist is a killer. And when Angelica asks Tricia to help clear her name and win the election, she sees little choice except to start snooping.

She soon uncovers a ballot box full of lies and betrayals, and a chamber full of people who had grudges against the victim. But were they serious enough to lead to murder? Tricia will have to do some serious sleuthing before she pulls the lever on a killer.

INCLUDES RECIPES

facebook.com/LornaBarrett.Author
facebook.com/TheCrimeSceneBooks
penguin.com

M1265T0213